C000116917

KISSING THE HIGHLAND

TWIN

AMY JARECKI

All rights reserved.

No part of this publication may be sold, copied, distributed, reproduced or transmitted in any form or by any means, mechanical or digital, including photocopying and recording or by any information storage and retrieval system without the prior written permission of both the publisher, Oliver Heber Books and the author, Amy Jarecki, except in the case of brief quotations embodied in critical articles and reviews.

PUBLISHER'S NOTE: This is a work of fiction. Names, characters, places, and incidents either are the product of the author's imagination or are used fictitiously. Any resemblance to actual persons, living or dead, business establishments, events, or locales is entirely coincidental.

Copyright © 2022 Amy Jarecki

Book Cover Design by: Dar Albert, Wicked Smart Designs

Published by Oliver-Heber Books

0 9 8 7 6 5 4 3 2 1

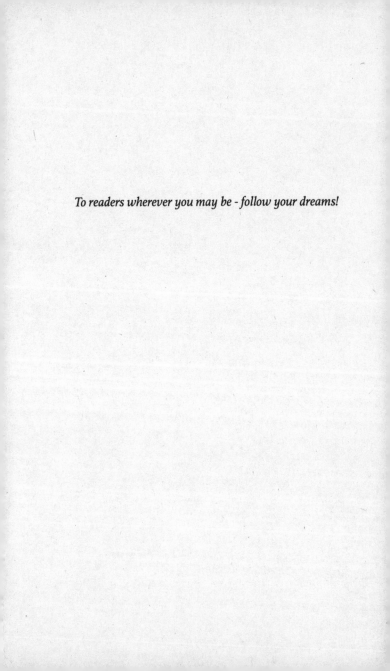

To readers wherever you may be - follow your dreams!

1

AUGUST 1816

From his perch on the red velvet armchair, Andrew studied the chessboard and plotted his options while making his brother wait. He rubbed his fingers together, relishing Philip's mounting tension as it charged the air to the point of combustion. Their Wednesday night games were as much an exercise in endurance as they were in strategy.

A hazy ring of obnoxious pipe smoke swirled above Philip's head as he feigned indifference, fixating on the ceiling's rococo relief. But Andrew knew better. His twin was never reticent or at ease in any way. In fact, Sir Philip MacGalloway's mind never stopped churning, not even in sleep. In the past five minutes, aside from growing impatient with Andrew taking an exorbitant amount of time to make his next move, Philip most likely had compiled and summed the month's cloth sales from all corners of Christendom.

Simultaneously, Andrew had categorized the vast differences in breasts he'd had the pleasure of fondling over the years. Large, medium, and small, round, oval, teardrop, pert. Regardless of the size and shape, he adored breasts, worshiped them, was in awe of them.

Alas, there were no breasts to be admired tonight.

Sighing, he batted the repugnant smoke away from his face. He hated pipe smoke. It not only stank, it made Andrew's hair smell like an ashtray as well as linger in the weave of his clothes. He might look like his brother, but that's where their similarities ended. Though he would defend Philip's honor anywhere at any time to anyone no matter their station, there was a chess game to navigate—one thing he enjoyed winning, especially when executing the fierce annihilation of his twin. Presently, however, with Andrew's king in check, they both knew he had but one move to spare himself from checkmate. "Knight takes queen."

Philip drew in another puff from his pipe before meeting Andrew's gaze. Their eyes were exactly the same shade of dark blue, the differences in their visages so slight, looking across the chessboard was nearly akin to staring into a mirror. "What say you to a wager?"

They'd been playing chess since their childhood tutor had introduced the game and, had they counted, each man most likely had won an equal number of matches, some upon which they wagered, but not all. Andrew examined the remaining pieces on the board. Given his last move, the odds for a victory now tilted in his favor. "What do you have in mind?"

Philip brushed a fleck of lint from his kilt before moving a pawn. "I need you to attend Mama's house party in my stead."

What the devil?

"Have you lost your mind?" Positive that he had indeed gained the upper hand, Andrew slid his queen horizontally. "In case you've forgotten, I have also been summoned to Stack Castle by our mother."

"Yes, but it would be much more acceptable if you didna attend."

"So, now I'm the insignificant second twin?"

"Nay. I was referring to Miss Radcliffe." Philip moved a chess piece, but Andrew was too outraged to take note of which one. "My intended would be unduly slighted if I were not there upon her arrival. Why must you always turn everything into a woeful tale about making an appearance to the world twenty minutes after me?"

"Because I continually seem to be the dupe who everyone leans upon, expecting me to act in their stead—and dunna deny it. Marty has appointed me to stand in for him in Parliament twice now. And *you*. Good God, I might as well change my name to Philip."

"Hogwash." Philip crossed his hairy knees, the cad. "I attended more than one class on your behalf at university. Come, Andy, I need you, just this once. Beatrice is running her first race in Perth and—"

"I kent it! You would rather watch an untried horse gallop around a track than spend a sennight with your betrothed." Andrew coughed out a guffaw. "You've made that woman wait three years. She'll be too old to bear children by the time you pull the stick out of your arse and manage to hobble down the aisle."

"Och, it'll only be for two days, mayhap three. Then I'll hasten up to John O'Groats and you will be able to take your leave early with no one the wiser."

"Aside from Mama and the rest of our kin." Andrew examined the board and again moved his queen, the taste of victory sweet on his tongue. With luck, only one more move and he'd secure a mate. "A wager, did you say? What will you do if I win?"

"You willna," Philip said, as he advanced his pawn to square D-8. "Queen me."

Andrew gaped at the board. For the love of Moses, the scoundrel pulled his attention away from the game to bamboozle him. "I call foul. You distracted me."

"No chance." Philip exchanged the pawn for a queen himself, then picked up his damned pipe. "Checkmate."

Andrew flicked his king at his brother. "I didna agree to the wager."

Philip eased back in his damned armchair. "Dunna tell me you're going to go soft and renege."

"How can I renege when I didna accept in the first place?"

"But we oft wager over our games. You ken as well as I."

"Aye, but this is your future we're discussing, not mine. You're the bloody bastard who proposed to Miss Radcliffe without ever having said a word to the poor lass. And now you've gone and made her wait three—"

"Many, many engagements last for years, mind you," Philip said with a billowing cloud of smoke puffing from his nose as well as his mouth.

Andrew waved his hand, futilely fanning the fumes away. "That may be so, but you have completely ignored your intended."

"I have not."

"Oh? When was the last time you wrote to her?"

"I've written."

"When?"

"Does it matter? I even breakfasted with her and her dragon of a mother the day after my proposal to allay any misgivings they might have had regarding the sincerity of my hasty offer."

"Oh, I'm certain that after three years, Baron Bedford and his baroness are completely at ease regarding the security of their daughter's engagement to you."

"God's stones, Andy. All I'm asking is for you to stand in for me for two measly days, three at most. Merely attend Mama's dinners, be cordial to Miss Radcliffe, then go hunting with Martin."

Andrew stood and moved to the mantel, looking up at the portrait of two of them commissioned by their father before they went off to university, God rest his soul. The painting would forever be displayed in a place of honor because it was a gift from the man who'd sired them both. "What if Miss Radcliffe kens 'tis me and not you?"

"How can she? We're identical. Even our mother has difficulty telling us apart. And, as you pointed out, the lassie hasna seen me in a trio of years."

"I still do not agree." Andrew turned from the painting and thumped his chest. "Besides, I have it on good authority that I am a better kisser than you are."

"No chance." Philip leaned forward and gripped his armrests as if he were ready to challenge him to a duel of fists. "Who uttered such a boldfaced lie?"

An alehouse wench from their days at university had confided such news when they were above stairs, but Andrew wasn't about to own to it. "I'm not one to kiss and tell."

Philip's eyes narrowed while his nostrils flared. "Regardless of if you are a mule-brained rogue, you will *not* venture to kiss my intended."

"Nay?" Andrew snorted at the ease in which he goaded his brother. "How do ye ken I willna?"

"First of all, you're uncannily adaptable. You're a chameleon—you can practically playact me better than I can act myself. Moreover, you are disgustingly honest and your loyalty is positively revolting."

Och, now the insults had begun in earnest. "So, as

I understand it, you believe I'm disgusting and revolting but you trust me nonetheless?"

"Exactly. I simply need you stand in for me whilst uttering as few words as possible." Philip tapped his pipe on the silver ashtray. "Please, just this once. Beatrice is going to be miraculous and I absolutely cannot miss her first start."

Andrew sipped his whisky, never once shifting his eyes away from his brother's pleading stare. He loathed saying no to any challenge, but in this instance he *needed* to say no. Besides, he'd been looking forward to a chance to do a wee bit of flirting. Mama always invited lovely young ladies to her parties in hopes that her sons might find one to marry.

Marriage. He shivered. That was one institution he had no intention of entering into any time soon.

However, if Andrew were to renege now, he'd never hear the end of how he'd turned milk-livered and wheedled his way out of a gentlemen's wager. He had no choice but to strike Philip in a place where he was vulnerable. "Verra well, if you need me so badly, then I must be compensated."

"Of course, anything."

This will stop his nonsense for certain. "I want Randolph."

Emitting a painful grunt, Philip knocked his tobacco pouch from the table, scattering the brown cut leaves onto the tartan carpet. "Have you lost your mind? My stallion is worth his weight in silver."

Tapping his fingertips together, Andrew waggled his brows while a sly smile spread across his lips. "Aye."

"Bastard." Philip's forehead creased, his lips twisting. "*If* I sign Randolph over to you, then I shall be entitled to unlimited breeding rights at no charge."

Dear God, the cad called my bluff?

Andrew meticulously reset his chess pieces on the board, placing each one exactly in the center of its square, this time drawing out his brother's discomfort while coming to terms with his own. In truth, he half-heartedly dabbled in horseflesh where Philip was completely obsessed with the vice. If his twin was willing to part with a prized stallion, the filly racing at Perth must truly be a champion in the making. Moreover, flirting at his own family's house party would have been awkward. Andrew rubbed the last piece between his fingers and handed it to Philip. "Done."

"You'll never have my jabot finished in time," Harriet snapped, her tone reflecting the irritation everyone felt, especially Eugenia. After all, this was the last day of their journey to the far northeastern tip of Scotland which had begun at Aubrey Hall in the English village of Bedford.

"You are aware this is a wealthy family of the Upper Ten Thousand we're visiting, not just your betrothed," Harriet continued. "There will be unmarried gentlemen present. Hopefully a great many of them."

The idea of seeing her intended made Eugenia's stomach squelch while her hands worked the threads faster. "Your jabot will be done and sewn to your evening gown's collar before supper."

"If your fingers don't fall off first." Huffing, Mama brushed an errant strand of cotton away from her lap. "This journey has been unbearable."

"Unduly tedious and tiresome," Harriet agreed.

Neither were wrong. The carriage ride had been excruciatingly arduous, especially given Eugenia's present company. Mama hadn't a good word to say throughout, and her sister yammered ad nauseum about her inadequate wardrobe and her dreadful dower funds, the sum of which had Harriet on the verge of hysteria. Not that either of them had been endowed with a horribly modest dowry. Modest, yes, but in Eugenia's estimation, the funds were satisfactory enough for any reasonable man to accept—especially if the man was smitten.

And now that Eugenia's younger sister had turned seventeen, Harriet would be introduced at court when the *ton* next assembled in London for the Season. Eugenia had heard her sister's woes thrice over. Harriet had convinced herself that she needed to be prettier, brighter, and more charming than all of the other debutantes just to entice the lowliest of suitors. The girl had made a list of every available bachelor and endeavored to uncover his annual income. Harriet insisted she not would accept a man who made less than four thousand a year. However, she had no idea the enormity of the competition she'd be facing in London once the Season began—the cattiness, the lengths to which young women would go to entice a husband.

"The problem is there are not enough dukes," Harriet announced out of the blue, as if she had suddenly discovered a cure for the ague.

"You're exactly right," Mama agreed. "Perhaps I shall ask your father to bring that quandary to the floor during the next session of Parliament."

Eugenia circled the cotton under, over, pulled, and tightened. Tightened, grit her teeth and tightened all the more. Heaven's stars, must every waking hour contain a conversation about finding the perfect match? "I'm not marrying a duke."

Harriet scoffed. "You're so shy, no one expected *you* to receive any offers whatsoever let alone one from the brother of a duke."

Though her sister's words were true, they stung like a slap to the face. Yes, Eugenia had endured two seasons with no prospects and a modestly suitable dowry. Her future indeed appeared to be mightily bleak when she'd attended the Dowager Duchess of Dunscaby's birthday party at the duke's London town house.

It began like most of the other parties she'd attended, but somewhere in the middle of the second set, Mama had sent Eugenia to the coat room to fetch a fresh pair of gloves from her reticule. To this very day, Eugenia remained mortified about the ensuing turn of events. As soon as she had stepped into the corridor, she'd stumbled on her hem, straight into the arms of Lord Philip MacGalloway. Of course, Mama had swept through the doorway and immediately accused His Lordship of salacious behavior and creating a scandal. She badgered the poor man into a hasty proposal, which Eugenia had no choice but to accept, no matter how embarrassed she'd been at her mother's impudence.

Philip's offer of marriage might have been hasty, but the engagement certainly had not been. Three years two months and five days had passed with nary a word from her betrothed, who was now Sir Philip because he and all four younger MacGalloway brothers had been knighted by the Prince of Wales for their gallant service to the crown. The papers reported that the men's efforts had enriched the kingdom's coffers with the importing of Irish sharecropper's cotton from the Americas, the manufacture of high-quality cloth, and the distribution of said cloth throughout

Europe. With their knighthoods, each brother had
opted to drop the courtesy titles granted them by the
dukedom and assume their honorifics.

In hindsight, Eugenia was certain the entire debacle at Her Grace's birthday celebration had been
staged by her mother. In fact, Eugenia highly suspected Mama of meddling with the hem of her dress
to ensure she did trip, though Eugenia needed little
help when it came to clumsiness. Still, upon inspec-
tion the ensuing evening, her hem had been tampered
with, and she had stumbled exactly at the right (or
wrong) moment.

Eugenia's stomach clenched while she pursed her
lips and worked the last few knots on the lace jabot for
her ungrateful sister. "There," she said, holding up her
work. "Finished."

Harriet smiled, the carriage jolting her forward as
she reached out to run her finger over the finely-
crafted work. "Do you think anyone will suspect that
you made it?" she asked, her tone condescending.

Gaping, Eugenia lowered the masterpiece to her
lap, but before she could reply Mama flicked open her
fan. "Of course not. If your elder sister had been born
into a commoner's family, she would have ended up
married to a renowned lacemaker. Though we shan't
ever speak of it outside family, she does have a talent."

Without adding her opinion, Eugenia shifted her
gaze out the carriage window. Little did her mother
know that she had already established herself as a
lacemaker of some repute. At least, she had begun to.
Once she'd received Philip's proposal and was granted
a modicum of freedom, she'd attended a few summer
fetes where she'd found a handful of patronesses who
paid her for her work. She'd used the pseudonym of
Miss Laroux, of course, because if anyone found out

the daughter of Baron Bedford tatted and made lace for coin, her entire family would be humiliated.

Though she'd saved the shillings and guineas she'd earned, Eugenia's independence was about to be quashed. She doubted Mama would allow her to leave Stack Castle without setting a date for the wedding, and then she'd be the lady of the manor in short order. Sir Philip's home was located on the River Tay near the MacGalloway Mill. It sat on twenty acres of riverfront property, which is about all the information he'd shared about her future home, aside from the fact that Sir Andrew, Philip's twin, also had a manor house nearby.

Presently, however, they'd traveled quite a distance north of the River Tay and it seemed they were about to arrive at the end of the earth. Last night they'd stayed at an inn in the seaside town of Wick and, since setting out this morning, there had hardly been any sign of humanity for the past four hours. The idea of being utterly isolated no sooner entered Eugenia's mind when as they crested a hill, the expanse of the North Sea presented the backdrop for the most enormous medieval castle she had ever seen.

Mama's gasp expressed Eugenia's own admiration. The immense curtain walls extended for ages, appearing expansive enough to surround an entire city. Evenly spaced guard's turrets rose above the wallwalk, with an expansive castle peeking above comprised of numerous towers all connected by stone masonry.

Harriet leaned out the window, partially blocking Eugenia's view. "My, it is larger than Alnwick."

"Word has it there are five hundred and twenty-one rooms," Mother added.

Eugenia busied herself with neatly folding her

work and putting it into her satchel. "Imagine what it must be like for the servants to have to clean such a place."

Mama smacked the back of Eugenia's hand with her fan. "Where did I go wrong in raising you? For heaven's sakes, the servants are paid to clean and up-keep the castle. Truly, my dear, you should be eyeing the tower where you might prefer your bedchamber to be located."

"I want one with a window overlooking the sea," Harriet volunteered. "Do you think I should ask His Grace to appoint me thus?"

Eugenia glanced to her mother's fan and considered using it to thwack her sister over the head, though she would never actually do such a thing. "No. You shall graciously accept whatever bedchamber to which you are assigned."

Harriet sat back and crossed her arms with a huff. "They'll probably give *you* the view."

Eugenia ignored the imp. After all, the carriage was swiftly approaching the guardhouse, rolling onto a cobblestone drive which made the interior shimmy and shake, the windowpane rattle. The driver urged the horses onward, beneath the sharp-toothed portcullis, rolling through an arched entryway.

A gargantuan wiry dog ran alongside them, frenet-ically barking, his eyes wild as if he were about to jump inside and bite Eugenia's nose off.

They stopped outside another archway, this one leading to a gargantuan door with blackened iron nail heads and a round knocker hanging from the teeth of a gnarled gargoyle. Eugenia dared to peer out the window and into the big dog's brown eyes. As soon as he met her gaze, he stopped barking and gave a happy yowl. "Goodness, 'tis as if we've traveled to the era of King Henry the Eighth."

The immense door swung open and Sir Philip, of all people, appeared looking as strikingly handsome as he'd done the evening she'd errantly stumbled into his arms. He wore a black leather doublet and a muted tartan kilt complete with sporran and a sash secured at his shoulder by a ruby brooch. "Skye, come behind, ye mongrel," he growled at the dog before smiling at her—or them—or in the direction of the carriage window.

Fanning her face with her fingers, Eugenia sat back against the seat, hoping the shadows hid her travel-weary face. Her gown was wrinkled and stray wisps of hair sprang out from beneath her bonnet. Where was the butler, the housekeeper? Why was her betrothed the first person out the door? They'd been traveling for over a week. She needed a bath and a change of clothes before she met Sir Philip.

To her horror, not only the butler, but the Duke and Duchess of Dunscaby filed out onto the portico to greet them.

Eugenia hastily tucked a few loose strands of hair beneath her bonnet. "I thought we might freshen up before greeting everyone," she whispered.

"Scots." Mama sniffed. "They always bend the rules far too much for my liking."

"But isn't the duchess English, the dowager as well?" asked Harriet.

"Shh," Eugenia managed to whisper before the carriage door opened. She waited and listened while Mama and Harriet were handed down by the footman, exchanging pleasantries and introductions. Evidently, the duke, duchess, and Sir Philip were about to take Skye for a stroll along the beach when the carriage was spotted.

Eugenia drew in a deep breath but before she scooted toward the door, Philip's smiling face appeared. The sunlight radiated around his thick auburn hair, giving him an ethereal glow—blue eyes as dark as a twilight sky on a cloudless evening, the corners crinkling softly with a warm, ever so friendly grin.

Eugenia stared.

I don't believe I've ever seen him smile before. But then again, I haven't seen much of the man at all.

"Miss Radcliffe," said the very handsome Scot with the pronounced burr that she did remember. He held out his hand. "I trust your journey was pleasant."

She placed her gloved fingers in his palm and was instantly at ease as he urged her down the steps. "It was long, but aside from throwing a wheel near Inverness, it was relatively uneventful."

"Excellent." The enormous dog slipped between them, pushing his nose into Eugenia's dress exactly where it had no business being. "Skye, come behind," Sir Philip commanded, and the dog immediately obeyed. He returned his attention to her and gave a saucy wink. "You must forgive the wee beasty. He's a tad too friendly with newcomers."

"I see that. He's awfully large." She let Skye sniff the back of her hand before giving him a scratch behind the ears. "What breed is he?"

"A Scottish Deerhound."

Eugenia was quite certain that Philip hadn't mentioned the dog before, though they had hardly conversed the night of his proposal, and he'd been stiff and reserved when he'd met with her in the parlor of her father's London residence the next day. And because that was the last she'd heard from him, she'd assumed he was aloof and indifferent. After all, he'd admitted that proposing to her had saved him a great deal of time on the marriage mart and he was relieved to have the whole ordeal settled.

Except as time had droned on, it appeared to Eugenia that nothing had been settled.

As the carriage rolled away, she realized the others had already gone inside and left her standing alone with Sir Philip. "Oh dear," she said, patting her hands over her bonnet. "I must look a fright."

"Not to worry, lass," he said, taking her arm and leading her through the enormous door into an expansive hall festooned with medieval armor and weapons. "Once the guards spotted your carriage, the housekeeper immediately tasked the maids with drawing baths. I understand the duchess has appointed you, your mother, and sister with a lady's maid as well."

He gallantly bowed over her hand and kissed it. "Please allow me to say how thrilled I am to have you here at last, my dear. 'Tis such a lovely day I trust you will consider joining me for a stroll in the gardens afore the evening meal is served."

Eugenia watched in awe as Sir Philip straightened, his blue eyes catching the sparkle from the candle-lit chandelier above. Upon the one and only time he'd ever kissed her hand, the moment had been rushed and devoid of emotion. His eyes had contained no sparkles whatsoever. And truth be told, over the years, she'd convinced herself that the Highlander neither found her attractive nor charming.

Though she couldn't put her finger on it, something was different. Had her memory played tricks on her? Perhaps the man preferred the cooler Scottish air? Perhaps time had mellowed her dearest betrothed?

2

"You wagered for a horse? Over a bloody chess game?" Martin MacGalloway, Duke of Dunscaby and the eldest of Andrew's brothers paced the enormous turreted library, complete with four stories of books, each with its own circular walkway, ladders, and reading nooks. His Grace was usually unflappable and open-minded, but today he'd donned an unseemly, stubborn demeanor. "My God, you are a man grown. When are you ever going to learn to say no to your brother's self-indulgent schemes?"

"Och, you werena there. I never thought Philip would sign over the ownership of his stallion. The last thing I wanted was to stand in for him, but what was I to do? And what would the family have done if Miss Radcliffe arrived whilst the cad was in Perth, watching a bloody horserace? The woman deserves far better."

Martin stopped, slamming his fist against a wing-back chair. "This is an untenable state of affairs."

Aye, Andrew had expected such a reaction. Because of that, he'd timed his appearance at Stack Castle to coincide with the arrival of the baroness and her daughters. He'd actually stayed at the same inn in the village of Wick, arose early and took his time ambling to the estate where his carriage promptly stopped in the courtyard a half an hour before the ladies, which gave him enough time to notify the family that he'd be stepping in for Philip, but did not allow them any chance whatsoever to thwart his plans.

Nonetheless, after the ladies had been shown above stairs to their awaiting baths, Andrew had been summoned to the library for this very chiding which he did not appreciate in the least. After all, he was the person most inconvenienced by Philip's irresponsibility. All their family members needed to do was play along with the ruse. "Please, brother, you're blowing this out of proportion."

"Me?" Martin gaped. "Forgive me if I appear a tad incensed. I'll have you know we received word yesterday that Prince Isidor from the ancient house of the Duchy of Samogitia will be here on the morrow—a bloody Russian, ye ken? And I also must inform you that our sister Grace turned down no fewer than ten proposals waiting for the royal arse to bend his knee. It goes without saying that your particular ruse is not only childish, your timing is *horrendous*. Playacting is the last thing we need to concern ourselves with at the moment."

The tension in Andrew's shoulders eased a bit. With a prince on the guest list, the attention would be drawn away from him for certain. "Och aye?" he asked with exaggerated interest, doing his best to change the subject matter. "If anyone can woo a prince, 'tis our sister."

"You're not wrong, and Grace is already about to drive everyone in the household mad with her frivolous demands." Martin gripped the wingback, sinking his fingers into the upholstery. "But enough about our sister and her prince. Your foolhardiness is sufficient to make the family the laughingstock of the *ton*."

Andrew batted his hand through the air. "Pshaw, even if this wee ploy were uncovered, Mama would ensure the whole thing was smoothed over before the Season begins. Mind you, I am not the one who chose attending a horserace over harkening to our mother's summons to spend an entire sennight with his betrothed."

"Mayhap not, but you did go along with Philip's harebrained scheme—you are the one who enabled him."

"Good God, 'tis only for two days—three at most," Andrew said, sounding exactly like his twin. "Then Philip will arrive and I will slip away with no one the wiser. No harm, no foul."

"Someone will err. Mark me."

"Agreed." Andrew gestured from his head to his toes. "Spend a few days in my ghillies. I am forever being mistaken for my twin, and Philip for me. Even Grace's prince will not be able to tell us apart. I swear, aside from Philip's brooding irascibility, there are only a handful of family members who distinguish one for the other."

Martin's expression grew sardonic. "I have no problem discerning the difference. I swear, Andrew, you are too good natured."

"Perhaps I am. Which is why I've stepped into Parliament on your behalf during the births of both James and Lily."

"For which I have been eternally grateful."

Finally, some words of gratitude. "Thank you." Andrew thumped his chest. "Though I am not a complete dupe in this endeavor. I did negotiate for the ownership of Randolph."

"Aye, but Philip can use the stallion for breeding any time he likes—not to mention the horse will be pastured a few paddocks away. 'Tis hardly a sacrifice on his part."

"I disagree. First of all, he will not be entitled to stud fees." It was one hell of a sacrifice, but Martin was six years older and Andrew highly doubted the duke knew exactly how obsessed Philip was with horses. "But that is not the crux of the issue here today. As I alluded to before, the issue is that had I not agreed to Philip's ploy, Miss Radcliffe would have been needlessly slighted, and a lass as bonny and patient as the daughter of Baron Bedford deserves far better."

"You're not wrong there, however I must caution you. Did I just hear a wee bit of admiration in your voice? You're not fond of Miss Radcliffe, are you?"

Taken aback by Martin's question, Andrew gaped. He might be a bit of a rakehell, but never when it came to family. "Not at all."

"You had better not be. I expect your behavior to be befitting the knighted brother of a duke. I'm not so much older that I'm blind to your jaunty appreciation of the fairer sex. You will be chivalrous, gentlemanly, and as aloof as you possibly can be."

"My thoughts exactly." Andrew rubbed his fingers over the worn leather binding of the family Bible, sitting where it had always been on the marble side table. After all, his discourse was akin to taking an oath. "I will take the wee lass for a chaperoned stroll or two, dance when appropriate, and engage her in idle chat."

Martin looked to the domed ceiling, a good sixty feet above. "God save us."

A knock came at the door, followed by a moment's hesitation and the clearing of a throat. Giles popped his head into the library. "I beg your pardon, Your

Grace." As Martin nodded, the elderly butler shifted his gaze to Andrew. "*Sir Philip*, you asked to be informed when Miss Radcliffe was ready to take a stroll through the gardens."

"Sir Philip?" Martin asked incredulously.

"Apologies, sir." Giles sucked in his gaunt cheeks, making himself look skeletal. "Sir Andrew gave the serving staff strict instructions to refer to him thus. He's even occupying his brother's bedchamber."

Martin's eyebrows arched so high, they disappeared beneath his fringe. "Are you now?"

"If I am to be Philip for the next couple of days, absolutely everyone here must believe it."

"I'll never believe it, nor will our mother." Martin looked to Giles. "Did you inform *all* the servants?"

"Aye. Most canna tell them apart, ye ken."

"I dunna see why not." The duke dropped into the wingback and crossed his knees. "One is a scoundrel, and the other is a numpty. Worse, we've no choice but to go along with this ridiculous ruse and see it through. Just pray Modesty can manage to keep mum. You ken as well as I our youngest sister has always been a chatterbox."

ANDREW MANAGED to make his way to the hall without encountering any of his family members, namely his sisters Grace and Modesty as well as his mother who, after he'd explained his wee switch with Philip, had gone above stairs to have one of her spells.

He stepped into the great hall and tugged down the sleeves of his doublet while spotting Miss Radcliffe standing off by herself, examining the 9th Duke of Dunscaby's coat of armor, complete with a hole caused by the spiked mace that had claimed his ancestor's life. The baroness and Miss Harriet Radcliffe were near the door, deep in conversation about something riveting, though as soon as they spotted him, they affected demure smiles that somehow imparted not an iota of warmth.

Andrew strode directly toward the elder Radcliffe sister who had not yet acknowledged his presence. "Have you an affinity for medieval armor, miss?"

The lass startled, making her freshly curled blonde ringlets bounce beneath the brim of her bonnet. Enormous azure eyes as blue as a winter sky on a cloudless day shifted his way. And with her wee gasp, she held his gaze. Dear God, what Andrew wouldn't do to stare into such eyes for an eternity. Dash Philip's uncanny luck. The woman had merely bumped into his brother which was all it had taken for him to secure a marriage proposal.

Once Andrew realized he was staring with his mouth agape, he gestured to his ancestor's suit of arms. "Armor and medieval weapons, have they captured your fancy?"

She pointed to the gruesome hole. "I was just wondering what caused such damage."

Och aye, the lass did have a gentle bird-like quality to her voice. "A mace as it were, swung by an English invader during the Wars of Independence."

"My heavens," said the baroness, moving across the floor. "I say, it is a very good thing the Scottish have done away with their harebrained ideas of independence and embraced Britain as one kingdom with one king."

Andrew's hackles stood on end. Yes, his family always bent over backward to support king and country, but if it were put to a vote, he just might opt to revert

Scotland to a sovereign nation. Members of the *ton* were forever downplaying the importance of the Scottish nobility as if their titles and lands were far more insignificant and less worthy. Moreover, having an English baroness refer to his countrymen as harebrained caused him heartburn.

But Andrew knew better than to rebuff one of his mother's guests. In turn, he offered his elbow to Miss Eugenia. "I see we shall have two chaperones on our stroll."

The lassie's cheeks blossomed with a delightful shade of pink while his attention was drawn away by the baroness gripping his other arm with the force of a wood-working vise. "After enduring a week in a carriage, we all can do well to stretch our legs."

"Of course," he agreed, leading the ladies forward while a footman opened the door.

It wasn't difficult to imagine why Philip had dubbed Eugenia's mother a dragon. However, Andrew was not about to allow the woman to irritate him. After all, he would be on his way soon enough, leaving his twin to charm his future mother-in-law forevermore. Whatever happened or was said in the next couple of days will ought to have no effect on him whatsoever.

"Where are you taking us, Sir Philip?" asked Miss Harriet, following closely behind.

He glanced at the lass. "Well, we have options. The maze is always diverting. The garden is splendid, especially the hothouse. My brother's stables are unsurpassed. The duke has a well-stocked loch. And if you are up for a trek down to the beach, I can certainly guarantee the discovery of dozens of seashells in the shadows of the Stacks of Duncansby."

Miss Eugenia's face took on a bright smile. "Oh, I'd love to—"

"I saw the cliffs from my window and the path to the beach is far too steep for my rheumatism," clipped the baroness, releasing his arm and pulling her youngest alongside them.

"Agreed," said Miss Harriet. "I think a stroll through the maze would be more suitable."

Andrew glanced to the woman on his arm, her smile had disappeared and, though she held her shoulders square, her eyes were focused on the ground. "Does the maze suit your fancy, my love?"

Good God, had he actually referred Miss Eugenia as love? He'd have to make a mental note to inform Philip, who Andrew doubted had ever referred to anyone as his love. But dash it all, this young woman was the most important person in the present party and it appeared that mother and sister paid her no mind.

Eugenia subtly jolted at the endearment, a wee gasp slipping through her delicate pink lips. "Ah...um...the maze ought to be fine, especially given it shan't be long before the evening meal."

"Verra well." Andrew patted the gloved fingers lightly gripping his elbow. "But we must endeavor to take a stroll along the beach on the morrow."

She smiled. The grin was shy as he'd expect from a woman who kept mum and focused her gaze on the path. Nonetheless, with the turning up of her lips, Eugenia imparted abounding emotion, including gratitude, affability, and dare he venture, awe? "I'd like that, thank you."

"I'm certain Her Grace must have the week filled with activities," cautioned the baroness.

Andrew gave the woman a dour frown. "I'm sure

she does. My mother loves playing the hostess, though she would never begrudge the granting of a wish to one of her guests."

The baroness tossed her haughty head. "Humph."

"I'm dying to know who will be here. After all, I am to be introduced at court this coming Season," Harriet chirped. "Surely the Dowager has invited a host of eligible gentlemen?"

Andrew shrugged. "Most likely. I believe my youngest brother Frederick is already here."

"And Sir Andrew?" asked Her Ladyship.

He gulped, fully aware that this question would arise. It wasn't in his nature to tell tall tales, even though he must do exactly that. "Unfortunately, my twin is indisposed and unable to attend." It wasn't a complete lie—just slightly misleading.

Harriet clapped her hands, touching her fingers to her lips. "Pray tell, who else might we expect?"

"His Grace only just informed me that Prince Isidor will—"

"From the Russian province of Lithuania?" The baroness snapped open her fan and cooled her face. "Oh, my."

"Oh my!" Miss Harriet repeated excitedly as if she were a nervous finch about to take to flight. "Are you aware that he is the most eligible bachelor in all of Christendom?"

"Is he?" On a sigh, Andrew looked forlornly at a raven flying overhead. If only he might sprout wings and fly away. Of course, Isidor must be a prized suitor. His sister would only set her sights on the best. In truth he ought to tell them the prince was already ensnared. But, then again, it might be fun to watch Grace in action, especially when she had a wee bit of competition.

Harriet clapped her hands over her heart. "I do not believe I brought a gown regal enough to be presented to a prince."

Andrew knew something of Baron Bedford's less than stellar financial situation and he highly doubted the chit possessed a dress regal enough for the Russian prince. And when did Eugenia's invitation to Stack Castle suddenly become Harriet's quest to nab a husband? Hell, she wouldn't officially be out in society until the Season started. The gel was still wet behind the ears.

Deciding to add a wee bit of fuel to the fire, he cleared his throat. "If you are in need of anything, might I suggest having a word with Lady Grace? I would say she is most likely the greatest expert on couture I have ever met."

Harriet tittered—aye, she was reminding Andrew of a finch more and more. "I knew your sister must be a kind soul. The papers reported that Her Ladyship has turned down dozens of suitors in her first season. Is this true?"

Andrew glanced to Eugenia who had released his arm and wandered over to a row of an assortment of brightly colored zinnias. "I believe *dozens* might be stretching things a wee bit."

The younger sister performed a pirouette. "Mama, we must return to the house at once and request an audience with Lady Grace."

"Yes, we must. At once." The baroness gathered her skirts as if preparing to run. "Sir Philip, I am afraid we shall have to cut our walk short."

"Verra well, if you wish." Andrew moved toward the zinnias. "However, if Miss Eugenia is amenable, I'd like to show her the gardens rather than the maze. My mother has some impressive roses—in plain sight of the castle, mind you."

Her Ladyship started away. "Yes, yes, that will be fine. Just ensure you return in plenty of time for my eldest to dress for dinner."

3

As she turned away from zinnias happily wobbling in the breeze with their magentas, reds, and yellows, Eugenia twisted a lock of hair around her finger, her toe pointing inward like it oft did when she felt out of sorts. Yes, Mama had said time and time again that Eugenia's face was passably alluring, but those words had never made her feel beautiful. In truth, she hovered in an unwelcomed state of awkwardness whenever she was away from home and especially when she had no lacemaking with which to busy her fingers.

"If you have something you'd rather do, my lord, I can return to the castle with Mama and Harriet."

The beautiful Scotsman planted his hands atop his kilted hips. Truly, the man was far more handsome than she remembered with wide, wild eyes. Striking features arranged as if a sculptor had a hand in his creation. "First of all, I no longer use the courtesy title afforded me at my birth. I am *Sir Philip* as I'm sure you are aware since you have already referred to me thus."

She immediately shifted her gaze away from those penetrating deep blue eyes and stared at his chest, clad in a leather doublet slashed by a tartan sash pinned at the shoulder by an enormous brooch, the bronze embossed with an eagle, and she'd never forget the rather large ruby in the center. "Forgive me. I misspoke. But..."

"Hmm?"

Good heavens, the Highlander's chest was broad. How did a man come by such brawn? "Are you happy with the change...um...in formal address as it were?"

"Verra happy." He caressed the brooch with the tips of his fingers as if the piece were very special to him. She marveled at the gentleness of his touch—such strong fingers, yet seeming to be incredibly tender. "It was an honor to be recognized on my own merits and those of my brothers. I suppose it was also an honor to be born into a dukedom, though I did nothing to earn the courtesy title aside from exit my mother's womb."

Eugenia gripped her hands together and tapped her knuckles to her lips. "Sir, you are quite direct."

"I've never seen much use in skirting around the truth." He used the crook of his finger to tilt her chin upward until she was looking him in the eyes. "And you may call me Philip."

She swallowed but this time, she didn't lower her gaze. She'd thought a great deal about what she might call him—*dear, dearest, my love*—though she'd never admit her musings to a soul. "Truly?"

He brushed her cheek, imparting the same tenderness that she'd just observed. "Aye, you seem rather surprised that I would ask my betrothed to call me by my familiar."

Absently, Eugenia moved her hand to cover the tingling sensation on her face. "Mama still refers to my father as Baron, though I imagine it is not too ter-

ribly unusual for people engaged to be married to use
the familiar."

"My thoughts, exactly. *Eugenia*."

She drew in a sharp breath as he enunciated her
name while continuing to gaze into her eyes as if he
hadn't a bashful bone in his body. Heavens, the utter
command of his presence made her feel as if he'd bent
down and kissed her on the lips. Truly, she had imagined him doing so oft enough. Though not out of
doors and not in view of hundreds of windows.

Philip grinned, looking quite content with himself,
devilishly handsome as well. "However, I digress. I did
have another matter to discuss after you suggested
you return with your mother."

Was he finally going to discuss the wedding? "Oh?"
she asked, hardly able to breathe. Hardly able to
think.

"Do you not care for flowers?"

With Eugenia's exhale, her shoulders fell. *Flowers*?
"I adore them."

"I thought as much after seeing you examine the
zinnias."

"You were watching me?" she asked, surprised, her
moment of disappointment waning.

"Of course I was. After all, we are engaged and, because of reasons beyond my control, I havena had the
pleasure of spending much time in your company."
Philip led her around one of the many corners of the
castle, then started toward a glass hothouse. "You
sound shocked that someone might be attentive to you
rather than your mother or sister."

"Well, they are both very difficult to ignore."

"I disagree. In fact, I am rather glad that they
parted company."

"Why?"

"I would think it ought to be as clear as the lovely straight nose on your face."

Eugenia tapped her nose—prior to this very moment, she'd thought it rather plain. At least no one had ever mentioned it before. "Is it *clear*?" she asked, uncertain of his meaning.

"When your mother and sister were with us, you not only kept your chin down and watched the path's crushed seashells pass beneath our feet, but you couldna get a word in edgewise even if you'd tried."

She cringed. "You noticed all that in how much time? Ten minutes at most?"

"Tell me, lovely Eugenia, are you shy, or do you merely choose to let those two females ride roughshod over you?"

"Sir—"

"Philip."

"Philip," she repeated, wringing her hands. "Let us first face the fact that you hardly know me."

He offered his elbow and changed directions, leading them away from the tall green leaves of the maze. "Verra well, I'll give you that, but tell me I'm wrong."

"Mama and Harriet are rather talkative and—"

"Overbearing."

Eugenia clapped her hand over her mouth. Yes, the pair of them could be downright supercilious, but she would never own to such a thing. "I prefer to keep my thoughts to myself."

As they walked, Philip regarded her out of the corner of his eye—long enough to make her bite down on her bottom lip and wonder if she had a smudge of raspberry conserve on her face. They'd enjoyed a snack of white bread with raspberry conserve after their baths.

"I reckon being somewhat reticent is a virtue," he said.

"Thank you."

"Ah, here we are." He gestured ahead. "Pink roses by the hundreds—my mother's favorite color."

"Oh my, these are Moss Provence." Eugenia cupped a fully opened rose. "They're stunning and bear such large blooms."

"I assure you, there will be plenty of them included in the house flowers—they're fragrant as well. You'll be sick of the smell of roses by the time the week has come to an end."

"Moss Provence are very aromatic, but I'll never tire of the scent of roses." Eleanor panned her gaze across the tidy rows. "And look there, the reds are Double Velvet."

"You are a rose connoisseur, I see."

"I know a little."

"Are roses your favorite flower?"

"Favorite? How can I choose a favorite when there are so many lovely blooms in the world? It would be unfair to choose a peony over a rose, or an iris over a lily. I simply cannot."

Philip bent down and plucked a pink rose—the bloom of happiness. Then he used his thumb to break off the thorns. Gallantly, he bowed and held out the flower. "For you. A true enthusiast."

"Thank you." She took the rose and drew it to her nose, breathing in the heady fragrance. "I say, after..."

"Hmm?"

She considered asking him what had changed. After all, it wasn't as if she knew him well. "As I recall, things had been rather tense when you proposed."

He looked out toward the sea and rubbed the back of his neck. "I suppose they were."

"I didn't expect you to be..."

"Please, my dear, feel free to complete your thoughts. Opposed to your mother and sister, I'm rather a good listener."

"Well, I thought you might be regretful of our hasty engagement."

He chuckled and gave her a sideways look. "It hasna been hasty."

"Not since you proposed, but the proposal itself was as hasty as one can be."

A shadow crossed Philip's face as if the sun had disappeared behind a cloud, even though the sky was unusually clear. He offered his arm. "I think we'd best return to the castle."

She slid her fingers into the crook of his elbow. "Very well, but tell me, why did Skye not accompany us on our walk?"

Grinning, he glanced at her out of the corner of his eye. "Do you reckon the baroness would have appreciated an oversized wiry hound rubbing against her? Mayhap bounding through the mud and planting his paws on her wee shoulders?"

"Mama? No, she would not." Eugenia chucked as the image of her mother batting Skye away with her fan. "She would have been appalled."

"But I take it *you* like dogs, madam?"

"Oh yes and Skye seems so well-behaved—hardly one to muddy his paws and jump on a baroness."

"He is a good laddie at that." Philip looked to the skies and sighed.

"Is something amiss?"

"I suppose I ought to inform you that Skye is my brother Andrew's deerhound."

"Truly? But did you not say that Sir Andrew is unable to be here?"

"That's right. He's...ah...um...he has urgent business dealings in Perth and asked me to take care of Skye in his stead."

"How very kind of you."

Philip gave her an oddly awkward glance as if he didn't believe he possessed an amiable bone in his body.

~

SITTING at Philip's writing table in Philip's bedchamber, Andrew dipped the tip of his quill into the inkpot, sighing as he started writing a list.

Eugenia not only loves roses, she loves all flowers and can distinguish one genus of rose from another.

She likes dogs and strolls along the beach. The lass particularly likes Skye because he is well-behaved (contrary to every negative word you have uttered about him). Also, I told her the dog was mine (Andrew's).

She is not the wilting wallflower you thought her to be. She merely chooses to remain reticent when in the presence of her overbearing mother and sister.

She is quite perceptive. I'd say far more so than you assumed. I think she's uncannily observant.

He rested the quill in the brass holder and read his notes. Andrew had thought this whole charade would be easy, but as soon as he left his brother's betrothed in the entrance hall, he headed straight for his twin's bedchamber which he'd opted to occupy to ensure there was no confusion between he and himself.

Good God, that even sounded ludicrous in his mind.

In less than an hour, he'd learned such a great deal about the lass, far more than Philip had ever let on. Moreover, if Andrew didn't start jotting down all the things he learned about Eugenia whilst he was impersonating his brother, Philip would be at an utter loss the first time he engaged the lass in conversation.

Sprawled in front of the hearth, Skye let out a sleepy grunt and opened his eyes.

"At least I made it clear that you do not belong to Philip. God forbid you have to move in with him. He detests dogs." Andrew patted his thigh, the cue for Skye to rise and come to his side. He ran his fingers through the deerhound's wiry fur. "Och, I had to tell the truth about you. Who kens, mayhap Eugenia will change Philip's mind about you canines, but I wouldna bank on it."

A soft knock sounded on the door. "Andrew?" asked a youthful female voice, decidedly that of his youngest sister, Modesty.

He turned in his chair. "What is it?"

She popped her head of flaming red curls around the timbers. "I have a question to ask you," she said, moving inside and perching on the settee like a proper young lady. Upon his arrival, he'd hardly had a chance to take a good look at her, but aside from the spray of freckles across the bridge of her nose, she looked as if she had grown into a woman since the last time he saw her. God save Britain, she even had sprouted bosoms.

Andrew ran a hand down his face, as he wondered how many slavering whelps he would be forced to fend off in her honor. "Pray tell, how old are you?"

"Sixteen." She twirled a red ringlet around her finger. "Soon I will be out."

"Imagine that," he mumbled dryly.

"Aye, and once I've found a match, Mama willna ken what to do with herself."

"I'm not certain about that, especially with all the grandchildren in the works." Andrew crossed his knees as well as his arms. "Now, tell me, what is this question you have to ask? Couldna it have waited until dinner?"

"Absolutely not." Modesty leaned forward and lowered her voice. "'Tis of a sensitive nature."

"Oh?"

"Aye. I want to ken exactly what is expected of me. All Marty said was to hold my tongue and call you Philip. Mind you, aside from wee James, I can tell you apart better than anyone in the family. He wears far too much pomade to temper his cowlick, though he is better at tying bows than you are."

"I didna realize that bow-tying was a critical necessity for elder brothers."

"Och, it certainly is." Modesty ran her hand over the red velvet of the settee. "So, *Philip*, what should I do if at tomorrow night's ball, I am dancing and my bow comes untied?"

"Back up a moment." Andrew's mouth grew dry. "Mama has planned a ball for *the morrow*?" Good God, he hadn't planned on dancing. What the devil? Mama always placed the balls on the last evening of any house party. Balls were the magnum opus. The final finality. To have one on the second evening was un-heard of!

"Aye, to commemorate the arrival of Prince Isidor." She hopped up, moved to his writing table, and tapped a sheet of paper resting on the corner. "Did you not read the Schedule of Events? Mama had one placed in everyone's bedchamber including mine."

Andrew shifted his attention to the agenda which he hadn't bothered to read. Indeed, it was entitled, "Schedule of Events."

"So, has your bow-tying improved in the past year?" Modesty asked.

"I can tie a bow as well as anyone. But where is Kitty? Can she not attend to your bows? Did she not come up with Charity and the earl? What about your lady's maid? I'd think at sixteen you have one, do you not?"

"My word, Andrew...I mean *Philip*, do you not ken anything? Charity and Harry decided that since wee Hyacinth is only one year of age, she is too young to travel, thus they sent their regrets. Mama has ap-pointed my lady's maid to Baroness Bedford and her daughters and that means I have to share with Grace." Modesty dramatically clapped a hand to her forehead. "Which will be a *disaster*. And alas, Kitty is still in Brix-ham, bored to tears, I'll wager."

If anyone could succinctly fill him in on the details of family matters, it was his youngest sister. "Are you still the best of friends?"

"Of course we are. Kitty and I are planning to spend our first Season together."

He leaned back in his chair and pretended to be shocked. "London will never be the same what with the sister of a duke and the sister of an earl joining forces."

Modesty laughed. "I believe you should dance with me on the morrow."

"Not allowed. I am your brother."

"But this is a private party, and Mama says you have no choice but to dance with me."

"Does she?"

"Aye. Furthermore, I think I ought not tell Miss Eugenia about how good Philip is at tying bows."

"But perhaps it might be best if you refrain from speaking to her at all."

Modesty patted her hand atop her chest and gaped. "How gauche, how utterly inhospitable."

"Well, I didna mean for you to ignore her—just find things to talk about that dunna include Philip, or me for that matter."

"Such as?"

"Interests? Embroidery? You do still have your pony, do you not?"

"My pony has been put to pasture." The lass flicked her red curls. "I'm riding a mare now."

"Well, then talk about the challenges of a new mare." Andrew moved to the sideboard and poured himself two fingers of MacGalloway whisky. "Talk about the food, the weather. What about the puffins? Are they nesting on the cliffs this summer?"

"Oh, aye. Grace and I rode out to the bluff and watched them just a sennight ago."

"See? There's plenty to discuss aside from me." Andrew sipped the excellent spirit distilled by his kin in the Scottish mountains. "Besides, if you stay nearby Grace, she never lacks for conversation—pray tell where is she now?"

Modesty drummed her fingers together, looking rather devious. "I imagine she's dressing Miss Harriet in sackcloth."

As Andrew tried his damnedest to hold in his laugh, the spirit burned the back of his nose. "'Tis that bad?" he asked, coughing, his eyes watering.

"Aye, ye ken Grace. When Miss Harriet told her that you had said *she* might help her find something suitable to wear for the ball because Prince Isidor would be in attendance, our sister turned utterly green." Modesty planted her hands on her belly and howled. "Och, you put a bee in her bonnet you did!"

"I thought it might be good for Grace to ken she isn't the only eligible lass here."

"Dunna try to delude me." Modesty drew in a deep breath as if trying to suppress giggles. "You did it to enrage Grace, and I for one thought it was capital. I could barely keep a straight face."

Andrew hid his smirk behind his glass. "You always were a handful. I see now that you're a wee bit older, you're cunning as well."

"Not anywhere near as devious as you, dear brother." She crossed the room and took the note he'd just written. "This is for Philip, is it not?"

"It is." Andrew snatched the paper from her fingers. "How else is he to change places without alerting Miss Eugenia?"

"Do you honestly think she willna notice the added pomade?"

"You are the only one who notices such a trivial thing—and dunna bring up the subject of pomade to *anyone*, not at least until Philip arrives."

"Verra well, brother, but the last item on your wee list does say the woman is observant. Mayhap you would be better chatting with her about anything rather than what Miss Eugenia likes and dislikes."

Before he could usher her out the door, it swung

open, revealing Grace's lovely, yet angry visage. "How dare you!"

Modesty gave a little wave as she slipped away. "I shall leave you now."

Andrew gaped at his middle sister. "Hardly the welcome I'd expect from a future princess."

She swept inside, her skirts brushing Andrew's ankles. "I *am* a future princess and do not forget it!" she said, sounding too English and very much like their mother. Grace had attended Northbourne Seminary for Young Ladies in the Cotswolds with the principal purpose of smiting her Scottish burr. "How could you tell Miss Harriet that the most eligible bachelor in Christendom would be here on the morrow?"

Andrew finished his whisky before he replied, "I did no such thing. I simply told her that Prince Isidor would be here. Miss Harriet compiled the rest of it on her own."

"Oh, dear brother, come now. You did far more than make mention of the prince. You told her to ask me for fashion advice—you practically insinuated that I'd be her damned lady's maid."

"Och, Grace, swearing doesna become you."

She stamped her foot. "I'll swear if I *damn* well please and when it *damn* well matters."

"Listen to me." Andrew took her by the shoulders as she stared at him with fury blazing in her eyes. Dear God, the lass had become a force to be reckoned with. If Isidor did win her hand, he would be a very lucky man. "You turned down how many proposals?"

"Ten. Do you have any idea the pressure placed upon women of the *ton*? I rejected ten very decent, highborn suitors because I kent I had Isidor on the verge of falling in love with me," she said, a hint of her

Scottish accent showing, despite her elite English education.

"I'm certain you did. Let me tell you, sister, your beauty surpasses that of every woman I've ever seen. You are the daughter of a duke. You are sophisticated and a graduate of the finest finishing school in all of Britain. Am I right?"

Grace nodded, the corners of her lips tight.

"Then you have absolutely nothing to fear from a plain daughter of a baron who hasna even experienced her first Season." Andrew pulled her into a brotherly embrace. "Dote on the wee imp for a time. Let her wear one of your superior gowns and play the gracious hostess I ken you to be."

Heaving an enormous sigh, Grace hugged him back. "You're right."

"Of course I am."

Andrew led his sister to the door and ushered her out. Though Grace was an iconic beauty with crystal blue eyes, blonde tresses, and a figure that filled a gown in a way that turned grown men into fools, she didn't have the unfettered, wholesome beauty he'd observed from Eugenia Radcliffe this afternoon. The two women were each lovely in their own right, but very different in most every other way. Grace had been molded into a woman who personified everything polite society held dear. On the complete opposite end of the spectrum, Eugenia seemed not to care an iota about putting on airs and acting to impress her betters. A fact which Andrew found quite refreshing.

Indeed, Philip had either chosen wisely, or he was damned lucky. Moreover, 'twas a good thing Eugenia was engaged to be married, else, Isidor might find he truly has a difficult decision to make.

4

"A very good morning to you all," said the Dowager Duchess of Dunscaby from her place at the center of the enormous dining table lined with people, many of them MacGalloway family members to whom Eugenia had been introduced. There were also several others she didn't yet know.

After setting her spoon aside, she dabbed her lips with her serviette. Her Grace appeared to be younger than her years. And though she moved with an unmistakable regal air, the dowager's expression always seemed pleasant and cordial as if she made it her purpose in life to be fair to everyone no matter their station.

"As you are all aware, we are expecting Prince Isidor to arrive today and we presently have carriages waiting at the pier in John o'Groats. Dunscaby has also stationed a rider at the lighthouse who, as soon as the ship is spotted, will immediately gallop to the castle and inform us."

Across the table from Eugenia, Lady Grace clasped her hands and absolutely glowed with happiness while murmurs of excitement swelled around the table.

The dowager used a spoon to tap a crystal glass. "If I might continue, please."

The hall once again grew silent while liveried footmen scurried about, performing their duties.

"Before his arrival, we shall gather in the great hall to greet His Highness. And that being said, if you have consulted with your schedules, you might have noticed that we will be playing lawn bowls directly after breakfast, and might I add the weather has behaved perfectly for our—"

"I beg your pardon, Mama," said Lady Grace. "But Miss Harriet and I cannot possibly idle away the morning playing lawn bowls. We have to find the perfect gown for the ball, and it obviously will need alterations."

Harriet, who was a tad fuller-figured than Her Ladyship as well as a few inches shorter, gave her sister a nudge. "I will be the belle of the ball," she whispered.

Eugenia couldn't help her snort and quickly raised the serviette, feigning a cough. Poor Harriet was so anxious for her debut, she seemed to have overlooked the fact that Grace was not only a stunning beauty with impeccable breeding, she was still unwed, even though only yesterday she had commented that Her Ladyship had reportedly turned down dozens of marriage proposals. Near the far end of the table, Sir Philip caught Eugenia's eye and they both exchanged subtle yet knowing smiles.

"Alas, I'm afraid Julia and I have promised James and Lily a jaunt to John o'Groats to see their Uncle Gibb's ship," said the duke who sat at the head of the table, smiling at his wife, Julia all the way down at the far end. It was a wonder they didn't need opera lorgnettes to see each other.

This morning, Eugenia's lady's maid had announced that Sir Gibb and his wife Lady Isabella had sailed up from their home near Musselburgh on the Firth of Forth and had arrived last evening. The couple had been introduced before breakfast and were sitting along the table near the baroness.

"My own children?" The dowager patted her chest, looking to her eldest son. "Goodness, Martin, both you and Grace have been in possession of the schedule of events for a fortnight."

"Aye," the duke agreed. "But that was afore Gibb and Isabella arrived. And your grandchildren were absolutely elated when their uncle offered a private tour of his eighteen-gun barque."

"Mama," said Sir Philip. "Mayhap we can play lawn bowls another day? After all, your excellently planned schedule does have the grand ball listed for this verra evening. Are there not a host of last-minute preparations you must see to?"

"Well, I wasn't going to be playing lawn bowls myself." The dowager offered a smile to Eugenia's mother, who most definitely would not be playing lawn bowls either, she'd said as much above stairs before they'd come down to break their fast. "But there are still plenty of people in attendance who—"

The duke raised a solitary finger, commanding as it was. "Forgive me, Mama, but I forgot to mention that Laird Buchanan will be accompanying us on the ship's tour."

Eugenia glanced down the table at the imposing, dark-haired Highland laird. The man seemed a tad rough around the edges as compared to the MacGalloways. He, too, carried weapons on his belt, but when he'd been introduced prior to being led into the dining hall, she got the impression that the man's weapons weren't for show. He gave Dunscaby a nod, holding up a fork speared with sausage, blood pudding, and egg.

"Also, I've promised a shell-finding excursion to my betrothed," added Philip. "And since the weather is fine, perhaps this might be the perfect day for such an adventure."

Eugenia busied herself with buttering a slice of toast, trying desperately to quash the swarm of butterflies that suddenly started flitting in the pit of her stomach. She wasn't particularly fond of lawn bowls because she never won. But more importantly, Philip had remembered his promise to take her down to the shore. *What a gentleman he is. How so very refreshing.*

"I'll wager it willna bet this sunny again for a fortnight," Modesty agreed. "You ought to see the puffins too."

"Would you like to act as our chaperone?" Sir Philip asked, glancing to the youngest MacGalloway.

"Me?"

Before Sir Philip could reply, the dowager gracefully lowered herself to her seat. "Well, I do believe it is decided. We shall all enjoy a free morning, but I expect *everyone* to be in the hall when Prince Isidor arrives. And that includes you, Martin."

"Agreed," The duke bowed his head to his mother. "We most likely will encounter His Highness at the pier, and if so, we shall give him a right royal escort to the castle."

~

"UNCLE ANDREEEW!" cried four-year-old James as he dashed into the entrance hall.

Andrew scooped the lad into his arms and gave him a spin while Skye looked on. "My word laddie, you are enormous," he said, throwing a panicked glance at his brother who was leading his wife and two-year-old Lily. "Mayhap it might be best to keep the wee ones in the nursery until my twin arrives."

Martin looked toward the grand staircase. "The carriage is waiting, but this is James and Lily's home. It is up to you to steer clear of them."

"But I want you to see my new toy soldiers." James tapped Andrew's brooch. "One even has a musket that he can raise up and down."

"And another rides a horse," added Her Grace who had proven to be a fabulous mother.

"'Tis a stallion," James replied, squirming out of Andrew's arms and scratching the dog behind the ears. "Da said so."

Modesty pattered down the stairs. "Och, thank heavens, you havena taken your leave."

"As soon as—och, there you are, Buchanan." Martin stepped forward and shook the hand of the laird who theoretically didn't exist, aside from appearances at private affairs such as this. After the '45, The Buchanan clan had been struck down by the crown and forced into hiding in the Highlands. Now more than seventy years on, few knew of their existence. Nevertheless, the Buchanans and the MacGalloways had shared bordering lands near Loch Tulla for hundreds of years and were fast allies.

"A moment," said Andrew, looking to Modesty. "Are you planning to go to the pier? I thought you were accompanying me and Miss Radcliffe to the beach."

"And miss a chance to see Isidor before Grace?" Modesty asked, a bit of deviousness dancing in her eyes.

Martin took his hat and gloves from Giles. "We'd

best make haste. Gibb and Isabella have already departed. And you ken how impatient the captain is."

"It will do him good to wait," said Julia.

"It seems everyone forgot about my need for a chaperone." Andrew had carefully planned this charade, and it definitely included an escort at all times, not that he in any way intended to take advantage of Miss Eugenia. Engaging a chaperone was a formality for her sake. "Modesty. Please, you promised to accompany us at breakfast."

"I did no such thing." Modesty donned her traveling bonnet. "Do you not recall? Before I could utter a reply, Mama continued with her discourse."

Julia patted Andrew's shoulder. "You're already engaged to the young lady, *Sir Philip*. I do believe it will not create any scandal whatsoever if you escort your betrothed down to the beach unchaperoned."

Wee James tugged on his mother's skirt. "But Mama, he's nay—"

"Wheesht!" said Martin, lifting his son into his arms and leading his family out the door as if he were a common father and weren't the most powerful duke in Scotland.

Andrew released a pent-up breath while giving Skye a pat. Dear God, James was only four years of age and far too perceptive for his own good. He would have to stay far away from the children until Philip arrived. The way things were progressing, his twin had best make an appearance sooner than later. What if Eugenia had been in the hall when James had run across the floor hollering Andrew's name?

I would have corrected him. After all, I anticipated being mistaken for myself. It happens often enough—not mistaken for myself, but for my brother.

To the sound of soft footsteps, he turned, his gaze

shifting to the landing. Eugenia stood there for a moment, her hand on the banister. Sunbeams cast a hazy glow from the window above, making her blonde locks shimmer like a halo. She'd changed since breakfast, now wearing a blue gown beneath a lacy pelisse —simple yet elegant.

Andrew raised his palm and beckoned her. "You are radiant, my dear."

He adored her unfettered smile as she donned her bonnet and tied it beneath her chin while descending the remaining stairs. Wagging his tail, Skye greeted her intimately, rubbing his wiry fur along her leg. Andrew couldn't deny his pang of jealousy. If only he were a dog, he might enjoy brushing up against and flirting with the lovely lass.

But he wasn't a dog. He was a damned imposter playacting a part to save his dear brother's arse. Now he had naught but to ignore the miserable palpitations of his heart and every single one of Miss Radcliffe's enticing wiles.

"Am I late?" she asked, a furrow forming between her delicately arched eyebrows.

"Not at all." Andrew bowed. "The duke and his family just left for John o'Groats. Had you been here three minutes ago, the hall was agog with wee James and Lily dashing about."

"Goodness, I'm sorry I missed the excitement. I love young children." Eugenia glanced from wall to wall. "And Lady Modesty? Will she be accompanying us?"

Feeling even more like a scoundrel since he wasn't truly engaged to the lass, Andrew focused on Skye and ran his hand along the dog's back. "It seems this fella will have to keep his eye on me."

She chuckled, the sound raising his spirits considerably. "I daresay I cannot see you as anything but a gentleman."

It was a good thing Miss Eugenia had been nowhere near St. Andrews during his university days. It was an undergraduate's rite of passage to outdo every one of his classmates in roguishness. If being a rake had been a course of study, Andrew would have received top marks. Indeed, it was during his university years when he'd become an exceptional connoisseur of female breasts.

But presently he had no choice but to be on his best behavior. Though it was a crime not to admire Miss Eugenia's breasts, he refused to allow himself an iota of indulgence.

Once out of doors, he did his best to eyeball the intense greens of the scenery, dotted with splashes of violet, white, and red flowers. Acting with utmost control, he led the lady out toward the edge of the bluff with Skye walking at heel, wagging his tail as if he were thrilled to be acting chaperone. The rising and falling rush of the sea swelled through the air as they neared the white post which marked the beginning of the trail.

The lass followed Skye around the bend northward. Andrew tugged her back. "That's the path to John o'Groats. Come behind Skye!"

"Truly?" she asked as the dog came to heel. "I thought the road northward from the castle went to the village."

"It does. This wee path skirts around the northernmost point of Scotland's mainland, and meanders along the coast until it ends at John o' Groats."

"Is it a great deal farther?"

"Not a great deal. 'Tis a pleasant walk, actually. Mayhap a mile or two."

As soon as they reached the bluff, the wind whooshed beneath Andrew's kilt, bringing with it a heady saltiness as well as the calls of the seabirds, diving for herring and sprat, swiftly taking their feasts back to the myriad of nests pockmarking the craggy cliffs.

Eugenia pointed to a bird in flight. "Is that a puffin?" she asked, her voice nearly as filled with youthful excitement as James' had been in the hall.

Andrew shaded his eyes with his hand, observing the graceful glide of the black bird with white markings on its wings. "'Tis a guillemot. They are always here in droves throughout spring and summer." Squinting, he scanned the sky until he saw one of the wee puffins flitting comically and diving into the surf. He wrapped an arm around Eugenia's shoulders and pointed. "There. He's just about to come up with his catch—if he's successful."

"Oh, look!" She clapped. "*Ooo, ah,* he's so small."

"Aye, puffins are not large. Highlanders call them the clowns of the sea on account of their bright orange bills and webbed feet. They flit more than fly, but make no bones about it, they are good fishermen."

She laughed, watching the bird head for the cliffs. "He does flit. He's adorable!"

Beside the post, Skye turned in a circle and yowled excitedly. Andrew gave the dog a nod and he disappeared down the trail.

"Skye seems anxious to comb the beach," said Eugenia.

"He loves galloping through the surf. Though the wee beasty doesna enjoy the bath afterward, however."

"Do you give him a bath yourself?"

"You must be jesting. It is far too much fun to

watch the lads in the stables wrestle with him." Andrew offered his hand. "Are you ready?"

She placed her fingers in his palm and craned her neck to peer out over the edge. "Goodness, it is a long way down. And steep."

"You're nay afraid of heights are you?"

She cringed, stepping away from the bluff. "Perhaps a little."

"Then keep a firm grip on my hand and dunna look down."

"All right," she said, squeezing his fingers so tight, Andrew's eyes watered.

"The path zigzags. This is the steepest section," he said, taking it as slowly as possible given he usually sprinted downward, catching himself on the rail at the first hairpin curve. "Once we get to the initial bend, the slope is far easier to negotiate."

Though it was a sunny morn, the cliffs were east-facing and the ground was still moist. The footing wasn't easy for Andrew, let alone a woman wearing delicate slippers. The first time Eugenia slipped, he merely urged her closer, but the second time, he wrapped his arm around her waist. "Hold on to me and I'll keep you steady."

She did as he asked, her fingers digging into his flank, as if holding on for her very life. "I'm afraid I am awfully clumsy."

"Not at all, lass." As Andrew glanced downward, she slid a foot forward and a tiny satin slipper peeked from beneath her gown. "Did you bring a pair of sturdy boots from Bedford?"

She tightened her grip, not painfully, but the woman held fast, leaning into him, somehow increasing his need to protect her. "Forgive me, but I didn't realize I'd need boots."

"Not to worry, only a few more paces and you'll be able to release me."

"Unfortunate."

The single word was uttered so softly, Andrew couldn't help but glance at her face. She wasn't looking at the path but smiling up at him—the length her body pressed against him as well. An unignorable soft breast plied his ribcage. And, heaven help him, he wanted nothing more than to stop right there and sample those pert little lips with a kiss.

Damnation, this is exactly why we needed a bloody chaperone.

They reached the hairpin curve none too soon. Andrew snapped his arm away as if he'd been burned.

With a gasp, Eugenia drew her hands beneath her chin. "Is all well? Have I done something in error?"

"Of course not." Andrew straightened his belt and spotted Skye. "See there. The laddie's splashing through the waves already."

"Oh, my. It does look rather fun." She gave him a mischievous grin—a smile so tempting, he'd never imagined shy Eugenia Radcliffe capable of such wiles. "Do you think it would be awfully scandalous if we joined him?"

Andrew threw his head back and roared with laughter while his next notation formed in his head—one sure to incite Philip's ire. "It isna a scandal if no one observes."

"I did not realize you had such a sense of adventure, sir." Giggling, the woman took her skirts in hand and negotiated the remaining path without assistance. And once she reached the beach covered with soft stones and sand, she dashed to the water's edge.

"You'd best remove your slippers and stockings,"

Andrew said, kicking off his boots, flashes, and rolling down his hose.

"Slippers, yes. But my stockings? What if someone sees us?"

Andrew gestured up to the top of the bluff. "Do you think a person two hundred feet up will be able to tell if you're wearing them or not? Furthermore, if you were wading through the water in your stockings, wouldna they think you're a wee bit silly?" He took her hand and led her to a large piece of driftwood. "Sit here and allow me to assist."

"You?"

Modesty had asserted Philip to be better at tying bows, but little did she know that Andrew had perfected the art of untying them. "Do you think I canna let loose a garter?"

As Eugenia looked back toward the path, Andrew followed her gaze as well. Except he was about to smack his head with the heel of his hand. How the devil had he ended up in this position, kneeling before Philip's bride-to-be, about to slide his fingers beneath the hem of her dress?

He dropped his hands to his sides. "Forgive me. I am being audacious. Would you prefer to remove your stockings yourself?"

When she met his gaze, she did so with a dark smolder in those fathomless blue eyes. The wee imp scraped her teeth over her bottom lip and inched her bloody hem upward. "If it pleases you, sir, by all means, do remove them."

Holy hellfire and brimstone. Andrew gulped, ever so grateful they were out presently of sight from the top of the bluff. Eugenia had the shapeliest ankles he'd ever seen in his life. His fingers trembled as he wrapped them around her slender calf and moved his hand upward—warm flesh, so very soft and feminine. Ever so slowly, he searched for the ribbon, inching higher, the fragrance of lavender and woman enveloping him, calling to him, making him breathe more deeply. He cupped his fingers over her knee and smiled, trying not to be charming or alluring, but wanting her to notice him all the same.

Wanting her to like him.

Wanting her to boldly lean forward and kiss him.

After all, his face was the mirror image of Philip's. If she found him pleasing to the eye, she'd do so with Andrew's brother.

As her lips parted, he found the silk ribbon just above her knee and tugged open the bow, then ever so slowly he rolled down her stocking. "Now that wasna too terribly unpleasant, was it?"

She blushed adorably. "Would I be horribly shameless if I said the experience was most stirring to the blood?"

Dear God, he ought to say yes. He ought to apologize and tell her to remove the left on her own. But he was supposed to be her intended. He was supposed to woo her. True, Philip had forbidden Andrew from kissing Eugenia, but he hadn't warned him off stocking removal. After all, what did his twin expect? Andrew couldn't exactly rebuff her. Not when he had come to Stack Castle for the sole reason of spending time with the lass.

Still, he was too damned close to overstepping his bounds if he hadn't done so already. With his own internal admonishment, Andrew opted to remove the second stocking with as much hasty indifference as possible.

Of course, the change in his demeanor brought on

a perplexed frown from the woman, but it couldn't be helped.

Andrew stood and offered his hand. "The North Sea awaits, my love." Hopefully the endearment assuaged any misgivings she may have entertained.

Excitement flashed through her eyes as she allowed him to help her up, then gathered her skirts and ran on the balls of her feet straight into the white foam of the surf rushing onto the shore. "Oh, my it is so cold!"

Following, Andrew marched in straight to his knees. "There's nothing better than Scotland's brisk water."

Not straying from the shallow, frothy surf, Eugenia kicked and splashed as if she'd never had so much freedom. She laughed aloud as she danced on her toes, ever so careful not to douse her hem. "Do you prefer the sea or one of the lakes I've heard so much about?"

"Lochs. In Scotland they are lochs." As a wave came rolling in, he hastened back to keep the hem of his kilt from being doused. "And there is nothing better than an icy dip in Loch Tulla in summer. Her brisk mountain water will turn a lad into a man for certain."

"It sounds like a rite of passage."

"Skye!" he shouted at the dog before answering. "Bloody oath it is. All MacGalloway men swim the Tulla while snow still crests the surrounding mountains."

"And you didn't catch influenza?"

"On the contrary. My ancestors believed icy lochs have healing powers, and I believe they might have been on to something." Ahead, Skye had stopped when he was called, but obviously had decided Andrew hadn't been serious and disappeared behind one of the Duncansby stacks. "Skye, ye wee beasty, come behind!"

That did the trick, the dog bounded through the water, a canine smile fixed on his face, his tongue lolling to the side.

Still ankle-deep in the water, Eugenia moved toward the deerhound. "He loves it here."

Andrew chuckled, following her. "If given the opportunity to drench himself in the surf, or wallow in mud, or roll in the foul-smelling remains of any rotting creature, he'll be utterly rapt." He expected the dog to come to heel, but when Eugenia clapped her hands, Skye changed tack his eyes wide like a crazed buffoon. "Nooooo!" Andrew shouted, breaking into a run while the deerhound bounded toward the lass, planting his paws on her shoulders with a happy yowl.

"O-o-oh!" she cried, just missing Andrew's outstretched hands, falling backward with a dunking splash, exactly when an enormous wave crashed into the shore.

"Eugenia!" he bellowed, tripping on a boulder as he stooped to help her. "Are you hurt?"

5

Pain knifed through Eugenia's backside but when she shifted her gaze up to Philip's eyes, her entire perspective changed. The concern etched upon his face was enough to ease the ache and replace it with a new, thrilling warmth in her heart. The man was stupendously beautiful, and there she sat, sand creeping under her skirts and up her legs with the crest of every drenching wave. Everything was wet, even the straw brim of her bonnet drooped, the curls once framing her face were now straight, plastered to her face, and dripping. *Could I be any less graceful?*

But the Highlander had asked her a question and by the worried expression crinkling his brow, she'd best answer. "Um...I do believe I've landed on a rather unforgiving stone." Skye licked her face and wagged his tail as she scooted off the pointy rock. "My heavens, your *wee beasty* is rather powerful, is he not?"

Andrew gave the dog a scowl. "Naughty laddie. Ye dunna go jumping on ladies!"

"Please do not chide him. I urged Skye to run to me. I just didn't realize how exuberantly he'd do so."

"Evidently he needs to learn some manners where

ladies are concerned." Philip offered his hand. "Are you able to stand, lass?"

She took just a moment to savor his Scottish brogue. "I think so," she said, letting him help her up. Pain shot through her buttock, and before she could stop herself, she hissed through her teeth. "Oof. Mayhap I ought to rest for a moment."

"Of course." Philip gestured to the driftwood log where they'd left their shoes. "Allow me to assist you."

"Thank you." Eugenia leaned on him so heavily, the Highlander bore the majority of her weight.

"Where does it hurt most?" he asked, sounding worried.

She cringed at the horror of admitting the exact location of her injury. In fact, her entire body tensed and curled inward in a fleeting attempt to make herself disappear. "I cannot say."

"You canna say or you dunna *want* to say?"

She glanced over her shoulder, downward to her throbbing behind. "Please, it is a delicate matter."

Philip gave her a pointed stare as if to say there was nothing on this earth that could baffle him. Then he shifted his gaze to her backside. "Good Lord, you've a tear in your skirts, lass." He moved behind her and bent down, giving her torn dress a much too familiar examination even if he was her betrothed. "You're bleeding as well."

Eugenia scooted aside. "'Tis just a bruise."

"Nay." He straightened. "Did you not hear me? Your right buttock is bleeding, my...er ...love."

She spun and faced him, moving her hands behind her back. "We mustn't speak of such things. Due to my clumsy nature, I took a spill onto my backside, and all will be forgotten as soon as I can return to my bedchamber and don a fresh gown."

By the twist to his lips, he wasn't convinced. "Can you sit?"

She glanced to the driftwood log and bit her lip. "I would prefer not to at the moment." Then she looked up to the top of the bluff, wondering how she was going to scale the long zigzagging path. "I believe it would benefit the dog a great deal if you asked Sir Andrew to introduce Skye to more ladies."

Philip's brows drew together and she could have sworn his expression was baffled, but only for a second. Within the blink of an eye, he nodded profusely. "I shall take it up with my brother at my first opportunity."

No sooner had Eugenia decided she could not possibly endure more humiliation when she brushed her fingers down the length of her day gown and realized the Holland cloth was not only soaking wet, it was clinging to her body. She tugged her skirts and flapped them only to have her teeth start chattering.

"You've a chill, lass," said Philip, removing his doublet and placing it over her shoulders.

As she pulled the coat around her, Eugenia turned her nose toward the soft collar. It smelled of spice and Philip and it warmed her inside and out. If only she were dry and they could stay on the beach for the duration of the day—but Prince Isidor would be here anon. And engaged or not, there would be an uproarious scandal if the two of them didn't make an appearance in the great hall.

"You're troubled," he said taking her hand between his warm palms.

She couldn't meet his gaze. "Look at me. The prince will arrive soon and I'm an utter mess."

"I wouldna say *utter*."

"I beg your pardon? I'm dripping wet, my dress is

torn, not to mention bloody. If my mother sees me return to the castle in such a state, she will accuse me of unmitigated clumsiness."

Stepping forward, Philip surrounded her in his arms—strong, comforting, masculine, laced with a hint of bergamot and spice. If only she could melt into him. By God's grace, the man was unbelievably kind and caring—so different than she had assumed him to be. Eugenia found it impossible not to lean into his warmth and rest her head against this chest, droopy bonnet and all. "Allow me to say, I'll be the first to attest that Skye is entirely at fault. But moreover, there's no need for your mother to see you until you've had a chance to change."

"But everyone will be able to see us as soon as we reach the top of the bluff."

"Nay, lass, that's where you're wrong." He rubbed his hand up and down her back, his strong hand ever so soothing. Heaven help her, she craved more. If only she could be so bold as to ask him for more. Eugenia dared to glance upward until her gaze met his lips, perfectly formed with the bottom a bit fuller than the top. A hint of stubble surrounded his mouth—masculine and ever so tempting. "'Tis an old castle—if ye dunna want to be seen, you willna be. My brothers and I used to slip down to the shore unawares by way of a secret passageway."

Eugenia swallowed back her urge to rise up on her toes and kiss him. Of course, she didn't want her first kiss to be when she was looking like a drowned waif and practically shivering to her toes. *A passageway, did he say?* "Goodness, this sounds like the start of a mystery novel." Deciding that mentioning she might presently be receptive to a kiss would constitute a critical error, she looked to the path. "Perhaps we ought to start back."

His hand slid down the length of her arms and grasped her fingers. "Do you feel as if you are able?"

Eugenia stammered while tingles skittered to her elbows, shoulders, and up both sides of her neck. No one had ever touched her thus—with such caring, such compassion, such (dare she think it) ardor. It figured. There she stood wearing soaking wet, sand-encrusted clothing while the man she had dreamed about for the past three years, two months and six days was looking at her as if she weren't a mess, but beautiful and worthy of his affection.

"I've no choice but to be," she replied with confidence she did not feel.

"Everyone has choices, lass."

Before she could refute his statement, Philip swept her into his arms and marched along the beach.

"Oh no, you cannot possibly carry me all the way up that horrible path. You'll collapse."

His gaze slashed to her face, darker now than it had been, making her blood thrum. "My dear lady, do you realize, you have just issued me a challenge I cannot possibly refuse?"

"I have?" she squeaked.

"Aye," he replied without a hint of strain in his voice, though if Philip managed to carry her all the way to the top, he'd most likely collapse from exhaustion.

~

SKYE BOUNDED AHEAD, his gait clearly one of a dog heading for a wee morsel at the castle's kitchen. Andrew didn't try to call him back, especially since once they crested the bluff, he needed to avoid a spectacle.

When he started the climb, Eugenia posed no strain whatsoever. After all, Andrew regularly challenged the laborers at the mill, hefting enormous bolts of MacGalloway cloth onto river wherries bound for trade across Britain and Europe. However, by the time he reached the portion of the trail with the steep slope, he was not only sucking in gasps of air, perspiration streamed into his eyes.

Eugenia placed a soothing palm on his chest. "You cannot possibly carry me the rest of the way. It is far too steep."

Andrew stopped for a moment to catch his breath and resituate his arms a tad. "Are you telling me what I can and canna do afore we are even wed?"

In such a short amount of time, he'd grown so accustomed to talking to her as if she were really his intended. Oddly, he had become quite comfortable with the idea.

A fact he must immediately excise from his mind.

Just as soon as he spirited her safely inside the castle.

And once he had safely delivered Eugenia to her bedchamber, he would take a moment of solitude and write down all the observations he'd made this day so that he could give the list to Philip. Once he did so, it would be up to his brother to either tell the truth or carry on with the ruse. Nonetheless, Andrew could scarcely wait to ride away from Stack Castle as fast as his horse could carry him.

He glanced at Eugenia's face—angelic, her blue eyes matching the hue of the sky. The lass truly embodied everything he'd ever admired in a woman. And she thought herself clumsy and plain? She moved like a doe, light on her feet, head carried high, slender limbs, a body...

God on the bloody cross, she's going to be my sister-in-law! I cannot admire her figure.

It did not escape his notice when down on the beach she'd fixated upon his lips. There was only one thing a woman wanted when she so studiously examined a man's lips.

Worse, he'd wanted to kiss her with every fiber of his body. Andrew had not been hewn from iron and stone. He was flesh and blood with a weakness for the fairer sex—a fact well known by his twin.

This whole charade had been a terrible idea. Andrew never should have accepted the wager. In fact, he hadn't. Philip had cajoled him, and now there he was, carrying his brother's intended up an impossible slope while his mind was consumed with all the reasons why he must not kiss her.

What did she taste like? Would she melt in his arms as their lips met? An innocent, she most likely would be timid at first—need a wee bit of coaxing, but once she caught on, the woman would turn into a seductress—a stunning, radiant, luscious hellcat.

Andrew moaned with the stirring of his blood.

Pain.

He must focus on the straining of his arms and the trembling of his tired thighs.

He gritted his molars and stepped up his pace, all but running, digging the balls of his feet into the soft soil until he arrived at the top. "Here we are," he growled, fairly out of breath.

An enormous oak tree hid them from view of the castle windows. Andrew carefully set Eugenia on her feet. "How are you feeling now, my love?"

She smoothed her hands down her soggy, sand encrusted skirts. "Much better, thank you."

He didn't believe a word. No one fell on a rock so hard they ripped their clothing and bled through layers of petticoats and fine muslin cloth. She'd be sore for days. "Take a few steps and see how you go," he urged.

Her lips pursed but she gave a nod and managed not to limp too much. "See?" She raised her chin triumphantly, though the flopping of her bonnet's brim and the disheveled state of her ringlets detracted from her attempt at bravery. "I'll be fine in a day or two."

Unfortunately, the not so curly ringlets plastered to her skin reminded Andrew far too much of a woman who had been thoroughly bedded, and not enough of the adorable, prim woman with whom he'd set out this morn.

"Verra well, I'll make a torch," he gruffly barked, using his dirk to hack off a thick green branch, and fashioning it into a two-foot-long rod. Then he rolled the tip in the pitch oozing from the tree where he'd removed the branch. "This ought to provide enough light to take us from one end of the passageway to the other."

"Amazing. I've never seen that done before."

"The making of a torch?"

"Exactly. All this time I've been wondering why you carry knives either side of your purse."

"'Tis a sporran. Not a purse." He leveled his gaze at her to ensure she understood. "And I carry a *sgian dubh* and a dirk—both Highland blades. The smaller is for cutting wee things like an apple or block of cheese." He sheathed his dirk. "This one is deadlier. Aside from making torches, 'tis for fighting in close proximity."

"Oh my." Her bright eyes filled with inquisitiveness. "Have you ever used it for such a thing?"

"Me da, the late Duke of Dunscaby made certain all his sons could wield a deadly dirk. But nay, I've not been called upon to kill a man be it with a dirk or broadsword or dueling pistol."

"Thank heavens."

"I suppose. Though I oft thought about leaving university and joining Wellington against Napoleon."

"But you did not?"

"Phil...um...my brother convinced me not to go, though Gibb, second to Martin, saw a great deal of action in the Navy." Andrew turned away and pretended to examine the torch he'd made. Damnation, he'd nearly erred and forgotten his own bloody ruse.

"Well, I for one am very glad that you didn't go off to war."

He didn't look at her. "Why?"

"Because you could have been killed."

At least someone was happy that he was alive... even though the lass thought him to be Philip. He took her by the hand. "Come, the entrance to the passage is behind the thicket."

"Do many people use it?"

"Not in the modern age. It was a crucial supply route to the castle during the Middle Ages when Scottish *birlinns* sailed these seas. Fortunately, our shores have not been invaded for centuries. But it was awfully fun for us lads when we were growing up. We could slip away from our lessons without the schoolmaster ever knowing where the devil we'd gone off to."

Andrew stopped outside the door to the tunnel. It wasn't as large as he remembered and the timbers appeared to be the worse for wear. "Here we are." He pulled on the latch, only to have it give way, leaving the door hanging from one hinge. Casting the handle aside, he tore off the remainder of the rotten wood. "I'll have to ask Marty to send out a carpenter."

Eugenia peered around him. "It looks haunted."

"Would you prefer to enter through the kitchens?"

A mischievous expression made the lass look adorable. "And miss the adventure? Absolutely not."

Andrew chuckled. He liked a woman who relished a challenge, who was amenable to leaving her parlor and her teacup and her embroidery and replacing those activities with something far more diverting.

He bit his bottom lip. *I am not going to allow myself to think about where else I might like her to be diverted because I am to become her brother-in-law.*

"Please hold this," he said, handing her the torch, then pulling a flint from his sporran.

"What all do you keep in there?"

"This and that." He gave her a wink as he unsheathed his dirk and set to making a spark and lighting the pitch. "Mostly coin."

Once the flame took, he removed the torch from her fingers and brandished it through the doorway, revealing hundreds of spider webs. Behind him, Eugenia gasped. "I'd forgotten about the spiders. Are you certain you'd prefer this route?"

"I'll be fine as long as I can hold your hand and your torch doesn't extinguish."

Andrew glanced to the flickering flame before gripping her hand. "Then we'd best make haste—that is if you're able."

"I'll just close my eyes and bear it."

"Verra well." He started in, waving the torch to and fro, clearing the webs as they made their way forward.

"Applying a right- and left-hand pearl and using ten bobbins..."

Andrew strengthened his grip on Eugenia's hand, though he didn't dare look back for fear of being encapsulated by a sticky web. "I beg your pardon?"

"'Tis a lace pattern. Reciting it is calming to my nerves."

"I'll take your word for it then."

"...turn to the plain edge, and in doing this, do not omit twisting the outside picot three times at the first stitch..."

She might as well have been speaking Greek, though if it kept her from hysterics, he was content to have her continue. If Grace or even Modesty were with him, they'd be hysterical for certain. Truth be told, Andrew didn't much care for the darkness or the moisture oozing down the walls in trails of green slime.

Suddenly, a spurt of water spewing from the wall doused the torch. "Are your eyes still closed?" he asked, unable to see past his nose, though there seemed to be a wee spring presently running onto his shoulder.

"Yes."

He led her around the water. "Then keep them thus."

"Why?"

"I didna use enough pitch."

"Oh dear," she squeaked, a tad of panic in her voice.

"Not to worry. As long as we move forward, we'll reach the cellar door in no time."

"Cellar?"

He gingerly proceeded, waiving the stick back and forth, praying he cleared most of the cobwebs. "Aye, the tunnel leads to the old storage cellars under the castle, of course."

"Are we nearly there?"

He had no idea. "Aye. Just a few more paces."

Andrew found the door when his stick scraped across it. "Here we are," he said, releasing her hand and running his fingers along the cobweb shrouded door until he found the latch. The first time he pulled on it, the damned thing didn't budge, but after pounding it with the butt of his dirk, he managed to wedge the door open far enough to slip through.

A sliver of light shone from the corridor, thank God. He reached for Eugenia's hand and tugged her inside. "The worst is over."

"And we weren't accosted by a single spirit," she said, astonishingly still in good humor after all she'd endured since Skye knocked her to her backside.

"Do you believe in ghosts?"

"Not really, though they're awfully diverting in books."

He led her through the labyrinth of cellars to the wheeled stairwell which was seldom used by anyone aside from the servants. "You read horror novels?"

"Sometimes. It depends on what is available in the Bedford library. 'Tis rather provincial, mind you, nothing like the library in London."

Andrew started up the stairs, the stone worn down by centuries of use. "I'd think not."

"Do you like to read?"

"For enjoyment?" he asked.

"Yes. Novels. Stories where good overcomes evil, where dashing young men fall in love with industrious women."

"Why are the men dashing and the women industrious?"

"Because I prefer an energetic and hard-working heroine as opposed to a simpering waif."

He stopped at the landing which led to the third-floor guest chambers. "Someone like yourself I'd venture?"

She tilted her face upward, her eyes catching the light from the window above. "I'd like to think I'm strong."

Despite his constant internal admonishment, Andrew's gaze slid to the woman's lips. Her mouth was pert and ripe and asking to be kissed. He dipped his head, nearing, his heart thrumming. With his next blink he was hit with a moment of sanity and stopped himself before he did something he'd regret. "After today, I dub you adventurous and brave."

"Truly?" she asked, not sounding convinced.

"After you soldiered on even though you were wounded? After you followed me into a spiderweb-infested tunnel, reciting lace patterns?"

Her eyes brightened, those delicate eyebrows arching. "It was rather frightening, was it not?"

"'Tis quite possibly the most dauntingly terrifying passageway Stack Castle has to offer."

"If there's one more terrifying, I think I'd rather give it a pass."

Chuckling, Andrew couldn't help but kiss her cheek. Feminine skin softer than silk. The fragrance of lavender mixed with a hint of the sea. All accompanied by a womanly sigh enticing enough to make his loins stir.

God save him.

I am utterly daft. A cad. Nothing but a dupe for the duke and my twin brother.

Andrew jolted, straightening his spine, and stepping away. He gestured toward the door. "You'll find your bedchamber right through there."

Bewilderment shadowed those lovely blues. "Oh."

She reached for the latch. "Thank you. I suppose I'd best change quickly before the prince arrives."

6

"**P**rince Isidor scarcely gave me a glance!" bemoaned Harriet, draped across the settee in Mama's bedchamber. The three of them had been assigned with separate rooms though they were accessed by adjoining doors. Unfortunately, their mother was in the middle chamber which meant her daughters must move about on the tips of their toes if they wanted any privacy whatsoever.

Luckily, however, when Eugenia had slipped into her bedchamber soaking wet, Mama and Harriet were not within and the lady's maid who had been so graciously provided by the duke and duchess had addressed the gash on her backside without the humiliation of having anyone else looking on and gawking at her clumsiness.

"You are overreacting," said Mama. "We were all queued up in a receiving line. Of course, His Highness had no choice but to shower his attention on the host family. Not to mention this is the seat of a dukedom." Mama pretended to flick some lint from her sleeve, her expression haughty. "Even though it is a *Scottish* dukedom."

Eugenia could only purse her lips at her mother's

misplaced disdain for the Scots. After all, she would soon be living in Scotland, soon to comprise a part of the duke's family.

Harriet ran her handkerchief across her eyes. "But h-he couldn't take his eyes of Lady Graaaaaaace!"

Content to be standing and not sitting on her throbbing backside, Eugenia rubbed her sister's shoulder. "You are aware as to why Her Ladyship turned down all those proposals, are you not?"

Harriet slapped Eugenia's hand away. "You are horrendous."

"I am truthful." She crossed to the bed where the most beautiful ballgown she'd ever seen lay atop it. "I say, Her Ladyship was quite gracious in taking you under her wing, giving you a gown fit for a duchess."

"B-but the only duke here is married," Harriet bemoaned as if she truly thought she was destined to wed a peer, let alone a duke.

"That may well be," Mama sat on the settee beside her youngest daughter. "However, the dowager has assured me there will be a plethora of gentlemen in attendance."

Eugenia replaced the gown and smoothed out the taffeta skirts. "Is this ball not supposed to be a dress rehearsal for you—a chance to practice your charm before you are introduced at court?"

Harriet dabbed her eyes. "But I intended to practice my charm on the prince and he scarcely acknowledged me."

Mama took the gel's hand. "My dear, you are lovely and you will find your prince charming in due course —far sooner than it took your sister to find *her* match."

Every fiber in Eugenia's body tensed.

"I don't want to settle for a Highlander or a stupid Scotsman." Harriet crumpled the lace handkerchief in her hands. "The men here are so barbaric, wearing absurd kilts, carrying those deadly weapons on their belts."

Eugenia slipped through the door to her chamber and quietly closed it, muffling her sister's and mother's voices. Heavens, she tired of their banter—always seeming to gouge at her either directly or indirectly. After two Seasons and no husband, according to them, she had "settled" for a Scotsman who was *merely* a knight. For the love of Moses, Papa was *merely* a baron. Mama constantly repeated that Harriet would do far better on the marriage mart because she was more approachable and less clumsy. At some stage while waiting for Philip to set the wedding date, her younger sister had become the golden daughter and Eugenia the elder, frumpy wallflower.

It isn't so easy to find a husband no matter how well you dance or how charming you are or how pretty your face might be. Not unless your dowry is worth a thousand pounds or more.

But it was never any use trying to impart her opinions or her experience. Harriet believed herself superior in every way and completely disregarded Eugenia's advice.

Fortunately, Eugenia would soon be shed from her sister's disregard. Besides, she quite liked the man wearing the kilt, dirk, and *sgian dubh* who had spent the morning with her. He'd conversed with her as if she were a person of value, as if her opinions mattered, as if he might actually enjoy her company.

Of course, she'd made a muddle of things by falling on that horrid rock exactly when a rogue wave crashed onto the shore. Though, even then, he'd been concerned for her welfare. For heaven's sake, the man had carried her up an impossible hill. He'd led her through a dank medieval tunnel just so she wouldn't humiliate herself whilst wet and bleeding.

Still, something unsettling clawed in the recesses of Eugenia's mind.

There had been a pair of instances when she was certain Philip might kiss her. Oh, how her heart had raced. She'd even tilted up her chin and attempted to give him every opportunity to do so. But as soon as his lips neared hers, he jolted away as if she were afire.

Did Philip not wish to kiss her?

Was she too frumpy?

Too clumsy?

Too English?

Perhaps too provincial, though Sir Philip lived in a relatively remote part of Scotland, quite possibly even more provincial than Aubrey House in Bedford.

Surely a kiss was allowable between engaged couples. Was it not? In London, the wallflowers had gossiped about engaged people kissing all the time—even those who were not betrothed.

Though perhaps Philip wanted to remain chaste until their wedding day.

If they ever had a wedding day.

She'd expected the topic to arise on their walk down to the beach. After all, they had been alone. Perhaps he was waiting for a better time? After all, the house party had only begun. There were still six days remaining before she climbed back into the carriage to endure the long ride home with Mama and Harriet.

Worse, if he didn't set the date by then, Eugenia would never hear the end of it.

Since the topic was not broached during the morning's walk, she couldn't be sure if he was ready to choose a date or not. Though he did seem attentive, even amenable.

How does one go about broaching the subject of setting a wedding date without actually doing so?

Eugenia rang for the lady's maid, opened her traveling trunk, and removed her lavender gown with the ivory lace overlay that she had spent the entire winter making. No, the gown hadn't been fashioned by an expensive London modiste, but it was elegant enough to have done so. It could have even been ordered from Paris. Of that Eugenia had no doubt. She'd made a similar pattern for a gentlewoman in Cambridge who'd told her as much and had paid her quite handsomely for the piece.

The maid stepped into the bedchamber. "Are you ready to dress for the ball, miss?"

STACK CASTLE'S great hall had been completely transformed into a summer garden. Of course, there were roses of every variety in enormous arrangements placed on every surface. Trees filled with exotic fruits had been brought in from the hothouse, and every lady had been given a dance card that opened like a fan, each blade fashioned in the shape of a tulip with the dances written on the stems.

The gala was every bit as opulent as any Eugenia had attended in London, except there were two problems. The first was that she still walked with a limp and doubted she'd be able to dance. The second was more concerning. Philip had yet to make an appearance and had missed the grand march.

Of course, she had made her excuses and stood aside during the march as well. Mama was a tad piqued, though Harriet had joined Lady Grace and the prince who graciously escorted the two ladies around the hall, showing off their extraordinary gowns.

As usual, Eugenia stood against the wall. Well, most of the time she sat, but tonight sitting was out of the question. When the orchestra started into the first set and Philip still hadn't made an appearance, her stomach levitated into her throat. How could she have been so clumsy? The man had most likely collapsed from the exhaustion caused by carrying her up to the top of the bluff.

Heavens, she never should have called the dog. Furthermore, she should not have removed her slippers and bounded through the surf as if she hadn't a care. Eugenia was no child. She had a great deal to fret about. If she did not leave Stack Castle with a date for the wedding, she'd be as good as snubbed.

Would she not?

By the time the orchestra started a quadrille, she was convinced that she had completely humiliated herself on the shore and now Philip was plotting how to gently rescind their engagement. For heaven's sakes, the back of her dress had not only been torn, she'd fallen hard enough to bleed all over her skirts. What must he think of her? Mama was right, she was clumsy. She had been fortunate to have received a single marriage proposal. But now it appeared as if that, too, might be dangling on a string.

What would she do if he did rescind? Go into hiding? Mayhap run away and make lace?

All the women had come out in fine style, and Lady Grace was like a beacon of light radiating everywhere she moved. No wonder Prince Isidor was smitten with her. And Harriet seemed to have recovered from her doldrums, as she was smiling and dancing with a handsome lord.

A footman came by with some ices. Eugenia took one and wandered down the corridor—at a slow pace. She couldn't sit. Standing made her look too desperate, and if someone did take pity on her and sign his name to her dance card, she didn't want to be put in a position where she needed to explain about falling on her backside.

Besides, this castle was so vast, she doubted she'd seen a quarter of it. Ahead, muffled voices filled the corridor.

Eugenia hesitated for a moment. "You must stay the course," said a voice sounding decidedly like the duke.

"I think you are doing splendidly," said a woman —definitely the Duchess of Dunscaby.

Taking two more steps, Eugenia peered through a crack in the doorway of a gargantuan library.

"And this is Scotland," said Her Grace, dressed in a jewel-encrusted ice-blue gown. "No one here will care if you forgot to bring your cutaway and knee breeches."

Philip tugged down the cuffs of a finely tailored black woolen doublet. "I dunna give a rat's arse, that's for certain."

"We've been away from the festivities for long enough. Regardless of your feelings, you must toe the line until your brother arrives." The Duke of Dunscaby's gaze shifted to the doorway. "Miss Radcliffe! Andrew...um...er...*Philip*, it seems, has forgotten his formal attire."

The duchess smiled so broadly, the corners of her lips practically touched her eyes. "And the silly man did not make it known until he sent a footman to fetch us after the grand march."

"Did your valet not pack on your behalf?" asked

Eugenia, quite happy with Philip's state of dress—especially since Harriet abhorred kilts.

"Aye." Philip moved toward her and bowed. "And after I had a harsh word with him, I doubt he'll ever make such an error again."

"I hope you weren't too severe. I'm sure the poor man didn't mean to err."

"Not to worry. Fergus has been serving the family for ages. I let Andrew have him after he graduated from university."

Eugenia stifled a laugh, offering an apologetic expression to her betrothed. "I beg your pardon, Your Grace, but did you not mean to say Philip?"

Dunscaby stood stunned for a moment, then roared with laughter. "Och, not even our mother can tell the lads apart." He took his wife's hand. "Come, my love. I want to show off your beauty to all the gentry in Caithness."

As the couple headed off, Philip offered his elbow. "Shall we?"

"Caithness?" Eugenia asked.

"'Tis the northeastern region over which the dukedom presides."

"Oh." She fanned herself with her dance card, making it flop and smack her nose. "I suppose I should have known that."

"Mayhap you would have if you'd been educated in Scotland." He took a step along the corridor, but stopped, giving her a concerned expression. "How is your...ah...your injury?"

"A tad tender, but nothing that won't heal in a few days."

"I suppose your mother thinks me an utter cad for allowing you to fall."

Goodness, this man knew how to be charming.

Had her mother known about the incident, she would have chided Eugenia severely. "Fortunately, she and Harriet were both out whilst the lady's maid tended... my um...*me*."

"I do owe you another apology. I would have caught you had I been a wee bit closer."

"No apology necessary. I was being clumsy and only I am to blame for the fall."

"Nay, you were skelped by a fifteen-stone beast."

Eugenia chuckled. She'd never heard the term skelped before, but it sounded like something from the Auld Scots dialect, a word only Philip would use. She like that about him—his uniqueness, even his brashness, wearing a kilt to a ball. The man hadn't even removed his weapons from his belt. "I thought you referred to Skye as a *wee* beasty."

"Aye."

"But he's not so small, is he?"

"He's smaller than me, though mayhap not you." His gaze shifted from her face as he fingered the sleeve of her overdress. "This is exquisite."

Eugenia's heart swelled in tandem with her smile. "Thank you. I..." Whenever someone complimented one of her designs, she always hid the truth.

He arched a single eyebrow. "You were saying?"

She shook her head. "You'll think me provincial."

"Me? I'm a Scot. I dunna believe anyone is *provincial*."

"Well, I don't want to sound boastful, but I made it myself."

"This?" His eyes grew round. "The lace?"

It warmed her to receive his approval. "Mm-hmm."

He leaned closer and examined her work very studiously, as if looking for mistakes. But then he own a mill that produced some of the finest muslin cloth in

Europe. "Astonishing," he said as if he were truly impressed.

"Thank you. I usually do not tell anyone when I'm wearing one of my own creations."

"Whyever not?" he asked offering his elbow.

"I'm sure you are well aware that being a lady and a lacemaker are not compatible."

"Och aye, heaven forbid you actually have a talent upon which some value may be placed—aside from embroidering cushions, mind you."

"It seems polite society has endowed a great deal of value on a woman's ability to produce an heir."

Philip stopped, a hint of red spreading across his cheeks. "May I sign your dance card?" he asked sliding the tulip fan from her wrist and opening it. A crease formed between his eyebrows. "This is blank."

"When I didn't see you I—"

"What?"

She clutched her hands together. "I suppose it doesn't matter. I cannot dance tonight. Not with my... ah...wound."

"Too sore?"

"A bit. I wouldn't want people to see me plodding across the floor like a clumsy ox."

"Hardly. In my observation, you are many things and clumsy is not one of them."

"Many things?" she asked, amazed. No one ever noticed anything about her, but since arriving at Stack Castle, Philip had proven ever so observant.

"Graceful." He again fingered her sleeve. "Talented, affable, curious, perceptive, and a connoisseur of roses."

"You've ascertained all that in two days?" she asked, wondering if he was indeed sincere, then why hadn't he mentioned the topic of their wedding date?

"Aye, and I imagine I'm just scratching the surface of the depth of your personality." Philip produced a pencil from his sporran. "What is one thing you would like to do whilst you're here?"

Eugenia glanced back down the corridor to the library, yearning to see more of it. "I think I'd like to explore the castle, with a lengthy stop in the library."

"That can be arranged."

"And there's one more thing," she said, biting down on her lip while a tremor shot through her body. Somehow she had to find a way to say it.

Philip's auburn eyebrows drew inward as he lowered his chin and looked her in the eyes. "Oh no, you canna pique my interest and then snap your lips together. What is it you wish to say, lass?"

"Well...um...ah..." *Now I've gone and put myself in a right royal muddle! Drat, drat, drat, I've no choice but to blurt it out.* "If you are planning to end our engagement, I would prefer it if you would do so before I return to Aubrey Hall."

7

F rozen in the corridor like a startled stag, Andrew
gulped.

He blinked.

He bit the inside of his cheek.

The pox to Philip and his damned obsession with horseflesh.

Every fiber in his body screamed at the absurdity of standing immobile while staring at Miss Radcliffe's winsome face without giving her some thread of assurance. After patiently waiting over three years, the lass had earned the right to be given a vow of colossal proportions. "I...I..."

For the love of God, what the devil should I say? If I'd known exactly how precarious this situation was going to be, I would have told my brother to keep his stallion and shove the horse up his arse! I cannot promise anything to this woman.

Andrew cleared his throat and took the lady's hand, plastering on an expression he hoped conveyed his utmost sincerity. "I give you my word that I have no intention of backing out of your...*our* betrothal."

With Eugenia's sigh, her shoulders relaxed as if he'd just relieved her of a heavy burden. This woman didn't deserve him. Hell, this woman didn't deserve Philip. She was kind and honest and could make lace to rival any tatter in London.

Andrew made a mental note to add this conversation to his growing list of details to pass on to his twin: *You need to set the damned wedding date, you miserable, unfeeling, selfish numpty.*

He slid the dance card from her fingers, moved to a hallway table and signed his name to every set.

Eugenia peered over his shoulder, making him incredibly aware of her nearness, her warmth, *her... everything.* "It would be scandalous if we danced every set."

"Scandalous, say you?" Andrew closed the tulip fan and returned it. "If you havena yet noticed, I dunna place much importance on what others think. 'Tis a privilege of being fifth in line."

"But there are so many people here. And I have no doubt your mother would be cross. Am I right?"

"My mother and I tend to disagree on a great many things." He patted his kilt-clad hip. "I reckon the Dunscaby matriarch will have a small spell when she sees what I'm wearing."

"Well, I like it. And your doublet is quite fetching, not to mention your valet has tied a pristine ballroom knot."

Andrew stretched his throat. "From the feel of my neckcloth, the sadist used at least a pint of starch."

"I believe that is something in which both of our mothers will approve."

"Which is why I'm tolerating the itchiness of it."

"Well, if it is any concession, you needn't worry about dancing. My injury has made skipping rather awkward, not to mention walking, climbing stairs and, most especially, sitting."

"Ouch. I'm so sorry." Andrew took her hand and kissed it. "But you cannot avoid dancing. This is Scotland. Posing as a wallflower in my country is simply not done."

"You're jesting."

"Nay, I never jest." Andrew oft jested, but Philip was too full of self-importance to do so.

"You do not want to be seen with a clumsy woman limping about like a lame ox. This is no simple family affair. There are over a hundred people here, not to mention a Russian prince."

"That may well be, but with royalty dazzling everyone's eyes, I'll wager no one will be watching the two of us."

"You are overconfident about that. Everyone notices when a young woman hobbles about the floor like a clubfoot."

"Verra well. I am grossly underdressed and your injury prevents you from regaling the Caithness gentry with your grace. Therefore, we shall dance unobserved by all the gabble-grinders in attendance."

"Objection. Do you not recall my mother accusing you of impropriety immediately after I bumped into you at the dowager duchess' birthday celebration in London? Mama is the worst gabble-grinder of them all."

Ah, yes, *The Dragon*, as Philip had so kindly dubbed Baroness Bedford. "You must immediately inform her that you have a megrim."

Eugenia looked stunned. "You want me to lie to my mother?"

Andrew gave her a playful snort. "Please, everyone tells tall tales to their parents on occasion, dunna tell me you have never done so. Besides, you have pain, it just doesn't happen to be located in your head."

A slow smile spread across the lassie's delicate lips. "Quite true, I am uncomfortable."

"Do you recall the secret passageway where I left you this afternoon?"

"Yes."

"Meet me there in twenty minutes."

ANDREW PACED the dimly lit landing on the third floor while jamming his fingers into his hair and pulling until it hurt. What had he been thinking? Inviting Eugenia for a wee interlude in the midst of a royal ball was the worst idea he'd had since donning his brother's mantle. In fact, it was as addled as Philip's harebrained scheme for them to trade places.

He must have experienced a moment of insanity brought on by a woman who not only was kind, gifted, witty, and in Andrew's estimation, she was the bonniest creature at the ball. Of course, he hadn't entirely lost his mind. After all, his valet hadn't packed his formal suit of clothes and if he promenaded onto the dance floor in a kilt as if he were attending a Highland ceilidh, his mother might have one of her spells. And he wouldn't want her to miss a single moment of this night, not with Grace being regaled by a prince.

Aside from the Prince Regent, Mama was most likely the grandest hostess on the isle of Great Britain, and tonight she had outdone herself. Andrew wasn't daft. He knew full well the importance of Prince Isidor's visit. Grace had been bred to be a *grande dame* and she would make an ideal princess. Though Andrew purposely wore kilts to express his Scottish pride, he did not want to do anything to make Isidor think less of the MacGalloway Clan or the Dunscaby Dukedom.

He ruffled his fingers through his hair to make it settle back into its stylish cut and stood a bit taller.

This plan of mine is purely in consideration of my family, and for poor Miss Radcliffe who is embarrassed about the limp caused by her injury...which was my fault. It is my responsibility to ensure the lass has an enjoyable experience. I owe her at least that.

With the muffled sound of approaching footsteps, Andrew's heart set to hammering like a woodpecker's beak. Tugging down the hem of his doublet, he faced the little door, shoulders back, expression set to reflect a picture of calm unlike his daft heart.

The latch rattled as if expressing a tad of uncertainty, then the door slowly opened, flooding the landing with a beam of light.

Eugenia stepped inside, holding a candlestick high. "You're here," she said as if surprised.

He bowed and gave her a wink. "And you've brought a wee torch."

"I wasn't sure if the sconces would be lit."

"The servants light them at dusk." He took the candle from her grasp and kissed her forehead. Dash the scent of lavender. Forever onwards, he'd think only of this woman when he smelled it, even if she was his brother's intended. A woman he never could have.

As his heart nearly thudded to a stop, he offered his elbow. "Shall we?"

"Where are we going?"

"You'll see." Andrew grinned, watching her out of the corner of his eye. "Was your mother terribly disappointed that you opted to retire?"

"Not really, though she asked after you—asked if you would be disappointed."

Together they descended the narrow, medieval spiral stairs, used by countless servants and MacGalloways over the centuries. "And what did you say?"

"I simply told her the truth, of course. Your valet made an error, and there was no time to bring in a tailor to alter one of the duke's suits of clothes and you didn't want to embarrass your family by wearing a kilt." She glanced downward. "Adorned with *barbaric* sharp weapons."

"Och, barbaric say you?"

"Not my words. Harriet's. In her opinion, kilt-wearing Scots are still barbarians."

At the second floor, Andrew pushed out into the corridor. He'd heard it before, Scots and their marauding, violent natures. Damn, he'd like to show a few English highbrows the extent of his violent nature. Unfortunately, however, he'd been born a century too late. "Would you prefer it if I removed my uncivilized weapons?"

"Oh no. I like them."

He stopped in the middle of the corridor and faced her. "You do?"

"I think they make you look rather virile."

Trying not to smile and utterly failing, Andrew surged forward, looking at the wall until the urge to thump his chest subsided. "Virile, aye?"

"Yes. Most definitely."

He adored the way she uttered the word "definitely" with such conviction. It made him stand taller, his chest broader. Andrew might not be his brother, but he posed a mirror image and Philip was as comfortable in his kilt as Andrew. Once this charade was over, he fully intended to find a woman like Eugenia—well bred, lovely, with a keen admiration of the wonders of the world around her—flowers, the sea, fine days. A competent lacemaker able to rival any proficient in Paris. Why, he wouldn't be surprised if she liked rainy days as much as fine. "Do you ever take walks in the rain?"

"I have, yes."

Andrew loved to walk in the rain with Skye. "Do you find them refreshing?"

"Summer rains, yes. Not so much in December with the droplets are icy cold."

"Fair enough," Andrew said, wishing it was raining this very moment.

When he opened the door to the orchestra's antechamber behind the gallery, a muffled minuet swelled through the air.

Eugenia's smile touched her eyes as he led her inside. "What is this place?" she asked, turning full circle in the center of the parquet floor.

He pointed to a pair of walnut double doors which led to the gallery above the ballroom. "This is where the musicians prepare for their performances and retire for intermissions."

She turned once more, taking in the enormity of the chamber, lined with ornate mahogany tables atop which sat opened instrument cases. Adjacent was a long table filled with refreshments that nearly looked as delicious as those served to the guests. Along another wall stood a white marble hearth, complete with statuary depicting mythical kelpies on either side. "It is quite grand."

"I believe during the eleventh century, this was actually the great hall." He chuckled, the castle had been added onto by every great man who had occupied it. "I suppose everything about Stack Castle is grand."

"After seeing the library this evening, I believe you."

Andrew took Eugenia's hand and bowed. "May I have this dance, madam?"

She curtsied in kind. "If you do not mind partnering with an inelegant clubfoot."

He moved beside her and picked up the minuet regally as the tempo dictated. "Hogwash. I hardly noticed your limp in the corridor."

The lady's steps were small and reserved and, not wanting to cause any further discomfort to her backside, Andrew matched her gait. "See? You're doing splendidly."

"I love to dance."

"But I thought you said you abhorred dancing."

"I believe I said I was not fond of dancing. But to be honest, I do enjoy it...and I don't." Eugenia followed his lead into a turn, clearly favoring her left side. "I do not care to dance in front of crowds."

He led her into a turn, changing hands. "Then I take it this intimate setting is more to your liking?"

A delicate blush spread across her cheeks while she stumbled only slightly as she twirled back to the other side. She was ever so bonny when blushing, it was a gift to watch her color thus.

Andrew pretended not to notice, mindful of keeping his steps smaller than usual. "I was wondering why a young woman as lovely as you would refer to herself as a wallflower."

Eugenia's eyes grew wide as if she had a great deal to say on the subject. "I much prefer the company of the young ladies along the wall."

He most certainly could believe that statement. When out on the dance floor, it most assuredly could be intimidating when trying to match up to someone as refined and well-schooled as his sister Grace for instance. "Then, might I assume a quiet country life is more appealing to you than the bustle of living in a city such as London?"

"Most definitely."

As the minuet ended, he bowed. "Then you ought to enjoy living on the River Tay."

She dipped into an elegant curtsy. "What is your home like?"

"I suppose it wouldna come as a surprise for me to admit the duke made certain his brothers were appointed with homes suiting their stations. Phil—ah —*Andrew* and I share a twenty-acre estate." For the love of God, when would this ruse be over? It seemed of all the people here who might reveal his true identity, Andrew would most likely end up the culprit. "The mill is on the River Tay just outside the village of Stanley. We have matching manor houses up on a hill that overlooks the factory—you can see for miles from my bedchamber's balcony."

"Are the houses side by side? Two twins standing together?"

"Nay. They are separated by seven acres of paddocks. Our houses border property lines one to the north and one to the south, and each have their own drive."

"And you like it there?"

"Verra much though..."

"Hmm?"

"I'm often called away." Andrew needed to stop talking this instant. He was oft called away, but Philip was not. Even though they employed an overseer, his twin preferred to immerse himself in the day-to-day operations of the mill while Andrew was always off meeting with exporters or handling some critical family affair for the duke. "Though Andrew is gone far more than I," he added for good measure.

Mercifully, the music began again—a waltz this time, requiring them to move closer.

To touch.

As he rested his hand on Eugenia's waist, Andrew's heart beat out of rhythm. And when she arched her arm over her head and grasped his fingers, her lips parted with her gasp. Ever so slowly, her eyes shifted upward and met his. Such a lovely shade of blue—so clear, so strikingly alluring. He could stare into those eyes for an eternity and never wish to look away.

The music enveloped them, tantalizing his skin, making him forget where he was and why he was there. All that existed in this moment was the two of them, dancing, swirling, floating. They moved like two swans on a glassy loch as if they'd been matched by a force beyond this world.

The waltz ended with a gradual retard, the final chord hanging on the air as if it might last an eternity. Somewhere during the waltz, Andrew had pulled the woman so close, their bodies were scandalously touching. Her breasts plied his chest with her every deep and steady breath.

But what captivated him most were still those blue eyes, watching him, lulling him, beguiling him.

Her lips parted as she tilted up her chin.

He dipped his.

Then, as if drawn by a magnetic force, their lips met.

Andrew's knees melted.

His heart expanded.

His mind drifted into oblivion along with the orchestra's final note.

Consumed by the power of emotion flooding every fiber of his body, he shifted a hand upward, cradling

Eugenia's head and lightly brushing his tongue across her lips, asking permission to taste her.

With a womanly sigh, she didn't disappoint, allowing him in. Allowing him to sample the sweetest mouth he'd ever imagined. She accepted him timidly at first, then mercifully, she became as ravenous as he. Their hands explored with frenzy. As his fingers found the scooped neckline of her gown, a womanly sigh rumbled from her throat.

The door to the gallery creaked.

Andrew snapped his hands away and jumped back, his eyes wide. Eugenia's eyes betrayed her shock as the members of the orchestra filed into their sanctuary.

What have I done?

8

The morning after the ball, breakfast was served not in the dining hall but in the breakfast room which had been arranged with several small tables dressed with white linen tablecloths, each with a posey of roses interspersed with wildflowers in cut crystal vases.

Eugenia ate with her mother and sister much the same as she did every morning even though they were not at home and there were dozens of guests sitting in groups of three and four. She said very little while pretending to listen to their banter and smiling at the right cues.

Except this morning was unlike any other. She wasn't reticent and taciturn. A glow of sunlit proportions radiated throughout her breast. At long last Philip had kissed her! His kiss had surpassed all imagination. It had been magical, transportive, and utterly wonderful. Her lips had tingled—were still tingling. Her entire body had gone limp and she'd lost all sense of reason...of course, until the orchestra interrupted the moment at which time both she and Philip jumped away from each other as if they had each been caught by the dowager duchess herself.

But how their kiss had ended mattered not in the slightest. It also didn't matter that he'd barely uttered a word when he escorted her back up the secret stairs. Yes, she'd hoped Philip might have kissed her good-night. But he did bow politely, handsomely, gallantly and bid her to sleep well.

Now, as the dowager duchess began to urge everyone out of doors for an archery competition, the Duchess of Dunscaby caught Eugenia's arm and held her back. "I was thinking, Miss Eugenia dear, that as a future member of this family, you might prefer a private tour of the castle rather than take up a bow and fire arrows at a target."

Eugenia looked to her mother and sister who were heading out, deep in conversation with Lady Grace and Lady Modesty. Then, she regarded the duchess. "To be honest, I've never been particularly fond of the sport, Your Grace."

"Neither have I." The woman smiled as she looped her arm through Eugenia's elbow. "And please call me Julia. After all, we are going to be sisters."

Eugenia instantly liked Julia. She had the most welcoming and expressive brown eyes, complemented by thick brunette curls. The duchess explained a bit of history about each room, moving in and out of one grand, opulently appointed chamber to the next.

"I couldn't help but notice that none of the men were at breakfast," Eugenia mentioned, turning full circle in a grand drawing room that she hadn't yet seen.

"August twelfth is the first day of grouse hunting season. They all nursed their megrims with a flask of whisky and an oatcake before heading out at dawn."

"Oh." Eugenia traced her finger along a carving of a serpent that spanned the length of a settee. "I'm surprised the shooting wasn't on Her Grace's meticulous itinerary."

"That's because my mother-in-law would have rather the men stayed for the archery contest."

"Is she often thwarted?"

"Occasionally, but as the dowager, she takes it all in stride." The duchess opened two enormous double doors and gestured inward. "This is the gallery with portraiture of the MacGalloway ancestors dating back to the Renaissance—prior to that the family has only artifacts and weapons to prove their heritage."

"Is that so?" Eugenia asked, moving into the hall, admiring the life-sized paintings of men and women, many of whom had auburn tresses similar to Philip's.

"Oh, yes. Above the fireplace in the great hall, there's a powder horn given to our ancestor by Robert the Bruce for valor in the Battle of Bannockburn."

"Astonishing. It is difficult to believe that centuries ago the English and the Scottish were oft at war."

"It is. And the last skirmish wasn't all that long ago —the Jacobite uprising with Bonny Prince Charlie and whatnot."

"Seventeen forty-five." Eugenia looked up at a portrait of a gallant man in Highland dress, not terribly unlike Philip. "Do all the MacGalloway men wear ruby brooches?"

"They do, but they're all slightly different. At least in Martin's generation. He and his brothers all have different animals embossed in the bronze."

"Odd. I thought the clans had specific crests that didn't differ."

"You are correct on that point. The MacGalloway crest is a Celtic harp on an ermine chapeau, which is also at the base of every brooch. However, the former duke had individualized brooches made for each of his five sons." Julia clapped a hand over her mouth, her eyes wide and shifting to the mantel clock. "G-goodness, look at the time," she said as if suddenly a bit flustered. "We must continue."

With the faster pace, Eugenia had a little more difficulty hiding her limp as the duchess guided her into the family chapel. "You hail from Brixham, do you not?"

"I do. My father was the Earl of Brixham. The earldom has fortunately now been bestowed upon Martin's sister's husband, Harold Mansfield."

"Oh my, so the estate is still in the family?"

"It is and I couldn't be happier."

"As an English gentlewoman, how did you find the transition to living in Scotland?"

With the sparkle in Her Grace's eyes, it seemed as if a dozen memories passed within the time it took to blink. "My story would take hours upon hours to tell, but I can say this: Since I took my wedding vows, I have been utterly welcomed into this family and have never regretted a single moment of my life here."

Eugenia knew exactly what Julia meant. Philip had made her so welcome she already felt as if she was part of the clan. They proceeded on to the library where Julia threw out her arms and turned full circle. "This is not only the oldest part of the castle, it is my favorite."

She looked up through the turret at the surrounding walls, admiring the four levels of balconies lined with bookcases and filled with countless volumes. "It truly is astonishing."

"At one time, this was the home of the first Mac-Galloway laird, appointed to guard the Kingdom of Scotland and protect the northeastern shore from the marauding Vikings, if you can imagine."

"It seems fantastical now, like something I might read about in a book."

"Fantastical, but very real." Julia placed her hand on an enormous globe of the world. "The castle has been expanded dozens of times, and once this wing was no longer needed to house and protect the family, the 9th Duke of Dunscaby drew up the architectural design for the tower to be transformed into what it is today."

"I am duly impressed."

Together the two women took a turn around the circumference of the room lined volumes upon volumes of leather-bound books.

"And how are you feeling now?" Asked the duchess. "Do you feel as though you're ready to join the family?"

"Ever so ready." Eugenia clasped her hands over her heart. "May I confess something very personal?"

"We are sisters you and I, and I want you to feel comfortable confiding in me," Her Grace replied, her smile ever so warm.

Though they had only been on this tour for about an hour, Eugenia already felt closer to Julia than she did to Harriet. Mayhap it was because the duchess listened—that their conversation was two sided. She wasn't certain why, but she was excited to come to know Her Grace better. "I must admit that during the journey up here I suffered more than a little trepidation."

"I can certainly understand why. Sir Philip has made you wait quite a long time—three years has it been?"

"Yes, and I feared he might have regretted his hasty proposal."

"Oh, no. I'm certain Philip doesn't regret asking

you to marry him." Smiling warmly, Julia urged Eugenia to sit beside her on a crimson settee. "Now that you have had a little time to get to know my brother-in-law, are you still apprehensive?"

She buried her face in her hands and giggled. How things had changed in just a few days. "He is so much kinder than I'd remembered. When Philip came to call the morning after his proposal, he was unduly serious and reserved. At the time, I honestly thought he was going to renounce the engagement right there in my father's parlor. He didn't, of course, but then when I did not hear from him for years, I had no choice but to assume my initial fears were founded."

Julia reached for Eugenia's hand and squeezed it. "But you are not feeling as apprehensive now?"

"All of my assumptions about Philip were wrong. He's not pompous or unsympathetic. He's caring and amusing and engaging."

Her Grace smiled, but then bit down on her lip, her expression seeming to be a tad befuddled. "I think I ought to show you the nursery. Have you met James and Lily?" Completely changing the subject matter, she pulled Eugenia to her feet with renewed exuberance. "We've so much to see—the doocot, the kitchens, the king's bedchamber, of course the nursery. My heavens, James and Lily will adore you!"

WITH HIS FAITHFUL deerhound at heel, Andrew strode beside Martin as they crossed the wide expanse of moorland sloping toward the castle. With Skye at his side and his Brown Bess flintlock rifle tucked beneath his arm, all seemed well with the world. Verdant grass stretched to the sea, the Stacks of Duncansby presided just off the shore, and the heavens were nearly as blue as Eugenia's eyes.

Well perhaps not everything was well with the world. First of all, he shouldn't be thinking of the woman's eyes. "I'll be glad when Philip arrives."

"We all will be," Martin agreed, chewing on a two-foot-long grass stem. "I abhor this charade and will give Philip a good tongue-lashing as soon as I have him alone."

The race in Perth had been run two days ago, which should have allowed Philip enough time to ride north. Andrew's stomach clenched. "Damnation, I hope he doesna make himself look like an arse."

"How so?"

"You ken Philip. He never minces words—hasna ever been terribly romantic either."

"Nay, which is why he let that poor lass wait so long."

"She feared he'd intended to call off the engagement."

"Not surprising. Were I in her shoes, I might have thought the same." Martin spat out his piece of grass and clapped Andrew on the shoulder as they stopped outside the gatehouse. "Your brother is a good man and he'll be a good husband, mark me."

Andrew used the iron boot scraper to clean the mud off his soles. "Mayhap when he decides he's ready to be a husband. 'Tis just…"

"Hmm?" Martin asked, cleaning his boots as well.

"I wish he weren't so bloody indifferent about Miss Radcliffe."

"Not to worry. I have no doubt that once he comes to know her, he'll realize what a jewel he has found."

"I hope so." *For her sake, I pray ever so much.*

They proceeded through the cobbled courtyard

and after handing his musket to his groom, Andrew gave Skye a scratch behind the ears. "What say you we wash up afore dinner?"

The dog wagged his tail and yowled—not to the washing up, but to the mention of a meal.

"Aye, I'm most likely as ravenous as you, laddie."

After bidding good day to the all the men in the hunting party, Andrew led the dog through the medieval hall and up the grand staircase, weariness weighing on his limbs. He hadn't slept well since arriving. Last night was the worst of course, tossing and turning while he'd relived the kiss with Eugenia over and over in his mind. He tried to downplay it. He tried to convince himself the kiss didn't matter. He tried to envision Philip kissing her and that had been the most infuriating thought of all.

At the second floor, he started for the bedchamber he'd been occupying since his arrival, passing the small parlor where his mother often took her afternoon tea and read because she said the light was best there. Since the door was ajar, he peered inside, surprised to see Eugenia within, her fingers working in a blur as she sat alone. Spindles of cotton thread hung from her design, quickly turning the knots into a work of art.

Andrew leaned on the doorjamb, Skye sitting beside him, pressing against his leg. "What are you making?" he asked, truly curious.

Eugenia's hands stilled as she looked his way. "Oh, you've returned." She smiled, holding up her work. "'Tis a veil for a lady in Cambridge."

He sauntered inside and studied her work. Truly exquisite, he could not identify a single flaw. But if his memory served, Cambridge was a good thirty miles from Bedford. Not an impossible distance, but far enough to be inconvenient. "Do you ken many ladies in Cambridge?"

"Some," she said with little conviction. "How was the shooting?"

"Good for Martin, though I've decided the sights of my musket need to be realigned."

"Oh, I am sorry."

"Not to worry." Andrew ran his hand along Skye's back. "This wee beasty was in heaven."

"I'll wager he was."

He craned his head and looked to her skirts. "How is your injury today? Better I hope?"

"Definitely better." She shifted slightly and showed him a pillow she'd placed beneath her hip. "Though I'm using a bit of extra padding."

Together they both chuckled. "I'll wager your mother is still none the wiser."

"My mother hasn't paid me much notice since you proposed, so that would be a no. Last I saw Harriet, she was still prattling about the ball and the gown Lady Grace had lent her, and how her dance card had been entirely filled."

"I'm sure the ball must have been invigorating for a lass about to make her debut." Andrew brushed his finger across the delicate lace that was coming to life. "Did you enjoy the archery?"

"Well, as it turns out, the duchess pulled me aside and asked if I might enjoy a tour of the castle."

A stone sank to the pit of Andrew's stomach. He had planned to show her the castle—the library at least. "I'm certain Julia must have been a verra good guide."

"She was remarkable, and so friendly. I never would have expected such graciousness from a duchess."

"Oh? I believe all duchesses ought to be gracious, though I ken many are filled with pompous self-importance."

"True. I have intimate experience with pompousness."

"As do I." Skye strode to the door, reminding Andrew that they'd been outside marching through bogs all day and were in sore need of a bath. Glancing down to his boots which were still dirty on the toes and vamps, he recalled how the housekeeper had once chided him for tracking mud all over her freshly swept carpets. "If you would excuse me, I must ready myself for the evening meal afore Mrs. Lamont comes after me with her duster."

Eugenia's lovely azure eyes popped wide. "She wouldn't do such a thing!"

"Och, the housekeeper had no qualms with disciplining the MacGalloway lads when we were young. Though now that Martin is her master, I imagine she goes about keeping him in check with other tactics." He bowed, then offered a grin. "But I digress, and I truly must take my leave, madam. I shall look forward to seeing you at the evening meal."

"Very well." Eugenia resumed her lacemaking while her lips curled upward. "And I hope you'll attend the parlor games afterward."

By the time Andrew pushed inside his bedchamber, the fatigue he'd felt earlier had been replaced with anticipation. The lass had told him there would be parlor games tonight. He quite enjoyed parlor games, especially when there would be one particular young lady present.

Except when he opened the door, he didn't plan on seeing Philip standing there, list in hand, his face red, his eyes wild with rage.

Andrew scoffed. "What the devil are you doing here?"

"This is *my* chamber, you lout. What the bloody hell are you doing sleeping in here?"

Beside him, Skye growled. "I'm supposed to be posing as you, you bull-heided numpty!"

Philip slapped his chest with the list Andrew had so painstakingly detailed. "Aye, but ye werena meant to be traipsing about the Northeast of Scotland with my intended."

How dare he accuse me of impropriety? "Traipsing? I've been doing exactly what you asked me to do, and keeping a log on your behalf, ye bloody ungrateful swine!"

"Swine? You're the swine. I told you to go hunting with Martin until I arrived."

Andrew gestured to his muddy boots. "Which is exactly what I have been doing all day."

"I beg your pardon?" Philip held up the paper, reading. "Miss Radcliffe likes flowers of all varieties and can distinguish one genus of rose from another? Strolls on the beach? She's perceptive?" he demanded, his tenor inching up with every statement. "She tats lace like a Parisian lacemaker and loves to dance but not in the presence of gabble-grinders?"

He swatted the list on the writing table, making his cowlick spring from the amply applied pomade. "This certainly doesna sound like hunting to me!"

Andrew's face burned as he rubbed the back of his neck. Perhaps he'd spent a wee bit more time with Eugenia than he ought to have done. Though as his mind raced over the past few days, their encounters could not be helped. It was most definitely a good thing he had not written about the softness of her hip pressing into him as he carried her up the hill or sweetness of her mouth when last evening when he'd succumbed to a moment of poor judgment. However, the wee kiss he'd shared with the lass would never again be thought of, let alone revealed to anyone. Not even the woman who shared in the kiss will ever know it was not Philip who gave it.

Blast his brother's pretention. "If ye didna want me to be gracious to your betrothed, then you should have come up here and met her yourself instead of putting me in an untenable situation and expecting me to stand idly by like the bleeding coat of armor in the great hall."

Philip threw the list, but the paper only managed to rattle and flutter to the floor. "You're a cad!"

"Och aye? Well, you're an uncaring buffoon!" Andrew grabbed his valise and gripped the door's latch. "Send my valet across the hall with my bath water. I'm done with this farce. I'll be leaving in the bloody morning." He paused for a moment. "You dunna deserve a woman like Eugenia Radcliffe. Not by half!"

Andrew slammed the door and marched across the corridor to his real bedchamber—the one containing the four-poster where he should have been sleeping over the three nights since he arrived. Once inside, he turned the lock for good measure. If it was a fortnight before he next set eyes on Philip, it wouldn't be long enough for him.

Blast my brother and his arrogant, highbrow snobbery. And damn him to hell for asking me to step in for him. Anything that may have happened between me and Eugenia was his fault. It is entirely his fault that I kissed her. Entirely his fault that she fell on the rock, my bloody brother is entirely responsible for me being forced to carry the lovely lass up the damned hill.

9

E ugenia carefully sliced a bite of roast lamb and swirled it in mint sauce before raising it to her lips. She couldn't help but shift her gaze to Philip, though he didn't look her way this time.

When the guests had gathered in the long gallery prior to being ushered into the dining hall, Philip hadn't arrived after until his brother Frederick had graciously escorted her to the table. Now her intended was seated at the far end where Prince Isidor appeared to be holding court.

That wasn't terribly odd, since she and Philip were often seated beside other guests, but after last eve, and their brief chat in the upstairs parlor, she was looking forward to engaging in conversation with him—she wanted to be near him, possibly to feel her leg brush his beneath the table. Alas, she must wait for her opportunity to rekindle the magic from last eve.

As Eugenia nibbled a bite of potato, she again glanced to Philip. Her heart gave a little leap when, while nodding in agreement to something the prince said, her betrothed reached for his wineglass and looked her way. As if sunshine had suddenly shifted to her face, she smiled more broadly than usual.

Philip didn't exactly return her grin, but he did raise his glass and give a nod before returning his attention to Isidor. Between the two gentlemen sat Lady Grace who continually glanced from one man to the other as if a spectator at a tennis match.

"I do believe my sister cannot get a word in edgewise," said Sir Fredrick, dabbing his mouth with his serviette.

The comment afforded Eugenia the opportunity to openly stare. Something was different—Philip's hair. Though the part was still on the left, he appeared to have used more pomade, slicking it down rather than leaving it wildly tousled. However, he did mention that he needed a bath. Perhaps there hadn't been time for his hair to dry? "I daresay if two gentlemen were talking over me throughout an entire meal, I might be a tad vexed."

"I'm certain she's fuming on the inside, though Grace is far too well-bred to display an iota of emotion and undermine her chances of marrying a prince."

Eugenia mulled over his comment while chewing her last morsel of lamb. This morning, Harriet had given a detailed account of the ball, gushing about how the prince had saved the two waltzes for Lady Grace and how perfect they were for each other. Now that Harriet realized her chances of enticing a prince were slim to none, she had reverted back to her original plan and decided this house party was an exercise in gaining experience. Thus she'd turned her attentions to flirting with Mr. Howard Hale, the son of the resident vicar, who was only sixteen.

Since Philip hadn't initiated another exchange from across the table, Eugenia regarded his younger brother. "How did you find the shooting this morning?"

Sir Frederick reached for his glass of wine. "The weather was fine and the dogs were excited to be on the hunt again."

Surely they would have taken dogs, but she hadn't noticed any on the estate aside from Andrew's deerhound who was definitely not a birder. "Did the duke bring in dogs?"

"Of course not, though you wouldna have seen the kennels, they're beyond the stables on the south side, hidden by a stone wall." Frederick sipped the ruby liquid. "In my opinion, the MacGalloway setters are the best bird dogs not only in Scotland, but in all of Britain."

She speared a slice of boiled potato with her fork while glancing at Philip out of the corner of her eye. "They performed quite well for you, did they?"

"Absolutely. The lead male is phenomenal. You really should have been there to watch how he stealthily crept through the tall grass. The birds hadn't a chance when he pounced upon them, setting them to flight."

"Philip said that luck wasn't with him today."

Frederick stared at her with a quizzical expression, a pinch between his eyebrows. "Philip?" He looked down the length of the table. "Och, aye. His aim was off for certain."

Eugenia followed his gaze, meeting Philip's blank stare. She smiled. He smiled back, though his grin held nowhere near the warmth it had imparted in the above stairs parlor before he left for his bath earlier today.

When dinner ended, the duke led the men to the drawing room as was customary, though before they disappeared through the sliding slot doors, the dowager duchess warned the gentlemen that they were only to be granted three quarters of an hour after which she would send Giles to fetch them for parlor games.

Eugenia joined the ladies in a withdrawing room where a lavish tea service had been set out complete with a spirit lamp, but otherwise the room had not been prepared for the evening's entertainment.

"We are playing parlor games, are we not?" asked the baroness.

"In the hall," said the duchess, picking up an ornate urn and beginning to pour. "There are simply too many guests present to have us all squeeze into this tiny chamber."

Stack Castle had several parlors, withdrawing rooms, and whatnot, this one being among the largest, which made Eugenia look from one wall to the other. She shrugged. Though this particular chamber was quite spacious, the hall was most likely a better option.

"Dinner was delicious," said Mrs. Hale, the wife of the vicar who sat in one of the armchairs.

"At least the food was good," said Lady Grace.

"Whatever do you mean by that?" asked the dowager, taking a cup of tea from the footman and helping herself to a meringue biscuit from another. "From my viewpoint, it seemed the conversation at your end of the table was quite riveting."

"It was—if arranging shipments of muslin cloth to Lithuania holds your interest." Grace waved off the footman's offer of a cup of tea, though she did snatch a biscuit. "The prince is a fine dancer, but his conversational skills are wanting."

"Oh?" asked the duchess. "After the gentlemen returned from grouse hunting, His Highness seemed quite engrossed in a conversation with Laird Buchanan."

"With a Highlander, who is a man." Lady Grace nipped a tiny bit of the meringue, making white sugary flecks rain to the carpet. "Isidor has hardly spoken to me—hardly spoken to any of us."

The dowager who was sitting on a scarlet fainting couch, delicately sipped her tea. "Men like the prince have a great deal of responsibility, and he will only be in Scotland for a short time. It is not surprising to see him engage in discussions that do not concern us."

"I, for one, can understand Grace's vexation," Harriet slid into the seat beside Lady Grace. "This evening I sat between Mr. Hale the younger and Lord Fiene and they, too, spoke over me as if I were merely a servant peeling potatoes."

The few times Eugenia had looked across the table at Harriet, she seemed to be either blushing or in conversation. She most certainly hadn't appeared to be talked over as Eugenia had noticed with Her Ladyship.

"Not to worry, ladies," said Julia, her smile as radiant as the sparking crystals on her gown. "After watching the prince dance both waltzes with my dearest sister-in-law, I personally witnessed the fact that Isidor could not remove his eyes from her. I do believe the man will propose by the end of the week."

"There is a reason why the gentlemen withdrew this evening—so they can discuss their politics and whatnot," said the dowager. "Believe me, there will be no opportunity for such bravado after they join us in the hall."

~

THE FIRST PARLOR game was Question and Answer, which Eugenia loved, even though the questions and

the answers were already on sets of cards. Half the unmarried guests sat on one side of circle who were
given "question" cards and the other half were given
"answer" cards. The gathering went through three it-
erations where a question was posed to the person directly across, then diagonally, then randomly. The
game was strictly adjudicated, however, and those
with the answer cards had to keep them face down on
their laps. If anyone tried to peek at their answers,
they were issued new cards.

Eugenia had been marshalled to the side of the
circle with answers while Philip sat with the question-
ers. Finally, during the third iteration, when it came to
his turn, he looked her way. "This question is for Miss
Radcliffe."

She moved to the edge of her chair, listening intently. "May I hope?" he asked.

She bit her bottom lip, praying for a coy response
before she turned over her final card. Heaven's stars,
this was only a game, but it would have been far better
if she'd received Lady Grace's last response which had
been, "*Only if you would escort me to the settee.*"

Or Lady Modesty's, "*Everyday!*"

Eugenia cringed as she looked up and met Philip's
stare. "*Ask the cats.*"

Everyone howled with laughter as she clapped her
hands to her face, her gaze shooting to the dowager.
"May I have another answer, please?"

But her request was lost in the laughter and
chatter while the dowager rang her little bell and
swept into the middle of the circle. She continued to
ring the bell until all mouths were shut and all eyes
were on her. "Next we shall have a game of forfeits."

Murmurs of excitement rose, especially from the

ladies, which caused another bout of bell ringing. "Each person will be given a slip of paper with a task which they must direct a lady or a gentleman, or both a lady and gentleman to perform—"

"Excuse me, Your Grace," said Prince Isidor. "But cannot a lady perform said tasks with another lady, or two men perchance?"

The dowager frowned, imparting an aghast expression that shook Eugenia to her toes. "Absolutely not." She resumed an air of utter unflappability. "Now, if the party should fail to perform their assigned task, then he, she, or they must forfeit something on their person."

"Scandalous," said Mrs. Hale which Eugenia didn't find odd coming from a vicar's wife.

"No," replied the dowager. "I fully expect all the perfectly able men and women present to carry out the tasks assigned. Besides, a glove, a fan, a handkerchief forfeited should not cause too much consternation."

It wasn't surprising when Sir Frederick was asked to impersonate a duck. Harriet was asked to partner with Mr. Hale the younger and pretend he was a park bench. He kneeled on all fours while she sat on his back and pretended to read a book, receiving a resounding applause for her acting.

Prince Isidor was asked to give a rose to Lady Grace and everyone demanded to know the color. To waylay any question, His Highness marched to a bouquet of house flowers and plucked a Double Velvet, which always produced blooms in a deep shade of red —the color of desire, of course.

How scandalous!

He gallantly bowed and offered the rose to Her Ladyship who accepted the flower with the appropriate blush in her cheeks.

Modesty's task was to imitate a lamb, which she did rather convincingly, especially since her red hair was piled atop her head in ringlets. If the young lady weren't the sister of a duke, she might make a superb player.

When Sir Philip's name was called, he was asked to dance the *Prince's Waltz* with Miss Eugenia Radcliffe. Though the tune only consisted of sixty-four bars, she hated to dance in front of others. Regardless of if they had danced in the orchestra's withdrawing room last eve, she would have much rather playacted a sheep, or a duck. Truth be told, Eugenia would make an excellent mollusk—if there were anything in the hall in which to burrow.

But dancing was better than suffering the humiliation of forfeiting an item on her person. In these games, forfeiture was considered to be the utmost humiliation. With the urging of Laird Buchanan who sat beside her, Eugenia rose and moved to the center of the circle. Philip met her there and he eyed her, his head held high, his lips slightly curved. He behaved differently here in the hall with so many eyes upon him—as did she. Was he also unnerved in crowds, or perhaps he acted more loftily when in the presence of his mother and the duke?

He placed his hand on her waist and she on his while the butler began to play the introduction on the pianoforte. As they joined their hands above their heads, Eugenia turned her head toward Philip's shoulder and coughed.

His eyebrows slashed inward as he regarded her. "Are you well, miss?"

She blinked in succession, her mind running

amuck. Thus far, she hadn't seen Philip smoke a pipe, but as sure as she was breathing, his usual enticing scent of bergamot had been replaced by the stench of tobacco. True, usually when men retired after the evening meal, they partook in gentlemanly activities of smoking and imbibing in a tot of brandy, but to know that he had just been smoking caused her a modicum of unease.

Goodness, he'd just inquired as to her health and she'd best reply. Offering a little smile, she nodded. "Quite well, thank you."

Unlike last eve, his dancing, though practiced, was stiff. And in response, hers was even more stilted given her backside still caused some discomfort. When he cued her for a turn beneath his arm, she stumbled over the tip of his toe. Gasping, she caught herself, barely breaking stride while she glanced downward. Philip had placed his foot too far forward. Goodness, anyone would have had to look down not to trip. Though Eugenia oft cast her gaze to the path when she was walking, no self-respecting lady ever looked to her toes when dancing.

When the music began to retard, Philip twirled her away without a stumble this time. She dipped into a curtsy and he bowed and kissed her hand. "My thanks, Miss Radcliffe."

Miss Radcliffe? Given the present company I expected formality, but everyone present has been calling me Miss Eugenia to allay any confusion with my sister.

She glanced at the others all looking on expectantly. She executed a second, albeit hasty curtsy, deciding that since there were so many high-ranking people in attendance including a prince, she'd best reply formally and in kind. "Sir Philip," she said, her gaze drifting to his ruby brooch.

What was it Julia had said about them? Did he have a separate brooch for formal gatherings?

The mantel clock struck the midnight hour as footmen arrived toting trays of wineglasses filled with madeira. The guests began to mingle and somehow, Eugenia found herself standing on the outer edge of the crowd, alone while sipping the sweet wine.

"There you are, my dear," said Mama, taking Eugenia by the arm and lowering her voice. "Has Sir Philip discussed setting the date for your wedding?"

"Not exactly as of yet," she whispered.

"I thought not, which is why I took matters into hand."

Oh dear. Eugenia's stomach roiled. "What, precisely did you do?"

"Nothing that any mother in my circumstances wouldn't have done. After all, it has been thr—"

"Three years, yes, I am painfully aware." Eugenia exchanged her empty glass with her mother's full. "Please tell me you did not pressure the poor man."

"No, though that isn't entirely out of the question. But after the hunting party returned, I happened to find His Grace in the library and prevailed upon him to intervene and exert his influence over Sir Philip's hand."

Eugenia glanced to Philip who was once again deep in conversation with the prince. "You didn't?"

"Of course, I did. It is my duty to do so." Mama retrieved her full glass and drank, then tipped up her chin with a victorious smile. "And the duke agreed the date must be set by the end of the week. Furthermore, he also promised to have a word with his brother at his first opportunity."

"Oh please. Sir Philip will set the date when he—"

"If that reticent man does not feel the weight of his brother's boot up his backside," Mama hissed, "I fear you will be well and truly an old maid before you take your vows. If you ever do."

Eugenia glanced around for the footmen. The glasses of madeira had been only a quarter full, and she truly could do with at least five more of them.

"Miss Eugenia," said the Duke of Dunscaby with Lady Grace on his arm. He offered his other elbow. "Would it please you to join me?"

Mama all but pushed her into the fellow. With a sigh, Eugenia took his arm. "I sense some meddling in the air."

The man glanced at her out of the corner of his eye. "This is my castle and I do not meddle."

"How dare I jump to conclusions, Duke," she replied dryly as they crossed the room.

Lady Grace tittered. "You do have an impressive backbone, Miss Eugenia."

"Whatever do you mean?" she asked, feigning an innocent, eye-batting expression and pretending she did not just show a duke her sardonic side.

Before anyone could reply, they arrived beside Philip and Prince Isidor. "Your Highness," said His Grace, bowing slightly. "My sister and Miss Radcliffe were just telling me how exhausted they are from the day's activities and, knowing it would disappoint you greatly not to have said goodnight, I thought it might be expedient of you to escort them to the grand staircase to bid adieu."

"Of course," said the prince, placing his wineglass

on a footman's tray and offering his hand to Lady Grace.

Philip followed in kind, offering his elbow.

Still smelling of pipe smoke, he led her toward the hall with a purposeful air as if he were rushing to reach the staircase. Eugenia squeezed his arm gently to slow the pace. After all, aside from their brief discourse in the upper parlor, she'd hardly had a chance to talk to him today. And things between them had been so magical the previous night. She wanted to rekindle the spark. "I daresay our waltz during the parlor games wasn't as vigorous as the one we shared last night by half."

"Och aye?" he asked, stopping in the middle of the hall, seeming a tad piqued. "On the contrary, I believe our waltz was executed to perfection aside from..."

She took a step away gripped her hands together. "What?"

"'Tis nothing."

"No, you were going to say aside from my stumble, were you not?" she asked, while the back of her neck burned.

"You did stumble."

"Because you slid your foot forward."

"I doubt that. I rarely err."

She looked him up and down, unwilling to discuss the matter further. After all, it was merely a silly dance, something not worth arguing about, and definitely not something she wanted her betrothed to hold against her when she was desperately waiting for him to discuss the establishment of the wedding date. "Forgive me." She curtsied. "As you said, I did stumble, and had I been watching where I was stepping, I would not have done so. Good night, Philip."

"Miss Radcliffe," he growled as if displeased with her use of the familiar.

Not stopping, she continued up the stairs. Good heavens, he didn't seem to be inebriated. Had something awry happened? How could a man be so incredibly affectionate one night and so snobbishly aloof the next? Was he having second thoughts? Was he disappointed by her lack of experience when they'd kissed?

10

"Uncle Andreeeew!" hollered James, running with open arms, his sister following, doing her best to keep pace with her elder brother.

"How are my two favorite wee bairns?" he asked, swooping them both into his arms and kissing Lily on the cheek. Since Prince Isidor had talked Martin into taking the men for another hunt, the ladies had all piled into carriages to pay a visit to Gibb's ship, still moored off the coast at John o'Groats.

"I'm no bairn," said James, jutting out his bottom lip.

Lily squirmed and patted her chest. "Me Lady Leelee."

"Indeed you are," Andrew replied, setting the children down and sitting on the floor so that they could talk to him eye-to-eye.

"Can you and Skye come watch me ride my pony?" asked James.

"I'm afraid I must take my leave."

"Why?" James thrust his fists onto his hips, looking very much like his father while Lily climbed on Andrew's lap.

His arms surrounded the child. "I have an important matter to attend." It wasn't a lie. It was of utmost importance for him to remove himself from Stack Castle to ensure one particular young lady did not become aware of the ruse to which he'd so foolishly agreed.

James flung his arms around Andrew's neck. "But I dunna want you to go anywhere ever again."

"Mayhap the pair of you can visit me on the River Tay. I have a very large manor house and if you come, I'll promise to hang a rope swing from the chestnut tree in the front garden."

"Can I bring my pony?" James asked.

"Of course, you can."

Behind them, a door creaked followed by a high-pitched gasp. As the hairs on the back of his neck stood on end, Andrew shot to his feet while James wrapped his arms around one leg and Lily the other.

He hadn't expected to see the lassie's face again for a very long time. The sun shone in from the window at just the right angle to make her look like a vision—such a lovely woman...who was not supposed to be here in the nursery. "Eugenia," he croaked, wondering why she hadn't boarded one of the carriages bound for the pier.

"Philip?" She glanced to his brooch, her eyebrows pinched. "Forgive me, the duchess said I could visit the children at any time. I...ah..."

"He's no' Philip," said James. "He's Uncle Andrew."

"Drew!" Lily echoed.

A crooked grin twisted his lips as he met her confused stare, praying she didn't realize that he was the cad who'd broken every rule he'd ever set for himself in his life and kissed her—betrayed her, betrayed his brother. He, the MacGalloway lad who everyone knew to be disgustingly honest who's loyalty...as Philip had so eloquently put it...was positively revolting. His brother had meant it as a compliment at the time, but Andrew had just proved exactly how revolting his deep-seated loyalty to family was.

"But I thought—" Her eyes darted from his hair, to his brooch, to his face, then she covered her mouth with trembling hands. "Oh God," she said, turning and dashing down the stairs.

Skye yelped and started after her. Andrew did as well. "Wait!"

"Stay away!" Eugenia shouted, her voice echoing through the old medieval stairwell, followed by the slamming of a door.

Andrew stopped, his dog returning to his side. He looked to his brooch with its eagle head embossed in the bronze. Philip's had a boar. She had obviously noticed the difference at some point. "Bloody, bleeding hell."

He jabbed his fingers into his hair and pulled. How the devil, when so many people continually confused him with Philip, did she immediately recognize their ruse? Damnation, he should have ridden away last night. Now Andrew had no choice but to find his twin and tell him their secret had been exposed.

Philip was going to combust. Worse, early this morning, Martin had taken the men on another hunt and they wouldn't be back for hours.

Making his decision, he slapped his thigh. "Come, Skye. We've a hunting party to locate."

NOT WISHING to be seen by anyone attending the house party, Eugenia slipped up the servant's stairs and hastened toward her bedchamber, her hands shaking, her chest so tight she could scarcely breathe. Did Sir Philip MacGalloway think so little of her that he thought nothing of sending his brother to act in his stead? At least James was honest. A babe uttering the truth.

Obviously, her years of waiting for Philip to set a wedding date had been in vain.

The years hadn't mellowed the man. If anything, they had made him stodgier.

By the time she stepped inside the bedchamber and locked the door, she knew exactly what she must do. Moving as quickly as possible, she willed her hands to stop shaking as she darted to her trunk. She pulled out the satchel with her lacemaking things, her reticule with the coin she'd earned from her labors, a change of clothes, and the lace overdress she'd worn the first night. After carefully rolling, then stuffing her clothing into the satchel, she hastened to the writing table, removed two sheets of paper from the drawer, dipped her quill, addressing one letter to her mother and one to Sir Philip.

She had made no mistake. The foppish, arrogant man she'd waltzed with last night had been the same lordling who'd proposed so long ago. As soon as she'd seen Andrew in the nursery, she knew she had been played for a fool.

Three years ago, the odor of pipe smoke had lingered on her gloves after Philip had kissed her hand, just as it had done last night. Given that Andrew had not been at dinner or the parlor games, she hadn't realized one blatant clue that distinguished the two men, but now she knew. Andrew's brooch had an eagle embossed in the bronze where Philip's had the head of a boar. Well, the man was a boar to be sure. Also, Philip used more pomade than Andrew as well.

Good Lord, she'd kissed Philip's *brother*. She had scandalously been alone with him many times since arriving at Stack Castle. And no one, not the duke, not the duchess, not the dowager—not a soul said a word or cautioned her in any way. Eugenia could have been salaciously compromised and they all would have merrily flitted about, behaving as if Philip and Andrew always played tricks upon unsuspecting young women.

Did the lout ever once intend to go through with the marriage?

How could those two devious twins have deceived her so? Heaven help her, she was not about to marry a scoundrel who thought so little of her. Nor was she going to allow her family to be at the receiving end of a scandal, humiliated in front of all polite society.

She set pen to paper. "I know what I must do."

ANDREW AND PHILIP pushed their horses hard with Martin in their wake. The remainder of the hunting party opted to stay out with Frederick as their guide. After all, they didn't need to be akin to the fact that the twins had conspired to bamboozle Miss Radcliffe. It was a wonder Andrew hadn't been shot when he'd pulled Martin and Philip aside to deliver the news. Of course, his twin had been fast to point the finger, demanding how Andrew could have been so careless as to chance a visit to the nursery to say goodbye to their niece and nephew.

He should have expected something like this to happen, even though the ladies had supposedly all gone to see Gibb's ship.

"Why didna she go with the others?" Martin demanded. "And who the devil gave her leave to visit the nursery?"

"I didna have the opportunity to ask why she hadna gone to the pier," Andrew barked over his shoulder. "And it was your wife who told Miss Eugenia she could visit the nursery upon her whim."

"Bloody hell. That might be all well and good when we're not trying to cover up the fact that the pair of you are worthless idiots, but of all the people in the family, wee James can tell the difference between you twins better than anyone."

"It never would have happened if Andrew had taken his leave last eve," Philip growled.

"On a moonless night in the rain, mind you." Andrew leaned over his horse's neck, demanding more speed. "I stayed away from all the damned frivolities and waited until the guests were gone afore I went up to bid farewell to the wee bairns."

Philip scowled. "Except all the guests werena gone, were they?"

"Shut your gob," Martin shouted as they cantered beneath the guardhouse archway. "You are as much to blame in this as your brother. Furthermore, it is you who must agree to a wedding date as soon as we walk in the bloody door. I'll entertain no excuses."

Philip kicked his heels. "If she'll ever talk to me again."

Andrew growled under his breath. If he were in Philip's shoes there would be nothing he wouldn't do to win back Eugenia's affections.

A footman met them in the courtyard and took their reins. "Your Grace, the ladies are awaiting you in the drawing room."

"They've returned from their outing?" asked Martin.

"Yes, sir, about a quarter of an hour ago."

The three of them hastened inside, but Eugenia was not within. Julia, Mama, the baroness, and Harriet were the only ladies present, and not a one was sitting.

"Where is Miss Eugenia?" Andrew asked.

The baroness slapped a letter into his chest. "I hope this tells us. We were about to open it."

Andrew glanced at the lovely penmanship while Philip plucked it from his fingertips. "It is addressed to *me*."

"What does it say?" Mama demanded while Philip broke the seal and unfolded the paper.

He cut her a look before pursing his lips and reading.

Unable to help himself, Andrew peered over his brother's shoulder.

Dear Sir Philip MacGalloway,

You scathing, despicable cad, I ought to thank you for setting me free. For releasing me from the chains of duty all women of my ilk are forced to endure. However, in my present state of shock, I am feeling no such gratitude.

I now know the unabashed, vulgar truth. You sent your charming brother to Stack Castle to trick me into falling in love with you because you are too concerned with your own self-importance to be charming or endearing toward a woman for whom you care nothing. I am not only humiliated, I *am appalled that anyone can think so little of me. Please allow me to make myself clear:*

I hereby rescind our engagement. I will never marry you. Never! Furthermore, I, at no time want to see you, your twin brother, or anyone in your convoluted family ever again.

Please do not search for me. Please do not dispatch anyone to search for me. To you I am deceased.

Most sincerely,

The former Miss Eugenia Radcliffe

P.S. You may conspire with my mother on the deceased point.

As Philip glanced up, the baroness snatched the letter from his grasp. "I demand you tell me what is going on forthwith!"

Snarling, Philip slammed a right hook across Andrew's face. "This is your fault!"

After careening into the settee, Andrew recovered his stance, raised his fists, and threw a jab aimed to crush his twin's nose, but just before his knuckles collided with sinew and bone, Martin parried the strike away, slipping Andrew into a full nelson and pulling him across the room. "There will be no fighting in my castle!"

Andrew struggled against the duke's impossible hold while glaring at his twin. "Me? That miserable fiend is entirely at fault—heading to Perth to watch a bloody horserace! You dunna care about Eugenia and you never did!"

"Och aye?" Philip thrust his finger at the letter, held by the baroness who stood dumbstruck. "And what the blazes was the lass referring to—falling in love with you, ye obnoxious rogue? You kissed her, I ken it in my bones. You preyed on an innocent lass, *my* bloody intended and—"

"Enough!" Martin shouted, shoving Andrew into a chair. "Stay where you are or I'll lay you flat myself."

"So now I'm the villain here?" he asked, while his mind came to grips with the words, "*You sent your charming brother to Stack Castle to trick me into falling in love...*" In three days had Eugenia fallen in love with him?

Truly?

He started to push to his feet, but Martin thrust his finger, indicating that if Andrew dared stand, there would be bitter consequences. The duke explained the sordid details of Philip's ruse while Andrew sat stunned, recounting every moment of the past few days from watching Eugenia alight from the carriage, her rapt interest in flowers, her unabashed love of Skye, how she played like a nymph in the water, how she danced with unfettered flourish in the orchestra's chamber—and finally how she'd kissed him timidly at first, but learning quickly, giving her all, showing him the passion smoldering deep within a proper woman's soul.

Andrew had not intended to do more than to provide an escort, to supply a modicum of polite chatter, to dance in the hall rather than in the secluded chamber...alone. Their walks were supposed to be chaperoned for God's sake!

The baroness presented another letter for all to see. "This one was addressed to me. In it my eldest daughter has asked that I preserve the reputation of the Barony of Bedford and tell everyone that she fell off a cliff whilst searching for puffins."

"Hogwash," Andrew bellowed. "She did not take a tumble from a cliff!"

The baroness looked surprisingly composed considering her daughter had not only disappeared, she had rescinded her engagement. "But in Sir Philip's letter my daughter does refer to herself as the former Miss Radcliffe."

"Because she's running. Do you not see?" Andrew stood, this time eyeing Martin with a hard stare of his own, challenging the duke to lay one more finger upon his person.

"She'll be ruined." The baroness looked to her younger daughter. "Harriet's chances will be dashed."

"Not if you follow Miss Eugenia's wishes," said Philip. Who the devil was he to utter something so callous?

Mama gripped her hands over her heart. "She could not have gone far. We must stop her before she creates a scandal."

"Do you have any idea where she might have gone?" asked Andrew.

"Aside from jumping off a cliff?" The baroness flipped open her fan and rapidly cooled her face. "All she has done for the past three years is bide her time, waiting for Sir Philip to set the date for the wedding."

"And make lace," Andrew added, an idea forming of what she might be planning. After all, she did have an extraordinary talent. But then again, pursuing it would be madness.

The stablemaster entered, his hat gripped in his

hands. "Beg your pardon, Your Graces, but all of the horses are accounted for."

"Do you hear that?" asked Martin. "She's on foot. We must find her at once."

Mama looked to the doors, her complexion pale. "And what am I do to with the other forty-six guests, including Prince Isidor who still has not proposed to Grace, mind you?"

"Carry on as if nothing has happened. After all, the men are theoretically still hunting," said Martin.

"She never wants to set eyes on me again." Philip removed his pipe from his inside doublet pocket and thrust it in Andrew's direction. "And she's fallen in love with this numpty."

"She was using a figure of speech." Resisting his urge for revenge and issue his twin a clock to the muns, Andrew gave the duke a nod. "I have an idea. I'll ride for John o'Groats to see if she boarded the mail coach while you send out a search party. I'll send word if she has been seen."

"Oh heavens!" The baroness drew a hand to her forehead as she dropped onto a settee. "How could Eugenia do this to me?"

Julia joined Her Ladyship, giving her arm a consoling pat. "But we were just in John o'Groats."

"You went to the pier, did you not?" asked Andrew.

"Yes, to see Gibb's ship," Julia replied.

"Tell me, Your Grace, had you not wanted to be seen by a certain party riding in the Duke of Dunscaby's shiny black carriages, would you have been able to avoid them?"

As Julia's eyebrows arched, Andrew did not wait for her reply.

11

Eugenia did not take the main road to John o'Groats where she might have been spotted by the ladies who'd gone to see Captain Gibb MacGalloway's ship. Rather, she followed the path along the edge of the sea as Philip...no, as *Andrew* had pointed out to her on the day they'd gone down to the shore. Sure enough, after rounding the northeastern most tip of the main isle of Scotland, she spotted the little village of John o'Groats nestled just behind the bluff.

Before stepping out into the open, she had surveyed her surrounds, taking note of the Duke's two carriages waiting near the pier while two skiffs laden with ladies were on the sea, being rowed toward an enormous three-masted barque. Had she not awakened this morning with a megrim, Eugenia might have been on one of those skiffs.

Unfortunately—or fortunately as the case may have been, after a few cups of tea and a slice of toast, the pain throbbing at her temples had cleared and she'd decided that it might be fun to visit Lily and James in the nursery and read them a story. Now, as she sat in the mail coach beside a brother and sister of far less lofty birth, Eugenia finally allowed herself to think about everything that had transpired.

Of course, as soon as she'd met *Andrew's* gaze, she realized at once that he had been the very man who'd showered her with attention, who had put her at ease, who'd charmed her. She should have realized from the outset that Philip for some unfathomable reason had traded places with his brother. But three years, two months, and eight days had a way of blurring one's memory.

Though she had seen Andrew MacGalloway at the dowager duchess' birthday celebration three years past, they had never exchanged words. Moreover, the only thing that had struck her as odd after arriving at Stack Castle was that Philip seemed so much easier to talk to. He wasn't as stiff and reticent as he'd been after his hasty proposal. Now looking back, she'd played into their ruse like a daft fool.

Though she'd like to demand they explain themselves before she pushed both of them off a cliff, she wasn't exaggerating when she said she never wanted to see anyone associated with the MacGalloway family ever again. Neither did she exaggerate when she thanked Sir Philip for releasing her from the chains of duty that bound every highborn young lady. Starting today, she was no longer Eugenia Radcliffe. She no longer needed anyone to support her. She wanted nothing to do with marriage, men, or highborn, wealthy families.

Well, she did need wealthy families, but for completely different ends than before.

All proceeded according to her hastily drawn up plans, when she gave the man at the tiny station the name of Miss Laroux and slipped aboard the coach. Beside her sat two children, a boy aged about twelve years of age with his fingers wrapped around the barrel of a musket, and a sister who looked to be a little older. Though it wasn't terribly odd to see a weapon inside a carriage, Eugenia hoped it wasn't charged. Their mother appeared to be a rather responsible sort, sitting across and wearing a simple day dress, her features weathered, her chapped and red fingers clutched around the handle of a basket.

Next to the mother was an elderly man who reeked of spirits. As soon as he climbed into the coach, he'd given Eugenia an unpleasant once-over before tilting his hat over his face and promptly starting to snore.

The ride to Thurso was slow as the carriage ambled along, negotiating ruts and mud from the recent rains. "Are you traveling alone, miss?" asked the lad.

Eugenia immediately tensed.

"Och, Tommy, that's no' something ye ask a lady of quality."

Eugenia looked from her doeskin gloves to her new pelisse, to her polished boots. Though she considered her costume to be muted and plain, it was far nicer than the threadbare clothing the woman and her children wore.

"Sorry," said the lad, turning to Eugenia and looking her in the eyes. "Me da says I have to be the man whilst he's away. 'Tis up to me to take care of me ma and me sister."

"Oh my." She caught a proud smile from the mother. "That is quite a great deal of responsibility for a young man."

"Aye. He gave me the musket he carried against Napoleon. And I'm not afeared to use it."

Eugenia took a longer look at the gun, black, sleek, deadly. "I daresay I hope we are all safe here."

"Wheesht, Tommy, or Miss Laroux will make you sit up top with the driver."

"Och, do ye reckon the driver would let me?" Tommy tapped the butt of the musket on the floor. "I could fend off highwaymen and scoundrels."

"Ye'd be more likely to shoot yourself in the foot," said his sister.

"What do you ken? Have ye ever fired a flintlock afore?"

"Enough, children." Mrs. Hay pulled aside the curtain and looked out over the rolling hills of green. "Did you come from the castle, Miss Laroux? The village was all agog to have a great many grand carriages come through. I'm told the duke was hosting a house party."

Eugenia didn't think of extending her story beyond giving the coachman a false name, but she needed to come up with a plausible tale straight away. Traveling from Bedford to Stack Castle had taken a week, and on a mail coach, it might be a fortnight before she reached her final destination. Moreover, telling people that she'd fled because her husband-to-be's twin had posed as her intended was too humiliating to own to. "Indeed, I was at the castle, but not as a guest. I'm but a seamstress, returning home now that the ball is over with."

"What's it like?" asked the girl, Lucy? Lilian? Eugenia couldn't recall her name. "It must be grand on the inside."

"Oh, it is, at least what I saw of it." If Eugenia were a seamstress she would not have been given a tour by Her Grace, nor would she have been invited into the dining hall...or the orchestra's withdrawing chamber for that matter.

"Did you meet the duke?" asked Tommy.

Eugenia thought for a moment. She hated lying, but she'd already started digging a hole. Nonetheless, it was best to keep her ruse as simple as possible. "Unfortunately, no. I was there on the request of Baroness Bedford."

Ruse.

Now she was the person making up stories. Fortunately, she'd never see Mrs. Hay and her children again. Moreover, her ploy would do nothing to humiliate or demean them. *I simply must conceal my identity to enable me to escape my miserable fate.*

"How far are you traveling? Do you take the mail coach often?" Eugenia asked, diverting the conversation.

Mrs. Hay looked beneath the cloth covering her basket which appeared to be full of apples. "Oh, no. We have a wee cottage in Wick..."

~

AFTER DISCOVERING the post office locked, Andrew found the postmaster in the tavern next door. Still wearing his scarlet coat with contrasting blue cuffs and lapels, the man accepted a pint of ale from the barman and turned to Andrew. "The reason the post office is closed is because the mail coach left Thurso three quarters of an hour ago."

Today, Andrew's luck had completely abandoned him. Once he had learned that a lass fitting Eugenia's description had boarded the coach in John o'Groats, he'd ridden like a sinner being chased by Satan, covering the nineteen or so miles in less than two hours —far faster than any mail coach was capable of traveling.

Then again, after he'd wasted time searching for

the hunting party and going back to the castle, reading the letters, and being lambasted by the baroness as well as his brother, the lass' head start exceeded hours.

"Did any passengers disembark?" he asked.

"One."

"A young lady, perchance?"

"Nay." The postmaster pointed across the tavern in the direction of a dubious looking soul, presently doing his best to drain the contents of a schooner. "That fellow over there."

"So, the rest of the travelers continued on to..." Andrew rolled his hand through the air.

"Wick, of course. Every Thursday, the coach travels from John o'Groats to Thurso to Wick, and the next day continues down the coastline on its way to Inverness."

Andrew ran his hand down his face and looked out through the hazy tavern windows. He'd tethered his horse beside a watering trough. And though the gelding could go another twenty miles, the laddie wouldn't be able maintain the same pace as before. Still, he had gained time and ought to be able to catch the coach before it arrived in Wick.

Once outside, he climbed aboard his trusted gelding and headed out of town, posting at a steady trot, his jaw set, his teeth aching from clenching them. Damnation, he knew he shouldn't have agreed to Philip's ludicrous plan and now this unmitigated disaster was his fault. It was one thing to trade places when they were at university, but quite another to deceive his brother's betrothed. Eugenia was such a lovely, kindhearted woman. And now she was fleeing to God knew where to do God knew what.

All because of him.

And Philip, of course.

But Andrew was as culpable as his twin brother and it was now up to him to set things to rights.

Eugenia deserved to be happy. And whatever she was plotting in that bonny head of hers was most likely going to ruin her, no matter what she desired.

In John o'Groats she had given the station master the name of Miss Laroux, but when the man described her English accent, blonde hair, blue eyes, and looking akin to a woman of quality, Andrew had no doubt Miss Laroux was Eugenia. After all, the village was at the end of the earth for all intents and purposes. He doubted the population exceeded a few hundred. As promised, he'd sent word back to the castle that he was following the mail coach and that she'd used an alias (that he did not divulge in the letter), which hopefully would put the baroness at ease. He also promised to bring Eugenia back, which he fully intended to do.

At long last, approximately two hours after he'd left Thurso, Andrew spotted the coach swaying from side to side as it crested a hill. His heart took to flight as he leaned over his horse's neck and demanded more speed. "Come on, lad. We can catch them."

The gelding snorted through his big nostrils, as they gained on the rickety coach.

"Stop in the name of King George!" Andrew hollered, holding up his hands to show the driver that he was not a highwayman.

The man glanced over his shoulder and scowled, slapping his reins as if he had no intention of stopping.

Growling under his breath, Andrew surged ahead and took hold of the lead horse's bridle, tugging with all his might. "Whoa!"

"What the devil are you on about?" asked the driver, his whip posed to strike.

"I have it on good authority that you have a stowaway aboard."

"I paid my fare, mind you!" Eugenia's voice came from within.

Thank God she was unharmed.

Andrew dismounted while a wave of uncertainty crashed over him. He'd ridden all this way, bent on finding her, but now what should he say?

I'm sorry I deceived you? I do not deserve to kiss the ground upon which you trod?

After opening the carriage door, he blinked to adjust his eyes as he held out his palm, leaning inside. "Please, miss, there has been a grave misunderstanding and I owe you my deepest apology."

"Do you want me to shoot him, Miss Laroux?" asked a lad whose voice had not yet changed.

"No, Tommy! For heaven's sakes!" Eugenia placed her hand in Andrew's and allowed him to help her alight, thank God. "Driver, I won't be but a moment."

"Where is Skye?" she asked, searching.

Andrew handed her down to the road. "You've fled from your betrothed, your mother and sister, and you're worried about my dog?"

"My *former* betrothed, mind you, and yes. Of all the beings I met at Stack Castle, aside from the duchess, the only one who showed me kindness without inflicting a mortal wound was the deerhound."

"Forgive me. I left him in the care of my valet. In truth, when I set out today, I did not realize I'd be chasing a carriage all the way to Wick. And honestly, if I'd wanted to travel to Wick, I would have taken the coast road and saved myself a good four hours or more."

"And we're no' there as of yet," bellowed the driver. "Ye'd best climb back inside, miss, or else I'll have to leave without ye."

Eugenia thrust her finger at the man. "Allow me a moment, if you please," she said as if she were the matron of the London hospital in charge of a great many beds. Who would have known such a shy lass was capable of putting a crusty old mail coach driver in his place?

Andrew swallowed his grin as she turned her ire to him. "Did you...ah...*Philip* not read my letter?"

"Yes, he read it as did I, but you were hurt when you wrote those things...understandably, and I—"

"Let me make myself *eminently* clear." She narrowed her eyes, her lips thinning. "I was not joking when I said in my letter that I want *nothing* to do with you or your family ever again. Case in point, I see Philip has sent his brother to act in his stead once more."

"Miss!" shouted the driver.

Andrew sliced his hand through the air. "The lady asked you to give us a moment," he growled, not shifting his gaze away and holding her hands so that she had no choice but to look him in the eyes, albeit hers were wide and fiery. "My brother is bereft by your rescinding the engagement. Though I cannot vouch for him, there was, however, one thing you said in your letter that convinced me that I cannot let you go."

Behind them a click sounded. "Release her now, mister, or I'll shoot ye dead, I swear I will."

Eugenia snapped her hands from Andrew's fingers and whipped around. "Tommy, no!"

As Andrew caught sight of a Baker infantry rifle's

well-worn barrel, he stepped forward, while shoving Eugenia behind the carriage, out of harm's way. "I only wished to talk—"

The muzzle flashed.

Boom!

Andrew dove aside, the shot grazing his arm. "Argh!" he cried, crashing to the ground.

"Tommy, what have you done?" Eugenia shouted, dropping to her knees beside Andrew.

"I thought he was hurting you," said the lad while the driver hopped down.

Andrew clapped a hand over his wound. In seconds, blood was seeping through his fingers. "I was trying to talk to her, you bleeding eejit!"

"Put that gun away and get your arse back into the carriage with your mother," said the driver before crouching beside Andrew. He tugged off his neckcloth and set to tying it around Andrew's arm. Tight. "Ye're lucky the wee laddie only nicked ye."

It felt as if the musket ball had burned a hole in his flesh and the fire was still ablaze. "Why the hell did you let him shoot me?"

The driver offered his hand. "I didna see the lad until it was too late."

"Andrew," said Eugenia, her voice lulling. "Can you make it back to Stack Castle?"

"Will you go with me?"

"I cannot."

12

E ugenia stood beside Andrew, chewing the inside of her cheek as they watched the carriage drive the horses around a bend in the road and disappear. The driver had left them alone, the heartless lout. Worse, Andrew had refused to climb aboard the carriage and continue on to Wick.

She might loathe the MacGalloways and desperately want to proceed with her plan, but Andrew had been shot. He had been wounded because of her and she wasn't about to leave him bleeding on the road. Who knew how badly he'd been hurt? The Highlander needed to be tended by a doctor.

Goodness, during the wars she had read reports of more than one soldier succumbing to a so-called flesh wound which had developed all sorts of complications. One she recalled quite clearly had reported that a man had bled to death in his sleep. Another's wound had turned putrid causing the need for the removal of the limb and the poor man died during surgery.

Of course, Tommy assumed he was protecting her. If only Mrs. Hay would have insisted her son stow the weapon with the luggage, this never would have happened.

"We'd best go," said Andrew, his voice edged with pain. "I reckon 'tis only a couple of miles until we reach the coast. From there, the ride to Stack Castle ought to only take two or three hours. Interestingly, by the time we arrive at the gates, we will have executed a perfect triangle."

Regardless of if the mail coach took her miles out of her way, it had been the only viable option for her escape. "I am not returning to Stack Castle." She pointed to the blood seeping from the bandage fashioned from the driver's neckcloth now dripping onto the dirt. "You need to be seen by a physician, and I'd imagine the closest one is in Wick."

He stretched the wing, the movement bringing a grimace. "The shot only grazed my arm."

"Is that why you're still bleeding like you've been sliced by a dagger?"

Andrew reached for the horse's reins and pulled the gelding away from the succulent grass growing alongside the dirt road. "I ken you were upset with Philip as well as me. I realize now that our behavior was unforgivable and, for my part, I am immensely sorry. But to pick up and leave without your mother and sister, setting out on your own is madness."

"Oh, you would say that," Eugenia spat with a sharp edge to her voice. "You're a man. And an arrogant one at that."

"I beg your pardon? What were you thinking when you left the castle alone? You could have been—could *still* be ruined."

"Do you not believe me to possess the intelligence to understand the precariousness of my actions? I told my mother to inform everyone I'd fallen off a cliff for a reason."

"Which was what, exactly?"

Oh, no, she wasn't going to divulge the details of her plan, lest Mama send someone to ruin everything before it began. "I do not intend on ever returning to that life."

Andrew puzzled as he cradled his injured arm. "A life of privilege? A life where you had a chance to marry a good man who could support you in high style?"

"A good man? Have you lost your mind? Philip thinks so little of me he convinced you to act in his stead, did he not?"

"Och, it was only supposed to be for a day or two whilst he..."

"What? Enjoyed the attentions of his mistress?"

"Nay! You need to understand my brother. Horses have always been his passion. Even at university he studied horse husbandry and I must admit he has developed an impressive racehorse breeding program."

"So, he was awaiting the birth of a prized foal?"

"Not exactly." Andrew kicked a stone. "He went to Perth to see the maiden race of a promising mare."

Eugenia scarcely could refrain from slapping him. Never in her life had she been so horridly insulted. "Sir Philip chose a horserace over spending a few days with his betrothed—a woman who has sat idly by, passing the time, her heart pattering with futile anticipation every time the post was delivered to Aubrey Hall?"

"I suppose time slipped away from him," Andrew replied, his expression sheepish, doing nothing to convince her that his brother cared for her with one fiber in his vainglorious body.

"Three years, two months, and eight days does not simply slip away from anyone." Eugenia tired of this banter. It was going nowhere and she was still stuck at the side of the road in the midst of one of the remotest parts of Scotland with no other passersby in sight. "Nonetheless, do you honestly believe marriage to your brother is what I wanted for myself?"

"Yes. You seemed happy enough with your lot when you thought I was Philip."

"Mayhap I resolved myself to my fate, but then when I discovered the magic of the week had all been a ruse, I realized..." Eugenia clutched her hands against her stomach. "Oh, why am I bothering to explain my feelings to you? You care nothing for me."

Andrew released a breath, his brow furrowed. "That's where you're wrong, lass."

Heaven help her, he sounded so disgustingly sincere. "Is it?"

"Aye." Andrew reached for her hand, but she turned away, her shoulder brushing his horse. "If I promise to keep your confidences, will you please tell me what this grand scheme is of yours?"

Eugenia brushed her fingers along the gelding's sorrel mane. "If I tell you, my mother will force my father to send someone after me."

"If you dunna tell me, I will throw you over my saddle and haul you back to the castle."

"Pshaw! With a wounded arm?"

Faster than she could blink, Andrew snatched her wrist and whipped her around, locking her arm painfully up her back, wedging her against his body.

"You brute!" she shouted.

"I am simply making a point," the man growled, his voice a tad menacing, yet stirring.

As he released her, Eugenia spun, aiming a slap at his face, only to have him catch her wrist and twist it even harder than before, practically making her drop to her knees. "I have no idea how I could have possibly thought you to be a gentleman."

"Why did you flee?" he demanded. "Are you suffering abuse at home? Is someone hurting you there?"

"No!" Eugenia tried to twist away but that only made the pain worse. "Release me and I shall tell you even though you are an undeserving wretch."

"Do you promise to be civil?"

How could the dastard ask me to be civil when he's the person doing the manhandling? "Just release me, you brutish fiend!"

Mercifully, Sir Andrew's fingers eased.

She briskly rubbed the spot where he'd grabbed her. "I need your word that you will never in your life repeat this to anyone."

"I give you my oath."

She glanced away, wondering why she ought to believe him, given his recent behavior. "If you must know, I intend to sell my lace creations."

"Och aye?" he asked, but his tone wasn't mocking in the slightest as she'd thought it might have been. "Have you experience with such a venture?"

Eugenia squared her shoulders and tipped up her chin. "I most certainly do. As you are aware, I've sold pieces at fetes near Cambridge."

"Yes, I am aware, though selling at fetes is quite a bit different than entering the trade," he said, again without a hint of mockery.

"If you dare divulge my secret to my mother, I will see to your most hideous death."

"Believe me, it is one of a man's greatest pleasures not to have to speak to your mama." Sir Andrew looked toward the horizon. "But it takes time to establish a thriving business. Do you have pieces to sell now? How do you intend to make ends meet?"

Eugenia had not expected such questions. He actually sounded as if he might care, though she highly doubted he possessed a compassionate bone in his body. Moreover, most any male she'd ever met would tell her she couldn't do it, but Sir Andrew had at least asked if she had a plan.

"I did have a trunk full of pieces to sell, but they are in my bedchamber at Aubrey Hall." She held up her reticule. "However, with the coin I've been saving, I have earned enough to let a room in a boarding house whilst I build an assortment of lace items before I open a shop." She pointed in the direction the mail coach had disappeared. "In fact, I must hasten to Wick forthwith because the coachman didn't bother to retrieve my things. They left with the satchel containing an unfinished a scarf as well as the overdress I wore to the ball."

Deciding it was time to take her leave, she dipped into a curtsy. "So as you see, Sir Andrew. I will not be returning to the castle, nor will I be returning to my former life. Good evening. Everything would be so much easier if you told our families that I literally fell to my death and my mangled body was swept out to sea."

With that, she started down the road, toddling in a rut worn deep by dozens of carriages which had traveled this way.

Except footsteps of both the human and equine variety sounded behind her.

"You willna make it to Wick afore dark if you walk." Andrew's deep voice made the hairs on the back of her neck stand on end.

Eugenia looked to the skies. This time of year in Scotland, twilight wouldn't be upon them until nine o'clock, though she'd lost track of time. For all she knew it might be well after the dinner hour. By the way her stomach growled, she surely felt as if mealtime had come and gone. "What do you care about it?"

"I care far more than you realize." He led the horse beside her. "Come, I'll give you a leg-up and we'll ride to Wick together."

She almost smiled. At least he'd agreed to take her where she wanted to go. "Astride?"

He glanced to her skirts. "I promise not to ogle your ankles."

"Oh, for heaven's sakes." She placed her hands on the saddle and bent her knee. With one hand, he provided a cup and hoisted her up, but she didn't miss his anguished grunt. Indeed, Sir Andrew was in more pain than he let on.

Nonetheless, he mounted, took up the reins, and together they set off at a fast walk with barely enough room for them both to fit in the saddle, and though Eugenia kept trying to shift her bum forward, she continually slid back against him. His thighs cradled her. The warmth of his chest radiating against her back, making her yearn to lean against him, but every time her shoulder blades came in contact with the man, she'd inch forward again.

After a mile or so, she scooted forward with such force, that the pommel of the saddle smacked her in a very private spot. Tears misted her eyes as she tried not to gasp.

"Enough," Sir Andrew growled, tugging her flush against his chest. "Ease back and breathe, dammit."

She didn't fight.

But she refused to admit it was far more comfortable to allow herself to rest against his chest. She most certainly would not ride with him again, nor would she enjoy doing so.

After they'd arrived in Wick, she would book passage there. With luck, the town would be large enough to have a ferry that traveled down the coast.

At least another mile passed before she asked, "Why did you come after me?"

"Ah..." The Highlander's groan rumbled in his chest, sending frissons of tingles through her blood. "I would have come after you regardless, but..."

"But Philip did not?"

"He was bereft."

"With such a foothold in the horseraces, I doubt he'll mourn for long."

"Nay." Sir Andrew shifted, taking in a breath as if he had more to say but couldn't find the words. Finally, he released an enormous sigh. "In your letter, scathing as it was, you said something that struck a chord...ah...in my heart."

As she realized what she'd written, Eugenia drew a hand over her mouth. This Highlander must never think that she had actually fallen in love with him. Besides, she had not. Most certainly, any affection she had experienced was purely an infatuation. The week had been a lie, and he had tricked her into thinking he was charming, chivalrous, handsome, kind. Most certainly not *bedeviled*. She needed to reassert herself before her heart completely melted her resolve. "I believe my final paragraph did make it clear that I never wanted to see Philip or anyone in the MacGalloway family again. And that includes you, Sir Andrew."

13

By the time they reached Wick, dusk had turned the masonry of the town's buildings blue-grey and hazy. They'd spotted her satchel through the post office's window, sitting alone on a bench. Unfortunately, both the door and the window were locked and there'd be no retrieving it until morning.

A small fishing village, the only inn was above the tavern in the square. After stabling his horse, Andrew led Eugenia inside the raucous alehouse, shoulder-to-shoulder with fishermen who wreaked of haddock, most of whom well on their way to drinking themselves into a mindless stupor.

All heads turned their way but no one was looking at Andrew. He pressed his palm into the small of Eugenia's back and inclined his lips toward her ear. "Stay close to me."

The barman wiped his hands on a dingy cloth, his gaze narrowing on the lass. "Women arena allowed."

Andrew glanced over his shoulder. *No wonder the sailors are staring.* "Have you a room for me and my wife? Mayhap two?"

"What, did ye pair have a wee stramash?"

"Nay, nay." Andrew pulled Eugenia closer. "Have you a room?"

"Aye. One."

"And a meal for us both. Two schooners of ale and a flagon of whisky."

The man reached for a tankard. "Ye want a fire in the hearth as well?"

Andrew nodded. No matter what time of year it was, the nights were chilly this far north.

"All that will cost ye one pound, forty-five pence," he said, drawing the ale. "Payment in advance."

Andrew pulled the coin out of his sporran and slapped it on the bar. "My thanks."

"Is there a doctor in town?" asked Eugenia.

"Thurso." The man looked to Andrew's blood-encrusted bandage. "You want I should send for him? He willna be here afore noon on the morrow."

Taking the tankards, Andrew shook his head. "Not necessary."

Eugenia raised her finger. "In that case, we need clean cloths and a pot of boiling water, if you please."

The bartender frowned. "What happened? Did the lassie take her shears to ye?"

The last thing to which Andrew wanted to admit was being shot by a child. "Och, 'tis just a wee scrape."

"I'll have the laddie bring your food and water up to the room." The barman slid a key across the bar, which the lass snatched up. "First door on the right. And remember, no ladies allowed in the tavern."

"Hell will have to spontaneously combust before I agree to share a room with you," Eugenia growled under her breath as they started up the stairs.

"Wheesht," Andrew cautioned. "We'd best make them think we're husband and wife else you'll have a host of drunken fishermen trying to break down your door."

"They wouldn't dare."

"Would they not? A woman traveling alone. A proper English woman at that—all the way up here in the uncivilized north of Scotland."

At the top of the stairs, Eugenia slid the key into the lock and opened the door. "I daresay everything about this country is uncivilized. Including your family." She eyed him before stepping inside. "You may wait out here."

He held up the frothing tankards. "But what of the meal and the boiling water you requested?"

The door closed in his face, making the ale in his hands slosh over his fingers.

FINALLY ALONE, Eugenia paced the floor of the tiny room, sporting only one bed, a table, a stool, and a chair. Near the window, a white chamber pot was stowed on the floor beside a tall washstand with an ewer and bowl.

Since boarding the coach in John o'Groats, she hadn't had a moment to herself. She needed time to think. Things were not exactly proceeding as she had envisioned. First of all, Andrew MacGalloway was thwarting all of her plans. And then the dratted Highlander had to go and get himself shot. Even if he'd only been grazed, the wound was bad enough to cause consternation. Should Sir Andrew succumb to a fever it would be entirely her fault.

And why the devil is there not a physician in Wick?

Things would have been so much simpler if she could have been able to leave the Highlander in the care of a doctor while she went on her way. But then again, it would have caused an uproar if she had waltzed into a "gentlemen's only" alehouse and asked for a room. She most likely would have been cast out before she opened her mouth.

Now that she had a place to sleep for the night, she must think of a way to elude Sir Andrew and carry on with her plan. And why was the man so tenacious? First of all, she was shocked that anyone had uncovered her ruse and followed her all the way to the Thurso-Wick Road. Moreover, she was doubly shocked it had been Sir Andrew. He didn't care about her welfare.

Of course, she'd told him about the lacemaking, but everyone knew she was skilled at the art. If her mother ever thought of anything aside from seeing her daughters married, Mama might realize that Eugenia did have an option aside from wedded bliss, not that anyone of her ilk ever shunned their birthright and risked life and limb to become a lacemaker of some renown.

Which is why I am now Miss Laroux.

She continued to pace, her mind darting from one calamity to the next. Of course, she needed to tend Sir Andrew's arm. In order to do that, she must allow him inside the chamber.

Unfortunate.

Both of them needed to eat something or they'd not be able to function come morn, yet another reason for him to be allowed inside. However, she wasn't about to allow him to remain within for longer than absolutely necessary.

He could sleep in the stables for all she cared.

Eugenia bit her thumbnail and looked to the door. *It might be best if he slept in the stable loft.*

She strode to the window and pulled aside the flimsy curtain. There was an overhang about three feet below the window, and farther along at the rear of the inn, a post-and-rail fence surrounded a small horse paddock.

When a knock came at the door, Eugenia jolted and dropped the curtain. "Come in."

"We have your supper, madam," said a serving girl carrying a tray, accompanied by a red-faced boy straining to carry an iron pot of water, sloshing it all over the floor. Andrew followed them inside, holding one empty tankard and the other half-full.

After placing her tray on the table, the maid blushed as she curtsied to him, batting her eyelashes as well, the tart. "Will there be anything else, sir?"

"No, thank you." He seemed not to notice the girl's flirting, pulled a couple of coins out of his sporran, and gave one to each.

Eugenia stared at the tankards. Perhaps she had been rather abrupt when she'd closed the door on his face.

With a shrug, Andrew set them down. "Forgive me. I had a thirst."

"I see."

He gestured over his shoulder. "Would you like me to fetch another?"

"No." The scent of warm food made her mouth water, reminding her that she might be on the verge of starvation. She sat in the chair and nodded to the stool, picking up her spoon. "Stew and warm bread, is it?"

"Aye."

They ate in silence. Well, in truth, they devoured the fare in silence, Sir Andrew appearing to be every bit as ravenous as Eugenia. She didn't even leave the requisite morsel behind, throwing away all decorum, greedily sopping up the dregs of her gravy with the delicious bread.

She guzzled the remaining ale as well, setting down the tankard with an unladylike belch.

Sir Andrew grinned. "'Tis nice to see a woman enjoy a meal."

"Forgive me. I was hungry, and given the present company, I saw no need to stand upon ceremony."

The corners of his mouth tightened as he glanced away. Certainly, she'd issued a barb, but one that was well deserved. In truth, if she issued dozens more it would not be enough, and she refused to feel badly about it.

"How is your arm?" she asked, dabbing her lips with one of the cloths the maid had left.

Andrew uncorked the flagon of whisky and poured a tot into his tankard since the barman obviously hadn't sent up any proper glasses. "I'll be better once I've had a tot of this."

Before he could cork it, Eugenia took the flagon and splashed a bit into her glass. She was no longer the daughter of Baron Bedford and could do anything she pleased.

"Miss Radcliffe, I am shocked," he said, his eyes teasing for the first time since he'd tracked down the mail coach.

"Henceforth Miss Laroux," she replied, raising the tankard in a toast. "As such, I am no longer constrained to the societal edicts obviously dictated by men over the centuries until they have reached the point where women are merely chattel, constrained by their stays as well as their childhood leading strings."

His gaze slipped to her breasts, his eyes growing darker as he once again sipped. "So, is it off with the stays whilst swilling potent whisky?" he asked, again meeting her gaze, his expression reminiscent of the calm one experiences before the onset of a ravaging tempest, powerful enough to steal her breath.

"I did not say that." Eugenia looked away and drank, gulping down far too large a slurp, the fiery liquid burning a track down her throat as if she'd swallowed fire. Coughing, her eyes watered as she rapidly patted her chest, trying to regain a modicum of composure. "My heavens, that is overpowering."

"Which is why whisky is to be sipped and enjoyed in small doses, lest you have an unbearable megrim come morn."

Feigning indifference, Eugenia stacked the dishes to make room for the pot of water.

Of course, as she reached for the handle, Andrew slipped it from her fingers and easily hefted it up. Then he sat on the stool watching her with the rapt interest of a housecat while she untied the sullied bandage and threw it into the fire. As she doused the cloth, she bit down on her bottom lip. Knowing what she ought to do next but feeling ridiculously shy all the same.

He took another drink of whisky while she stood back and stared, cloth in hand. Ever so slowly, he set the tankard down then shrugged his injured shoulder. "I reckon we ought to inspect the damages, aye?"

Exactly. "If you would remove your doublet and shirt, sir."

He flicked the hole in the leather. "This is my favorite coat, I'll have you know."

"Something tells me your coffers will not be hurting overly much when you replace it."

"I suppose not, though a man doesna always like to part with things to which he's grown accustomed."

He slipped it off, untied his neckcloth, then whipped his shirt over his head."

Holy persimmons, Lord help me now.

Eugenia quickly doused the cloth again, wringing it out as if she must extricate every drop of liquid from its fibers. Yes, she'd seen men without their shirts. On occasion the laborers who came to Aubrey Hall for the harvest might remove their shirts on a particularly hot day or to take a dip in the lake. But never in her life had she seen a man's chest up close. And this one was incredibly virile—auburn curls blanketed a particularly unignorable set of sculpted pectorals.

No wonder the man was able to overcome me with one arm.

His creamy skin was dotted with very masculine looking freckles, all the way down to his...

Goodness, I've never seen abdominals ripple before. Is he flaunting his masculinity to me on purpose?

Andrew...*Sir* Andrew cleared his throat and pointed to his right upper arm. "I do believe I was shot over here, miss."

Snapping her eyes away from their ogling, she focused on a very angry-appearing and jagged wound. "Oh dear, this looks far worse than you let on. I do wish I had a salve."

She pulled over the chair and began to dab around the beastly cut. *This man willfully deceived me and I shall not allow myself to admire anything about him.* "Does this hurt?"

"Nay."

She dabbed a bit harder. "Unfortunate."

"Och, lassie, it may please you to ken this will." He took her cloth, doused it with whisky, and held it against the wound, hissing through his teeth while his face literally blanched.

Gaping, Eugenia drew her fists beneath her chin. "Why in heaven's name did you do that?"

"An auld Scots remedy," he growled, giving a strained grin and tossing the rag on the table. "It ought not go putrid now."

She glanced to his arm, now looking even angrier than it had done before. "You're bleeding again."

He reached for the rag, but she moved it away from his grasp. "Allow me. With a fresh cloth or would you prefer another go with the whisky?"

"I reckon I've endured enough pain for one day." He took the tankard and guzzled rather than sipped his remaining drink.

She took the last cloth and rolled it diagonally to give it the greatest length. "Hold out your arm."

He did as she asked and she set to tying it in place, trying her best not to watch the rise and fall of his chest out of the corner of her eye. If only he weren't breathing, his magnificence might be easier to ignore.

Sir Andrew might be easier to ignore as well. For heaven's sakes, she'd kissed the man and had enjoyed doing so. Even though he wasn't who she thought he was at the time, she had to admit, he was quite good at kissing, not that she had much experience with which to compare. However, Eugenia had overheard enough gossip in the lady's withdrawing rooms at the dozens of balls she'd attended over the years, and her ears always perked up when a lady spoke of a man who was thus skilled to make her knees weak.

"Are you finished?" he asked.

Eugenia blinked, realizing her hands had stilled and she'd been staring again. At least this time the object of her focus was the bandage she'd just tied, already showing the seepage of blood. "Ah, I am." She folded her hands in her lap. "That is, I am finished tending your wound."

He reached for his shirt and pulled it over his head. "My thanks."

Her gaze trailed to the soiled cloths as she steeled her resolve. "I must request that you sleep in the stables."

"Verra well," he said, slipping into his doublet and wincing.

"Before you go, could you tell me something?"

"I suppose it depends on the question."

"Why did you do it?"

"Come after you?" He fastened the top button on his coat. "I thought I already—"

"No, no! What I'm asking is why did you play along with Philip's scheme? Did you also believe that the horserace was more important than spending a few days with a miserable spinster who has been tatting lace up to her eyebrows while waiting for a letter—for some communication from a man who'd asked for her hand?"

Sir Andrew frowned and shook his head. "We oft play chess. Every Wednesday to be exact."

"Oh?" Good heavens, that made as much sense as watching leprechauns dance on rainbows. "I do not understand."

"Well, it isna unusual for one of us to suggest a wager," he said, cringing like a schoolboy caught pulling a maid's plait.

"You deceived me because you lost a bet?"

"Well, I did try to make it impossible for Philip to commit to the agreement."

Eugenia crossed her arms as if doing so could protect her from the pain of being snubbed. "How so?"

"I told him that I'd need to be compensated if I were to stand in on his behalf."

"I hope you were handsomely compensated, lest my self-image shall surely take yet another tumble."

He reached out, but then drew his hand to his throat where his neck cloth ought to be. "Though the compensation was extraordinarily extreme, I fear there is nothing worth the sullying of your dignity, madam."

Eugenia's stomach turned while she regarded him. His words were sweet, his Scottish brogue lulling, but she was not about to allow herself to be seduced by him. "Do you oft pretend you're Philip?"

"Not so much since our university days." He stood and took her hand. "You must know I gravely regret agreeing to the wager."

She snatched her fingers away. "Then why did you do it?"

"Because he's my brother and..."

"Hmm?" she demanded, flinching as she steeled herself for a cutting barb.

"I did not feel it would be fair to his intended if you arrived at Stack Castle and he wasn't there to greet you."

Eugenia's shoulders dropped. Well, that certainly wasn't the explanation she was expecting, even if it had merit. "I daresay, Mama would have made quite a fuss."

"Aye, and you would have been needlessly thwarted."

"Not needlessly. Perhaps aptly. Perhaps I could have spared myself more pain." As soon as the words left her lips, Eugenia knew she would have been upset no matter how Philip had chosen to snub her.

Andrew rubbed his arm beneath the wound. "My

twin isna a bad man. Though his priorities sometimes can be a wee bit questionable."

"Wee bit?" Eugenia asked, but decided the topic was not worth arguing over. Philip MacGalloway was a despicable scourge and his brother was not far behind. "I have one last question."

Giving a nod, Andrew tucked the flagon under his arm.

"What did you wager?"

The man's shoulders slumped. "Philip's prized stallion, Randolph."

Another horse? She was deceived by both men because of smelly horses? She thrust her finger toward the door. "Out!"

14

Considering the shoulder-to-shoulder crowd of intoxicated fishermen making a boisterous clamor down below, there was no chance Andrew was about to leave Eugenia alone and toddle off to sleep in the stable's hayloft. After she'd so unceremoniously cast him out, sleep hadn't come easily what with the throbbing ache in his arm and the unforgiving hardwood floor.

Initially, he'd sat against the wall for hours, nursing the flagon of whisky, giving in to its mind-numbing effects. Once or twice, he'd heard Eugenia moving within, which brought a host of unwanted images. What was she up to?

Removing her gown?

Certainly she'd removed her stays. How any woman could bear such contraptions he couldn't fathom

The lass ought to be sleeping in her shift, no doubt, especially since the satchel presently locked away in the post office was hardly large enough for a change of clothes. Add to that a lace scarf or two, and it was a wonder she had managed to fasten the buckles.

For a time in the wee hours, he'd indulged himself in idle fantasy, imaging her unbound breasts beneath a sheath of thin cotton. Or was it silk? She might warm herself with her back to the hearth. How he longed to open the door just to see if the glowing coals illuminated the supple curves of her body.

He had audibly moaned when that thought made his loins stir.

After all, Andrew considered himself a connoisseur of breasts. And it had been far too long since he'd properly examined a pair. Not that he ought to ever think of Miss Eugenia's breasts. Though now that she'd renounced her engagement to Philip...

No. I will not allow myself to fixate on the woman's breasts. Even if they are astonishingly admirable. Eugenia deserves a man who worships her, bows to her, loves her above all else.

Had she released her hair from its chignon? Did those honey-yellow locks cascade in waves past her hips? Did she carry a brush or comb in her reticule? Was she missing the services of her lady's maid?

Andrew's knuckles curled into a fist when he considered knocking and asking if he could be of assistance.

But she wouldn't want that. Eugenia didn't want him. She had made it imminently clear that she didn't want anything to do with his twin or the entire family, which was one of the oldest, most established clans in Scotland. The MacGalloways could trace their ancestry back to the dark ages. The dukedom of Dunscaby carried with it the highest honors in not only Scotland, but in the Kingdom.

And Eugenia Radcliffe nee Laroux had spat on it all.

Though everyone at Stack Castle had been up in

arms with her departure, Andrew didn't blame the lass a bit. The only reason he'd gone along with Philip's ruse was to prevent her from feeling jilted.

A great deal of good that did.

If she wanted to assume a new name and make lace, he ought to support her.

Except he couldn't.

Well, he could very well support her endeavor, but he could not in good conscience allow her to slip away on her own and face hardships she had no idea lurked around every corner. The woman was well-bred and far too naive when it came to the ways of the world.

Traveling alone?

Unheard of.

If she had arrived in Wick this evening without an escort, Eugenia would have been pounced upon by the first nefarious scoundrel who set eyes on her. Whether or not she chose spinsterhood, she needed an escort. All spinsters of her ilk traveled with escorts be they a lady's maid or at least an elderly, widowed aunt.

Sometime in the midst of his thoughts he'd fallen asleep. Now as he stirred, his temple grinding into floor. He sat up, a crick in his neck stabbing him, making it difficult to straighten his spine. Groaning, he rubbed the knot.

This morning he absolutely must talk some sense into Eugenia and take her back to Stack Castle where she would be able to rejoin her mother and sister. To help her come to her senses he would suggest that if she is bent on starting her lace endeavor, she might allow him to make some introductions first. She also needed to put some thought into naming a companion for any of her future travels to ensure she did not fall into an unsavory situation. Though not even Andrew could convince himself that the baroness would allow her eldest daughter to settle for spinsterhood.

Wouldn't it be better than feigning a premature death and being estranged from one's family for the rest of her days?

He swiped the sleep from his eyes and brushed himself off before knocking on the door. "Miss Eugenia?"

Receiving no response, he continued, "I thought I'd go below stairs and order breakfast. Do you have any requests?"

Again, she did not reply.

Andrew knocked louder. "Miss Eugenia!"

He rattled the knob. "Are you awake?"

When not a peep came from within, he lowered his shoulder and burst inside. "Miss—"

Good God.

He turned full circle, seeing nothing but an empty bedchamber and the curtain gently billowing with the breeze. He dashed to the opened window.

"Fie!" he bellowed, flicking open his pocket watch, only to realize he'd overslept by two hours.

His heart in his throat, Andrew barreled down the stairs and across the bustling street to the post office. Pushing inside, his gaze darted to the bench where her satchel had been. The vacant seat sent his miserable heart plummeting to the pit of his stomach.

He thrust his finger at the bench and glared at the postmaster. "The woman who left her satchel on the mail coach. Where has she gone?"

The man glanced up with a blank expression. "Pardon me, could you please repeat that?"

"The woman whose satchel was on the bench overnight—where is she?"

"Sir, I'm no' at liberty—"

"For the love of all that is holy!" Andrew slammed his fist on the counter. "Ye dunna understand this is a matter of life and death!" He might be stretching things a bit, but if Eugenia set off on her own, it might very well be her life that was at risk.

The man's eyes shifted eastward. "I told her that since the southbound mail coach had already left for the day she might have better luck catching a transport to Inverness."

Andrew thought better than to ask when the next ship was sailing. He sprinted to the wharf, dodging barrowloads of manure and men carrying heavy casks on their backs.

He caught a lad by the shoulder. "The transport to Inverness?"

"I beg your pardon?"

Bloody hell was everyone in this town hard of hearing? "The transport! The one sailing to Inverness. Where is it?"

The boy pointed to a ship in bay. "The schooner at anchor, but the last skiff just cast off."

"I cannot miss that boat. Do you know of anyone who can ferry me to her? Perhaps a fisherman going out to sea?"

"Dunna ken." The boy twisted out from beneath Andrew's grip. "I canna stop. Me da sent me to fetch the net. Ours has a hole in it."

"Where's your father?"

"The wee wherry just across."

Andrew let the boy go and marched over the pier to the wee boat equipped with oars as well as single-masted sail. He picked the lad's father easily enough —watching him intently with squinting eyes and a scowl. "I'll pay for your entire day's catch if you can ferry me to that transport."

"I reckon that'll cost ye ten quid."

Andrew figured the tar most likely made but ten quid in an entire season, but he had no time to quibble. He hopped into the boat. "Done."

The sailor held out his palm. "I'll be taking payment now."

He reached for his sporran but didn't slip his fingers inside. "I have a horse housed in the inn's stables —a gelding. The lad's worth fifty pounds or more. He's sound, well-broke, and can double as a carriage horse. He brought me here from the River Tay. He's yours."

"He's no' lame?"

"I wouldna lie to the likes of you. Can we cast off now?"

The sailor scratched his unkempt beard. "I'll need maintenance for the wee beasty."

"Ye drive a hard bargain." Andrew pulled out a golden guinea—worth twenty-one shillings and most likely five and twenty times more than the man earned from a day's catch. "This will keep him in hay for a good year, mayhap two."

The coin disappeared faster than he could blink. "Cast off men, we're taking this gentleman to the Inverness transport."

Andrew stood in the bow, his eyes straining to make out the myriad of individuals aboard the schooner, most of whom were seamen, scurrying about unfurling sails in preparation for the voyage.

He spotted the billowing skirts of a couple of women, but as the wherry sailed nearer and the small figures became life-sized, Eugenia was not among them.

Dear God, what if the postman was wrong? What

if she had taken his horse from the stables and was already heading south? She could be set upon by highwaymen. What if the horse threw a shoe? What if he spooked and threw her?

Andrew waved his hands over his head like a madman. "Hold the ship!" he hollered wondering if he was going to have to swim back to shore.

One of the sailors signaled back and cast a rope ladder over the edge as the men rowed the wherry alongside the much larger ship. Andrew grabbed the ladder and started his ascent, looking to the sailor at the top. "Have you a passenger aboard by the name of Miss Laroux?"

"I beg your pardon?"

Damnation, must everyone in the Kingdom be afflicted with deafness today? "A Miss Laroux?" he shouted, surging upward.

"Och aye, she's aboard, sir."

Relief filled him, though it was rapidly replaced by anger at the fact that he'd nearly lost her yet again. The dashed fool woman had no idea how much she needed him, and that quandary was going to end immediately.

EUGENIA HAD PAID for a small berth furnished with nothing but a cot. Nonetheless, it was better than sleeping below decks in a hammock which had been the cheapest option. Besides, now that she had joined the ranks of the common folk, she needed to become accustomed to going without comforts. Baron Bedford may have not been wealthy by the *ton's* standards, but he was far more well-to-do than most commoners.

A light tap came at the door.

She pressed her hands her hammering heart and looked to the timbers. She mustn't be so jumpy.

"Your satchel, madam," said a youthful voice.

Smiling, she opened the door. "Thank—*you*?"

A very angry-looking Sir Andrew ushered the lad aside, pushed past her, and shut the door. "You shouldna have left without me."

"And since when were you appointed to be my keeper?"

"Since I told your mother and the Duke of Dunscaby that I was going after you and promised to bring you back."

"You what?" Eugenia's mind raced. She hadn't told anyone where she was going or what she was planning. She'd been elusive in her letters to ensure it would be too late before anyone figured out where she'd gone. Except she hadn't counted on Andrew's involvement. As far as she knew, the few days she'd spent in his company were completely false. He'd proved himself an actor worthy of playing a role in London's Theater Royal.

Andrew threw out his hands, his hair disheveled and mashed on one side as if he hadn't a comb in the mysterious sporran he carried over his loins. "I sent the castle a message from John o'Groats—told them you had taken the mail coach, that I was following, and that I'd be bringing you back forthwith."

"Well, you were mistaken. Moreover, you had no grounds upon which to speak on my behalf. I told you I'm not going back to Stack Castle. Not ever. Nor will I be returning to Aubrey Hall."

"I'm beginning to realize you are quite determined on the matter."

"Furthermore, I—" Eugenia dropped her hands to her sides. "I beg your pardon?"

"My oath, everyone has gone a wee bit deaf today?"

"Did you just agree with me?"

"I did."

"So why are you here?"

Andrew set her satchel on the cot. "Because you are a *gentlewoman*. I canna in good conscience allow you to travel all the way to Cambridge alone no sooner than I can allow one of my sisters to do so."

So now he thought of her as a sister? Well, that stood to reason, Eugenia nearly became his sister-in-law. Though the idea of being one of Andrew's sisters did not bode well in the slightest.

"I see."

"Do you?" he asked, sounding irritated as a brother might be with a sister. "This transport is going as far south as Inverness, nearly five hundred miles north of Cambridge—Cambridge is where you intend to settle is it not?"

"Yes."

"Tell me, what mode of travel are you intending to use after arriving in Inverness?"

"I thought I'd take the mail coach to—"

"I will not allow it."

How dare he? Eugenia's spine shot ramrod straight. "I am not your sister nor am I any kin to you whatsoever! You have no right to prevent me from doing as I please."

"Forgive me." Andrew shoved his fingers into his thick auburn hair. "You are correct, you are completely able to ruin yourself however you see fit."

She placed her palm on the wall to steady herself against the listing of the ship. "I am not ruining myself."

"You're traveling alone. That in itself is enough to

create a scandal from which you might never recover. Furthermore, not only would you ruin your chances, your sister would be gravely ruined as well."

"Do you not realize I am painfully aware, sir? Have you not for one minute stopped to think as to why I asked Mama to tell everyone I'd fallen to my death?" Eugenia paced, stumbling a bit when the ship rolled to starboard. "I'll have you know the story isn't terribly farfetched. The cliffs where the puffins nest are perilously high and craggy. If anyone were to fall from them, they most certainly would perish."

"But this is madness. Even if you do not want to marry Philip, you are a stunning beauty and—"

"Pshaw. Lady Grace is stunning. I am merely passable."

When Eugenia turned, Andrew stepped into her path, making her bump into his enormous chest. "As a man, I stand to differ on that topic. Yes, my sister may have been the jewel of the Season declining marriage proposals whilst waiting for her prince, but the only thing Grace has over you is her desire to fit into the mold expected of her."

"See? I do not want to be one of those darlings of the *ton*. I do not want to flit around London's ballrooms, holding my head high because I've been born into one of the oldest baronies in England. As if by some act of God my birth has made me superior to someone like my lady's maid who works her fingers to the bone and eats in the kitchens with the rest of the servants. I hate the class system we've inherited and I cannot abide another Season where my mother parades me around London's marriage mart like a trussed hen."

"So, you are changing your identity and setting your sights on new horizons."

"Exactly."

"With no coin, and no references."

"I have money, you know I have sold a few pieces."

"But you have never been in *business*. You have never tried to sell your lace to a merchant who can see to it your items are placed in the finest shops in Cambridge and beyond."

"Well, I haven't had the chance—"

"I'll wager you havena thought about what success may look like, and the need to bring on more lacemakers. Or worse, what might come if you face hardship— face the prospect of not being able to afford your rent, or buy food, or—"

"You are saying these things to convince me to return home and seal my fate in a loveless marriage."

"No I am not." Andrew slammed the side of his fist against the wall. "What I'm saying is that you need help, just as anyone does when they're starting out. Philip and I were fortunate to have Martin as our benefactor when we opened the mill, and now we have become the most powerful manufacturer of muslin cloth in Great Britain."

"So, what are you implying? Now that I've rescinded Philip's engagement I ought to ask the duke to be my benefactor?"

"I'm merely asking you to allow me to be your escort to Cambridge, mayhap make a few introductions once we arrive."

Oh, good glory, now the man who fooled me deigns to be my mentor? "How can I trust you?"

"Because putting the poor decision I made to impersonate my brother aside, I am the most trustworthy and honest MacGalloway brother. Additionally, I promise you that I will treat you respectfully with utmost chivalry."

Eugenia shifted her fingers to her lips. Lips he had deceptively kissed...although with a great deal of passion and gentleness. Even after all that had transpired, the kiss didn't seem forced or false. "All I have to say is that you are from a family of cheats and scoundrels."

"Do you honestly believe that?"

She didn't, but she should. Also, Eugenia would be foolish not to accept his assistance regardless of if the man had become her sworn enemy. She wasn't a fool. It was dangerous for any woman to traveling alone.

"You do realize I can hardly stand to be in your presence?" she asked for good measure, even though it wasn't exactly true. The truth was that despite her baffling affinity for Andrew, she shouldn't tolerate being in his presence. She also still wanted to wash her hands of the MacGalloways and put this whole debacle behind her. To do that she needed to divest herself of this Highland rogue.

As soon as I arrive in Cambridge.

To her question, he gave a stoic nod.

"Very well," she said, her words careful. "But I shall accept your assistance as an escort only. And I refuse to pose as your wife. If anyone must know, we'll tell them that you are my *brother*. Since you already said you wouldn't allow one of your sisters to travel alone, it stands to reason that we are brother and sister, does it not?"

15

The fare aboard ship was medieval at best—
everyone including the crew received a wooden
bowl of pottage accompanied by a hard, tasteless ship
biscuit that needed a pint of ale to enable anyone to
chew it. There weren't many passengers, but the few
aboard were crouched on the midship deck. At least
Andrew was able to find a couple of half barrels for
them to sit upon near the bow.

"I canna believe the sea is so calm," he said, taking
a bite from his wooden spoon.

"Have you sailed much?" Eugenia asked, now
somewhat civil since she'd agreed to allow him to provide an escort.

"A bit. Took a trip to the Americas with Gibb a year
ago."

"Oh, my. I've heard such frightful things about
sailing the high seas, I'd be afraid to leave Britain's
shores let alone sailing all the way across the Atlantic
and back."

"The life of a sailor isna for the faint of heart, that's
for certain, but I trust Gibb. In my opinion, he pos-
sesses the skill to sail his barque through any squall
God can throw at him."

"Were the seas often rough on your voyage?"

"We faced our share of tempests, though it could have been worse, for certain."

Eugenia shuddered, then attempted to bite into her biscuit, not even causing a mark.

"Careful ye dunna break a tooth."

"I wonder how long ago this was baked," she mumbled, dipping it into her pottage. "Forgive my poor manners."

Andrew bested her and dunked his biscuit in his ale. "I doubt anyone from the *Gazette* is aboard. You ought to be spared embarrassment from the gossips."

With her smile, her face lit up as if the idea made her truly happy. "From now and forevermore if all proceeds to plan."

As he finished his meager meal, Andrew watched her out of the corner of his eye. She was so damned sure of herself, yet the only experience she had was selling a few measly pieces of lace at a fete or two.

Ever since he'd graduated from university, he had been embroiled in industry, from the procurement of cotton harvested by free men—not an easy feat given that the American south still used slave labor which was unacceptable to anyone in his clan. The MacGalloways had contracted with Irish sharecroppers, but the relationship was tenuous at best. Their crops didn't always yield the highest quality and their lands were often preyed upon by plantation owner's hired henchmen—which was why Andrew had sailed to America. He needed to make certain that his mill would be receiving the shipments they'd ordered lest upset all the dozens of customers who were expecting superior MacGalloway muslin.

Miss Eugenia didn't need to understand every facet of running a mill. She did, however, need introductions. Aye, her work was excellent, but she was going to be in competition with lacemakers from all corners of Christendom. As far as he could tell, even if she had her trunk, she had little or no inventory to begin with. She had few references, if any, and fewer prospects. The lass not only must have introductions, dare he think it, she needed a benefactor.

If he uttered a single word about helping her, she might try to run again. Andrew may have allowed himself a moment of weakness when he was flirting with her at Stack Castle, but now she had become his responsibility. Not only was she the daughter of an esteemed baron, she was his brother's betrothed—albeit former betrothed. Nonetheless, Andrew had been instrumental in Eugenia's decision to flee, renounce her family, and start anew. Thus, he was responsible to see to it that she did not end up in some Cambridge gutter whether she wanted his help or not.

He took their empty bowls and set them on the floor. "What say you to a wee turn about the deck?"

As she looked toward the bow, a wisp of blonde hair swept across her cheek. For the first time since he intercepted the mail coach on the road to Wick, she didn't try to argue.

The upper deck was alive with seamen tending sails as well as other passengers milling about while the twilight western sky shimmered with pinks, oranges, and the darkest of blues.

"'Tis a good eve for a stroll," hailed the captain from the helm.

Andrew tipped his cap. "That it is."

"We've been fortunate to avoid a bout of seasickness," said a passing sailor. "Och, once one passenger hangs their head over the rail, the rest always follow."

"What a vulgar man," Eugenia whispered while Andrew led her away.

The tar wasn't wrong, though there were far more delicate topics to discuss when in the presence of a lady. "Shall I challenge him to a duel of fists?"

"Heavens, no."

Honestly, Andrew would relish picking a fight about now. Damnation, a brawl would do him good—allow him an opportunity to release all his pent-up frustration. "Do you reckon I'll lose?"

"Please, I've already been made squeamish by imagining myself bent over the side of the ship, do not make matters worse."

"Forgive me."

"Have you ever succumbed to seasickness?"

He looked to the canvas sails overhead, straining and full of wind. "Only once."

"Was it awful?"

"Aye." As a boom shifted, he led her to the opposite side of the ship. "At the time I thought if given a choice between seasickness and death I'd chose the latter."

"I'm glad you didn't."

He stopped and faced her. "You are?"

She pursed her lips and looked across the North Sea. "I shouldn't have said that."

"No?" He suddenly took an interest in the sails overhead. He'd best not smile—he'd best not show her any sign that his stomach had launched into a leaping sword dance.

"No," she said most pointedly.

Andrew ran a hand down his face. "Och aye, I ken you want to be rid of me as soon as practicable."

"Most definitely."

He offered his elbow. "I canna blame you for that,

lass."

"I'm glad you're beginning to see my side."

By their fourth or fifth turn around the deck, the sun had set and the gentle waves reflected a shimmering glow from the full moon. Eugenia stopped outside the door to the berths and opened it. "I think I will turn in for the night. Besides, I need to work on the lace caps I'm planning to make for quick sales."

"Allow me to—" The door shut in his face.

He stood for a moment wondering who'd seen him stopped so abruptly. Shaking his head, he mumbled, "sisters."

There—that ought to placate any gabble-grinders. Andrew had three sisters. Any one of them could have shut the door in his face, especially Grace who had perfected the art of haughtiness.

He rubbed his neck, still sore from the crick he'd received by sleeping on the hardwood floor last eve, though it wasn't nearly as sore as his arm which seemed to have acquired a thrumming, relentless beat of pain.

"Care to join me in a tot of rum?" asked the captain.

Andrew glanced to the hatch leading below decks where the only thing he had to look forward to was a hammock that was certain to compound the stabbing pain. "Dunna mind if I do, sir."

～

NOT LONG AFTER BREAKFAST, the schooner dropped anchor in the Moray Firth across from the shipping district of Inverness. After a skiff transported them to the shore, Eugenia sat on a bench under the eaves of the harbor's maritime office while Andrew went inside

to pay their fares to London, reasoning that from the
city they could use one of the duke's London carriages
to take them to Cambridge which was a little over fifty
miles to the north.

Eugenia couldn't argue with Andrew's reasoning.
The mail coach would take at least two weeks to travel
from Inverness to Cambridge. And since the city was
inland, a few days sailing to London followed by a carriage ride north seemed like the most expedient
option.

She sat watching a team of laborers unload countless barrels from a ship's cargo, transferring them to
wagons pulled by mules. Eugenia had been there for
quite some time when the last barrel was wheeled
down the gangway and the plank was pulled inside,
she craned her neck and peered through the office
window. Back in a far corner, Andrew sat at a writing
table, wielding a quill.

She gripped her fingers tightly around her reticule. *I should have known better than to trust him with a
task as simple as reserving two berths on the next transport
to London.*

She hastened inside, the eyes of dozens of clerks
shifting her way while she marched directly to the
scoundrel. "What, exactly are you doing?" she demanded, folding her arms and staring at him
pointedly.

Andrew glanced up, his face as innocent as it had
been on the day he'd asked her about her favorite
flowers, pretending to be his twin, and feigning interest in her reply. He placed the quill in the holder
and sighed. "I'm writing a letter to Dunscaby. Contrary
to what you may believe, there are a host of people
who are worried about you and it is my duty to let
them know you are well."

She snatched the sheet of paper off the table. "And thwart my plans?"

Now his expression looked more apt—a grimace, followed by the biting of his bottom lip.

Without reading a word, she tore the page in half, then proceeded to make little squares, sending them fluttering into the waste basket.

With long huff, Andrew reached for a blank sheet. "We canna set sail this afternoon without sending word."

"No? What of the letters I wrote before my departure from Stack Castle? Why are they not enough?"

"You ken exactly why. Philip, your mama, and more or less everyone at the house party is worried out of their minds."

She flicked her hand through the air. "Move."

"I beg your pardon?" he asked, standing.

"I'll write it. Have you purchased the tickets?"

"Two berths for Mr. MacGalloway and his sister."

"Why MacGalloway?"

"Because that is my name," he replied as if he were as righteous as the Bishop of Canterbury.

"Oh, is it, *Philip*?"

Eugenia didn't wait for the backstabber to respond. She took up the quill and dipped the tip in the ink, addressing the letter to her mother.

Dear Mama,

Sir Andrew caught up with me and contends that you and his family are all distraught by my abrupt decision to rescind the engagement. Since the fiend cannot force me to return to Stack Castle, he has insisted I write to you yet again. I am very sorry if I caused you consternation, but I have made my decision and stand by it. I will not marry. I will not be used as a pawn to be paraded about the marriage mart ever again. Dearest Mother, you cannot in good conscience assume that I might possibly agree to be the wife of a conniving, deceitful man such as Philip MacGalloway. Please honor my wishes. I have decided to sell my lace creations and will be letting rooms in an undisclosed location and using an undisclosed alias.

No one in the family need suffer from my decision. I am not ruined. I am simply dead to you.

Sincerely,

Andrew leaned over her shoulder. "You ought to say that I am ensuring your safe passage as a gentleman ought."

"Should I?" Eugenia signed her name. "Should I also mention that you're now posing as my brother, once again taking on a false mantle in the name of doing the right thing?"

"How did such a demure English rose turn into a hellcat?" A flash of ire darkened the Highlander's eyes. "Never ye mind. I shall send proper word to Martin once we arrive in London."

16

Scotland, being renowned for its weather changes, shifting from fine and balmy to freezing and blowing a gale within hours, it came as no surprise when as soon as the ship sailed outside the protection of the Moray Firth, a squall swept down from the northwest, bringing spitting rain and rough seas. Andrew had to open the tiny window in his berth for a moment and take a few gulps of air to allay the onset of queasiness. Fortunately, the hint of unease passed about as fast as it had come on. Fortunately, this ship was twice the size of the schooner they'd sailed from Wick, thus the enormous hull made the rough seas nearly as tolerable as Gibb's barque. Besides, he'd endured worse.

Once certain the nausea had passed, Andrew reclined on his bed and opened the newspaper he'd brought along from Inverness. Fortunately, he'd found a shop not far from the wharf where he was able to acquire a few necessities for the journey including a brush and powder for cleaning his teeth as well as a cake of soap. To his delight the store carried MacGalloway muslin and he was able to convince the shop's tailor to fashion a pair of smalls and a shirt which were delivered to the ship before it sailed. The items were meager but would suffice until they reached London.

When he'd mounted his horse and hastened away from the castle, he only intended to ride as far as John o'Groats, mayhap Thurso at the farthest. Now that he had accompanied Eugenia aboard a ship sailing down the eastern coast toward London, he doubted he'd be visiting Stack Castle again within the year. As a duke, Martin had a great many residences, and tended to reside in the draughty old castle only during the hottest months of summer.

Andrew turned the page, finding an article about how corn had unseasonably frozen on the stalks northwards of the Potomac River in America, but before he read past the headline, an agonized moan rumbled through the wall of the adjoining berth.

He lowered his newspaper and leaned forward. The unmistakable choking from a heave roiled, followed by coughing and whimpers of utter misery. Though the seas were rough, the ship's rocking was nothing compared to the tempests he'd faced on the voyage to the Americas. But the lass was no sailor.

He set the paper aside and stepped into the corridor, knocking gently on her door. "Eugenia?"

After an agonized moan she managed to cry, "Go away!"

Andrew gulped. If only he would have hired a coach in Inverness, her misery might have been avoided. From there it would have taken a day or two to travel to Stanley on the River Tay where he could have arranged for his coachman to drive them the remaining distance. Even though such an option would have taken at least a week longer than sailing, the lass wouldn't have to suffer seasickness.

"Is there anything I can fetch for you?" he asked, wringing his hands. "A sip of water? A dry biscuit?"

"I said to go away!"

He glanced at the latch. Had she thrown the bolt? *'Tis best not to push her.*

When it was clear Eugenia was not going to open the door, he returned to his cabin, took his seat, and read the article about the unseasonable cold that hit the northern American states. Fortunately, the share-croppers who supplied his cotton were in Virginia and had been spared from the frost. Though it did make him wonder if the harvest might be affected this year.

By the time he'd finished reading the report, the grunts, heaves, and moans from the adjoining berth had doubled to the point where bile began to burn Andrew's throat in commiseration. Unable to withstand her misery a moment longer, he headed out to the deck, having to lower his shoulder into the door and force it open against the wind.

Stepping outside, the rain stung his face while the gusts of wind forced him to grab the rail. Shouts resounded from seamen with ropes tied around their waists, anchored to masts and booms. Clipped orders hailed from the helm, as the captain fought the tempest, trying to keep the sails billowing with wind and the ship heading into the frothy swells.

"Och, ye'd best head below and hunker down in yer berth," shouted the boatswain, making his way toward Andrew, sliding the hemp rope around his waist along the rail as he neared. "Ye're likely to be cast overboard. If anyone falls in this squall, there'll be no chance to save him."

Andrew locked his arm around the nearest post, holding it at his elbow as he'd learned on the voyage to America. "My sister is violently ill. Have you anything to help her?"

The man unhooked his tether, and stumbled forward, grabbing the door's latch. "Follow me," he bellowed over the howling wind.

The door slammed, shutting out the deafening wind and rain. The boatswain pattered down the steps. "I've only a moment."

"Will we need to seek safe harbor—divert into the Firth of Tay?"

"Possibly, though this time of year, I'll wager the seas will calm afore we reach the Tay." Keeping his knees bent with the sway of the ship, the boatswain led Andrew aft until they arrived at the galley, finding the cook sitting on a stool with his feet either side of a bucket, using a knife to pare potatoes. Every sailor was well aware that the kitchen's hob was never alight during a squall.

"Mr. MacGalloway needs a tincture," said the boatswain.

Andrew didn't bother correcting the man even though he'd not often been referred to as Mr. MacGalloway. As he'd told Eugenia, he preferred Sir Andrew, though there were those who still referred to him as Lord Andrew.

The cook eyed him with a scowl. "Ye dunna look green to me."

"'Tis is for my sister."

"Aye, the fairer sex always succumbs first." The cook stood and opened a crate, pulling out a stoppered glass bottle. "This will cost ye."

"How much?"

The man looked at the MacGalloway brooch. "That a clan pin?"

Andrew tapped the ruby, worth more than the

cook would make in his lifetime. "'Tis not for sale. 'Twas a gift from me da, God rest his soul."

The cook turned the bottle in his meaty hands. "Ye ken this wee tincture will set her to rights. Make her sleep through the worst of it, at least. What else have you?"

"A few shillings." Andrew shrugged. He didn't know these men from the swindlers who loitered about the taverns in St. Andrews. If he told them he had a sporran full of gold guineas, he'd most likely be robbed in his sleep. Feigning nonchalance, he slipped his hand inside, letting the coins roll over his fingers until he found a shilling, then held it up. "This ought to more than pay for a wee draft of laudanum."

The cook snatched the coin from Andrew's fingertips. "Och, this is me special recipe. Nothing like it is available in all of Christendom."

So say you. Andrew took the vial from the man's hand. "As long as it helps my sister overcome the sickness and doesna poison her, I'll be a happy man."

"Och, Cookie would never poison a soul," said the boatswain.

Andrew headed for the door. "Good to hear, friend."

~

IT REGISTERED that the bolt had been unlocked by someone outside her door, though Eugenia had no strength to even raise her head high enough to see who.

She lay across her bunk, her face precariously on the side of the mattress, the chamber pot directly below as she waited for the next round of heaves—either that or death. She'd lost all sense of time, though there was no light shining through the small, round window above. Initially she had vomited the contents of her luncheon, followed by everything she'd eaten from breakfast to last eve's dinner. In the end all that remained was sickly yellow bile, a sure sign that she would perish soon.

At least she hoped so. Never in all her days had she felt this ill or wished for death to relieve her from such unbearable misery.

As a footstep sounded on the floor, she managed to open the eye not presently pressed into the mattress. "Go 'way," she garbled, her throat dry and raspy.

"I'm here to help." Andrew replaced the chamber pot with an empty one, moving the soiled somewhere beyond her one-eyed view.

He closed the door and pulled the wooden chair beside her. "I've brought you a tincture as well as a wee sip of water."

Eugenia's stomach roiled. "I cannot withstand a single drop."

"Come now, I'll help you sit up, just a bit. Let us see if you can keep the water down first, shall we now?"

"No," she complained, helpless to fight the hand lifting her upward. A cup touched her lips and as she opened her mouth to protest, water gagged her. Sputtering and coughing, she batted her fingers, but Andrew pulled the cup away before she knocked it from his grasp.

"That's it, you're doing well," he soothed, being nice and sweet yet *horrid*.

"Go," she said, her command sounding as convincing as a newborn kitten's mew.

"Och, lassie, you may hate me to my core, but I'm not going anywhere until you're feeling better."

Crumpling against his chest, Eugenia sobbed. "I feel awful!"

"I ken," Andrew wrapped his warm arms around her and pressed his lips against her temple. It felt too comforting to try to fight him, not that she had the strength. "We shall go slowly. Do you think you might be able to have a wee sip? Just a tiny taste of the tincture on your tongue?"

"No, nothing. Please, nothing."

"Verra well," he whispered, holding her ever so tenderly.

Eugenia closed her eyes, the swaying of the ship making her shudder. Her only comfort—the only thing preventing her from succumbing to the heaves were the arms surrounding her. "Don't let go."

Andrew did as she asked, embracing her, kissing her, swirling his fingers through her hair.

After a time, he brushed his knuckle over her cheek. "Allow me to open the window to usher in some fresh air."

"Now?"

"I reckon it will help, lass."

Eugenia nodded, immediately overcome with a wave of dry heaves.

Cool air flooded the room as Andrew paid no mind to his injury, lifted her into his arms and carried her to the small opening. "Breathe deeply," he urged. "Open your eyes and stare at the horizon."

A few cool drops of rain peppered her cheeks as she looked out across the sea, her stomach still queasy, her head still swimming. Though Andrew had been right, breathing in air untainted by her sickness helped.

"It looks as if the worst of the storm as passed."

Eugenia focused on where the clouds met the dark swells and prayed he spoke true.

"Can you take the tincture now?" he asked, gently setting her on her feet.

Gulping back bile, she shook her head.

"Keep staring at the horizon," he said, shaking the vial, then running the cork across her bottom lip. "Just a few drops at first."

The medicine made her lip numb, it tasted sweet with overtones of ginger and peppermint.

"How's that?"

Eugenia didn't dare shift her gaze. "Well, it didn't make me gag."

"I hope not. The ship's cook prides himself—says 'tis a secret recipe." Andrew nudged the bottle into her hand. "He said it'll make you sleep and when you awake, the queasiness will be gone."

She grasped it. "Truly?"

"True enough, lass, though I'd be lying if I didna say I reckon there's a healthy dollop of laudanum mixed in that wee potion."

She tried to hand the vial back. "I'm not sure I want it."

He brushed a lock of hair away from her face and tucked it behind her ear. "Och, a dram willna cause harm."

"If you think I should."

"I think it will ease your pain if you can sleep."

She glanced to the bottle, only to be hit with a wave of nausea. "Anything ought to be better than this."

Andrew rubbed his hand up and down her back as she drank the potion and tried not to gag.

"Is it awful?" he asked.

She couldn't help but cringe, handing him the bottle. "I believe raspberry ices would be intolerable at the moment and—" She heaved, and coughed, her body shuddering as she frantically relocated the horizon. "Raspberry ices are my favorite."

"Of course they are," he whispered beside her ear, his arms slipping around her waist. "What else do you like?"

"Please don't ask me to talk. 'Tis terribly taxing."

"Then do not." Andrew stood silently beside her for a moment, his strong hands supporting her and most likely the only things keeping her upright. "Are you beginning to feel drowsy?"

"A bit," she said, leaning on him more heavily. "But I don't want to leave the window."

Again, he swept strands of hair away from her face and kissed her temple. It felt so inexplicably good, as if he truly did care for her.

"I never meant to hurt you, lass," he whispered, his words finding a frisson in her heart and seeping into it. "I ken you'll never be able to forgive me, but you must know I truly enjoyed the moments we shared."

Eugenia had enjoyed them, too. "It wasn't real."

Andrew didn't reply, his warm breath skimming her face. And though she knew she ought to push him away and tell him to remove himself from her cabin, she was simply too weak to do so. Though as soon as she regained her strength, she would tell him never to wrap his arms around her like this again. She'd demand that his lips never kissed her, that he never stood so close that she could feel his breath—or the strength of his arms, his fingers, his...*presence*.

"I've never felt so foolish as I did the moment our gazes met in the nursery," he whispered. "You may have believed me to be my brother, but the man with whom you strolled through the garden, walked on the beach, danced in the orchestra withdrawing room...was me."

Eugenia's eyes fluttered closed, the world still spinning, though now she wondered if it was caused by the seasickness or by the words she so desperately wanted to believe. As she drifted in and out of sleep, Andrew swept her into his arms and carried her to the bed.

She rolled to her side and curled into a ball. A soft blanket lightly draped over her. Warm lips caressed her forehead. "I adored every minute I spent with you."

Was she dreaming?

17

B y the time Eugenia began to feel spry enough to take a turn about the deck, the ship had sailed up the Thames and moored in the Pool of London.

After they disembarked, Andrew hired a hack which took them straight to the Duke of Dunscaby's enormous Mayfair town house. Inside it was so eerily quiet, the home seemed as if it might be haunted. The only time she had been there was the night Philip had made his hasty proposal. They were celebrating the dowager's birthday and the house was alight with hundreds of candles and adorned with fantastical arrangements of flowers. An orchestra dressed in gold livery played, serenading countless guests dressed in their finest.

Presently, the house was staffed only by a housekeeper and a contingent of maids who kept it tidy while the duke was in Scotland. There was only one sconce lit in the entrance hall, making it seem dark and uninviting. Eugenia wrung her hands, the corridor catching her eye—the one leading to the ballroom—the one where Philip had dropped to a knee and proposed.

"Why did he do it?" she asked.

Andrew turned away from the housekeeper. "I beg your pardon?"

"Why did Philip propose?"

Andrew sputtered. "As I recall, your mother accused him of scandalous behavior."

"But everyone knew I hadn't even been away from the ballroom long enough to create a scandal."

"Sir Philip is a man of his word," said Mrs. Purdy, the housekeeper. "A man of honor."

Andrew groaned while Eugenia stifled her urge to snort. "Oh, is that what you call asking your twin to impersonate you for the purpose of entertaining your betrothed whilst you attend a horserace?"

The woman's smile fell. "He didn't?"

"Och, ye ken Philip. When it comes to thoroughbreds, he's obsessed." Andrew gestured to the marble staircase. "Mrs. Purdy, would you please show Miss Radcliffe to her bedchamber?"

Eugenia bristled. "Miss Laroux, mind you."

"Perhaps but you're no stranger in this house." He handed her satchel to the housekeeper. "After you've had a good rest and a warm bath, I'll wager you'll be feeling much better. I'll take you to visit the modiste on the morrow."

Eugenia didn't want to visit a seamstress, she wanted to hasten to Cambridge and wipe her hands clean of Sir Andrew once and for all. "Modiste? I do not have the means, sir."

"Aye, but I do, and if you're planning to become a lacemaker of some repute, you'll need more than the dress on your back."

"I have clothing," she said motioning for the housekeeper to continue upward.

Andrew followed. "You must have an entire wardrobe."

She stopped at the landing and turned abruptly. "But that will take weeks."

"A few days is all," he said, two steps lower, yet they were almost eye-to-eye.

She motioned to the housekeeper to continue upward. "You've done enough already. Must you continue to meddle?"

"Yes. Most definitely. Not to mention I need to visit my tailor as well."

"I didn't realize they made kilts in London."

After reaching the second floor, Mrs. Purdy opened a door and stepped inside. "I'll have your bath drawn forthwith, miss."

"Thank you," said Eugenia, following the woman into the bedchamber and shutting the door, ever so happy to leave Andrew in the corridor. She raised her chin and regarded Mrs. Purdy, challenging the woman to pry.

But the housekeeper simply smiled as if she hadn't a care in the world. As if it were perfectly normal for one of the duke's brothers to miraculously show up on the town house stoop with his former sister-in-law to be in tow. "Would you like to take your evening meal in here or dine in the hall with Sir Andrew?"

"I'll eat in here, thank you." Eugenia balled her fists while the woman stepped toward the door. "Are you not curious?"

Mrs. Purdy turned an ear. "I beg your pardon?"

"Did the duke send word that we were coming?" she asked, though even if Dunscaby had sent a missive, there was no chance it would have arrived by now. First of all, Eugenia's letter had to wend its way from Inverness to Stack Castle. And furthermore, she had made no mention of their plans to stop in London.

"No," Mrs. Purdy replied. "But we must have the house ready for visitors at all times."

That may well be, but the circumstances of her appearance in the presence of Andrew MacGalloway could potentially create a scandal even to the most eccentric of families. Mama always said it was best to quash idle chat among the servants before it began. "Well, to allay any gossip below stairs, I'll have you know that I rescinded my engagement to Sir Philip because he convinced Sir Andrew to impersonate him at the castle's house party."

A wry smile spread across the woman's lips. "Those boys are still at it, are they? Few can tell them apart."

"I say, I now am an expert on distinguishing between the pair." *Philip is a pompous boob, and though Andrew seems to have a kind heart, the man either does not understand how to say no, or he cannot distinguish between right and wrong.*

"How interesting." Mrs. Purdy tapped her finger to her lips, her eyes widening. "Since you have taken me into your confidence, would you mind too terribly if I asked a question?"

Eugenia rocked back on her heels. "I imagine you are brimming with curiosity at the moment."

"Quite." The housekeeper lowered her hand to the doorknob. "Tell me, how is it you have come to travel all the way to London when you were attending Her Grace's house party at Stack Castle?"

"Well, you couldn't expect me to stay after I discovered that Philip thought so little of me, now can you?"

"No, I suppose not."

"So...I walked to John o'Groats and caught the mail coach which I was planning to ride all the way to Cambridge."

"Oh." Mrs. Purdy smiled—a knowing smile, perhaps that of a woman who knows the family she serves well. "'Tis quite interesting, however, to discover that Sir Andrew obviously is the twin who chased after you."

"Obviously?"

The housekeeper opened the door. "Is that not why Andrew brought you here, miss?"

Eugenia's face burned as Mrs. Purdy took her leave. In all honestly, she'd never spoken to a servant at such length about personal issues, though gossip was an ugly thing. Many family secrets were leaked to the papers by servants—or so Mama said often enough.

She reached into her satchel and pulled out her spools. It was high time she started working on the caps for which she'd designed a new pattern before Harriet had asked her to make the silk lace jabot to adorn her new gown. She needed to think, and the best way to focus was to keep her hands busy.

For the love of daisies, the past four days had borne a whirlwind of confusion. From the moment when she met Andrew's gaze in the nursery up until now, Eugenia had been out of sorts. First her heart had been torn from her chest. Then she'd suffered awful seasickness. Now here she sat in the Duke of Dunscaby's town house, her fingers working in a blur.

I feel as if I'll never be able to get away from the Mac-Galloway family and their deceit.

Well, Julia had been ever so kind.

So had the dowager.

And the duke seemed like an affable chap. His children were certainly darlings.

Perhaps just the twins were tainted.

But every time she thought back to how kind

everyone had been, she remembered that the entire family had played along with Philip's ruse.

Eugenia looked to the window, her hands stilling. *Andrew wants to take me to a modiste? I cannot allow it. He already paid my fare to London. I cannot allow him to pay for a new wardrobe and then take me to Cambridge in one of the duke's carriages.*

She set her work aside and clenched her fists. If the servants spread gossip about her, she would have brought it on herself just by remaining in this house. Enough was enough!

The mantel clock clanged five times, announcing the hour. Of course, there wouldn't be a coach leaving for Cambridge at this time of day, but come morning, she intended to be on the very first one. And this time she would make certain one tenacious Highlander didn't follow her.

With renewed determination, she marched out of the guest bedchamber and down the corridor. As she recalled, the second floor contained the library which happened to be the very place she found Andrew sitting in a wingback chair reading a book, his heels propped atop an ottoman.

Looking up, he sprang to his feet, putting the book aside. "Miss Eugenia, is all well?"

"No, all is not well," she said, slipping inside and closing the door.

"Is your bath water too cold?"

"They haven't brought it up as of yet."

He gestured to the bell pull. "Shall I—"

"No!" Eugenia clapped her palms together and closed her eyes, willing herself not to shout. "I don't want you to do *anything* for me. Yes, I am grateful to you for helping me when I was too ill to hold my head up, but if I had followed through with my original plan I never would have been seasick."

Andrew rubbed the back of his neck and nodded. "I did not intend—"

"Of course, you didn't. But I did not ask you to come after me. I made it explicitly clear that I never wanted to see you again, yet for the past four days I've seen little else but you."

"I only—"

"I know, you're trying to help me." She shoved the heels of her hands against her throbbing temples. "But for one minute did you ever think that I might not want your help?"

He heaved a breath as if he were about to reply, but Eugenia wasn't finished. "I will *not* be going to the modiste tomorrow."

"If that is what you wish." With a slight grimace, Andrew rolled his injured shoulder. "Shall I—"

"I also will not be riding in a carriage with you to Cambridge." She tried to stand taller, chin up, affecting an expression of unflappable seriousness. "Come morning, I will leave this house. I will henceforth pay my own fare, after which I truly hope to never set eyes upon you again."

"Please, you canna mean that." Andrew reached for her hand, but she took a defiant step back. "You ken we made a connection. A powerful connection, one that two people may not experience in their entire lifetimes."

"But it was not real!" Clenching her fists, she stamped her foot. "Can you not understand how wretched I feel whenever I am in your presence? Every time I look at your face I am reminded that the man for whom I—I developed *feelings* was playing a ghastly trick on me and—"

"I did not mean to hurt you in any way. You must believe that—"

"The only thing I have to believe is the truth."

"Verra well." His eyebrows pinched as if he was in pain. "But tell me one thing, do you have a place to stay once you arrive in Cambridge?"

Her lips thinned. "That is none of your concern."

"I believe that it is very much my concern since I am the one who caused you to flee in the first place."

"You did not cause me to do anything. You simply were the catalyst to enable me to act on my dreams—to do something for myself for once in my life."

"Well then, I shall ask the coachman to have the carriage ready at dawn."

"That is not what I want. You go ahead to your tailor and I will make my own way to Cambridge. It is time to stop pretending that we're something we are not. We're not married as we told the barman in Wick. We are not traveling as brother and sister. I am taking my things and leaving at dawn and you cannot stop me from doing so."

"Eugenia, be sensible." Andrew stepped toward her but did not reach out this time. "Do you mean to tell me you would rather ride sixty miles to Cambridge in a stuffy, cramped mail coach than spend a day riding in one of Dunscaby's beautifully appointed, spacious carriages?"

"That is exactly what I'm saying. And I am being more sensible now than ever before," she replied, her voice stern, her chin high, her eyes unwavering. Then before she did something entirely nonsensical like breaking down into a sobbing heap, she turned on her heel and fled for the sanctity of the guest bedchamber.

ANDREW JOLTED when the library door slammed. Never in all his days had anyone shut doors in his face as often as did Miss Eugenia Laroux nee Radcliffe. In fact, he decidedly was a complete imbecile for putting up with her rebuffs. He should wash his hands of her. She wanted to be left alone.

So, why can I not grant her wish?

He dropped into the chair and groaned.

Truly, he hadn't imagined the connection they'd experienced at Stack Castle, nor had he imagined how well they'd danced together, or how utterly magical their one and only kiss had been.

Yes, she was right to be angry with Philip, but to push Andrew away as well was insanity. He needed to change her mind, to prove to her that he wasn't a cad who played tricks on unsuspecting maids and laughed behind their backs.

No matter what Eugenia thought, he wasn't a callous, uncaring man. Moreover, he'd all but groveled on his knees in the past four days to prove his sincerity. To prove his devotion. To prove his trustworthiness and loyalty. What were the words Philip had used to describe him? *...you are disgustingly honest and your loyalty is positively revolting.*

If only Eugenia looked upon him thus, and not as some rapscallion who loitered in the gutters of hell.

Unable to come up with a single solution to this conundrum, he moved to the sideboard and poured himself three fingers of pure MacGalloway whisky.

"Sir Andrew?" Mrs. Purdy asked from the doorway. "Will you be taking your supper in the library this evening? Miss Radcliffe has decided to dine in her chamber."

He took a healthy swallow. "Yes, here, please, though I've not much of an appetite."

"I'm sorry." The housekeeper brought in a tray and set it atop the writing table. "It seems the young lady's feelings have been hurt."

"Aye, and it is my fault."

"After she confided a bit about the cause of her disappointment, I believe the blame is more apt to be placed on Philip's shoulders, is it not?"

He sighed. "I only wish she'd see it that way."

"Perhaps Miss Radcliffe needs time."

"The lass most likely does, but I dunna like the idea of her traipsing off to Cambridge by herself. It is perilous for a woman of her ilk to be traveling without an escort of any kind."

"I agree, yes, it is dangerous for any woman to travel alone." Mrs. Purdy put a white serviette beside the place setting. "But you won't allow her to do so, will you?"

Andrew slid into the chair and finished his whisky. "Of course not."

18

A long the arduous northward ride, Eugenia made every attempt to tat lace, but due to the constant jostling, she ended up ripping out nearly as many knots as she made. Regardless of if the coach from London was cramped with passengers sitting with shoulders, thighs, and elbows touching, she grew more certain of her decision to set out on her own with every passing mile.

Of course, the drawback of riding in a mail coach was that they made frequent stops. A private carriage ride to Cambridge would have taken approximately eight hours or a long day's journey. The mail coach, on the other hand, within ten hours had only traveled as far as Standon, approximately halfway to her destination.

To everyone's surprise, however, the innkeeper announced that all passengers on the mail coach were to be given complimentary meals as well as accommodation. When she asked the driver if the innkeeper often was so generous, he replied that she ought to keep mum and be thankful.

Suspecting that Andrew could have intervened,

she watched the door of the dining hall, waiting for him to make an appearance, but the handsome High-lander was nowhere to be seen. She shared a room with two other women who were grateful to have a private place to bed down for the night.

The next day of traveling progressed faster than the first because the farther they traveled from Lon-don, the greater the distance between villages. None-theless, by the time they arrived in Cambridge, the time on the clock in the town square was seven min-utes past six and Eugenia was not only tired, she was famished, hot, and felt as though she'd spent the past two days tossed about in a bowl of dust.

As the coach moved away, the old horses tired and ambling, Eugenia tightly clutched her satchel and turned full circle. She'd never been in the middle of Cambridge's town square. Yes, she'd gone to a few fetes nearby, but fetes were never in the center of town. She had stayed with family friends who lived closer to Bedford than to Cambridge. Though it looked like most any English village, she felt lost. Alone. And suddenly cold.

A dry fountain stood in the middle of the road. Across was a tavern, the lamps within casting an amber glow through the windows. Laughter rose and fell while the hum of voices carried on the breeze.

Unfortunately, the two women with whom she'd shared a room at the inn the night before had disem-barked in Newton. Though it would be nice to have Harriet with her, or a lady's maid, Eugenia needed to stand on her own two feet. After all, this is what she had wanted. She had no right to feel lost and alone.

Beside the tavern, a shingle outside advertised an inn. It made sense to spend the coin on a room for the night, even though she needed to watch her outlay. On the morrow she'd find a boarding house and promised herself to watch every farthing with utter frugality.

"Ye look as though ye're lost, luv," said a man weaving toward her. He had dark hair and unshorn whiskers peppered his cheeks, his smile crooked. And when he stopped beside her, he stank of sour beer.

"Not at all," she replied, heading across the road.

His dirty fingers wrapped around her wrist as he reached in and tugged at her satchel. "Allow me to be o' assistance," he slurred.

She tightened her grip and pulled the bag away, but the lout refused to let go. "I said I do not need your help."

Gnashing his brown teeth, the scoundrel wrenched the leather strap from her grasp. "So ye fink ye're the Queen of Sheba, do ye now?"

"No. Please I—"

"Stop!" bellowed a man, barreling out the tavern door and dashing across the street.

Andrew!

The drunkard wrapped his arms around the satchel as if it were filled with silver. "The wench tried to rob me!"

Andrew lunged forward, reaching for the bag. "She did no such thing. From that verra window, I watched you take it from her hand."

Twisting away, the man started to run. "Ye're a liar!"

"And you're a thief!" Andrew shouted, tackling the dastard to the cobbles and slamming his fist across the man's face.

"Don't hurt him!" Eugenia cried, shielding her eyes with her hands yet peering between her fingers.

Ignoring her, Andrew tore the satchel away from the man's grip and tossed it beyond his reach, then drew back his fist. "Do ye want another click to the muns or will you be on your way, ye filthy, vile, shameless skiver?"

"I'm but an ole man. Please don't 'it me again."

Standing, Andrew thrust his hands onto his hips. "Be gone with you, but if I ever hear that you so much as utter a single word to this woman, I'll thrash you within an inch of your worthless life."

Eugenia inched toward her satchel, her head filled with questions. Something was terribly off, expressly the fact that Andrew was there after she'd made it clear in no uncertain terms that she still wanted nothing to do with him.

The Highlander hastened to her side. "Are you hurt? Are you shaken?"

Breathing deeply, willing herself to stop trembling, she watched the drunkard retreat. In truth, she ought to be grateful, but to show gratitude now would sabotage her independence. "I am fine. I had matters in hand before you burst into the square and attacked that man."

"Attacked?" Andrew snatched the satchel from the ground and held it toward her. "He was stealing your bag."

In truth, the lout did seem to have gained the upper hand, but Andrew didn't even give her a chance to set things to rights before he took charge like he always seemed to do. Well, Eugenia could play the simpering damsel no longer. "Thank you for your unbidden assistance." She snatched the satchel from his fingers. "What, pray tell, are you doing here?"

"I ken..." he cringed like a naughty boy. "I am fully

aware that you dunna want my help, but I could not in good conscience sit idly by while you embarked on your own, arriving in Cambridge in the evening hungry, with no place to stay. And, case in point, it is not safe for any woman to arrive alone in a strange town, especially at night when kindly folk have turned in."

Eugenia wanted to scream. Why did she have to be set upon as soon as the coach had pulled away? True, Andrew had already deduced that she needed to find a boarding house. "How do you know I'm hungry?" she asked, ignoring all the other points he'd made.

"Because you were on the mail coach. You would have been lucky to have found a bread roll for your luncheon."

He wasn't far from wrong, but she would not give him the satisfaction of saying so.

Andrew gripped his hands behind his back. "I hope you dunna mind overmuch, but I rode ahead and arranged for you to stay at Mrs. Spencer's Boarding House for Ladies."

Eugenia held up her palm. "Stop. This is ridiculous."

He blinked dumbly. "That I rode ahead or that I booked you into Mrs. Spencer's?"

"Both. Yet again you paid no mind to my wishes. How many times must I tell you that I do not want your help?" She shifted her satchel over her shoulder. "And I do not appreciate your constant meddling."

Andrew rubbed his injured arm and winced. Most likely he'd jarred it in the skirmish with the drunkard. "Verra well, if that is what you truly wish, I shall take my leave now that you've arrived at your destination relatively unscathed." He pointed to a Y in the road. "You'll find the boarding house up Market Street on the left. Mrs. Spencer has a shingle outside her door. You canna miss it."

"Thank you," she said, no matter how much it hurt to do so.

He cupped her cheek, his gaze sliding to her lips. Eugenia's stomach fluttered as she thought for a moment that he might kiss her. Turning her head, she couldn't allow it. He knew as well as she that any chance at romance between them had been shattered, never to be resurrected.

"Goodbye, Sir Andrew. Have a good life."

THOUGH ANDREW HAD LET a room at the inn in Cambridge, he didn't stay. Instead, he rode to the town of Bedford and slept in a copse of trees until dawn.

Still quite early, he found Aubrey House on the outskirts of town, lazy smoke fluttering from the largest chimney, a sure sign the cook had started a fire in the hob. He rode around back to the servants' entrance where deliveries would be made.

He knocked on the old wooden door which was opened by a footman dressed in moth-eaten livery. "May I help you, sir?"

Andrew handed the man his card. "I'd like to have a word with Miss Eugenia Radcliffe's lady's maid if I may."

"I do not think she is—"

"Dunna *lie* to me," he seethed. "Miss Eugenia didna take her lady's maid when she traveled to Stack Castle with her mother and sister, and I am quite certain the baroness has not yet returned."

The man narrowed his gaze then examined the card. "MacGalloway...?"

"I am the duke's brother."

"I see." The footman gave a stiff bow. "Please remain here for a moment."

Andrew paced while he waited, but eventually a small, middle-aged woman stepped outside, wiping her hands on her apron, her expression bereft. "We've received word that Miss Eugenia has perished."

Andrew looked to the dark clouds above, threatening rain. So, the baroness had decided to give in to Eugenia's wishes? He should have realized her mother would have preferred to avoid a scandal than to chase after her wayward daughter. "What I am about to say must be kept in utter confidence."

The maid glanced over her shoulder, then gave a nod.

"Can I trust you?"

After closing the door and leading him several paces away from the house, she whispered, "Miss Eugenia's not dead, is she?"

"Nay, but she wants to build a life for herself."

The woman's brown eyes glistened with hope. "Selling her lace?"

"How did you know?"

"Ever since Miss Eugenia realized that her talent was exceptional, she wanted to be a lacemaker. She hoped her husband would support her endeavor. *You* were her betrothed were you not?"

"No, my twin brother had that honor, though together we ruined it." He ran his fingers around his brooch reminding him both of his family, and of his own independence. "But that doesna matter at the moment. Miss Eugenia needs her trunk of lacy items —things she's made and was saving to sell at the next fete. Can you fetch it for me?"

She rubbed her palms, looking back toward the

house. "I might need Michael to help me—the footman who opened the door."

Andrew shook his head. "I dunna want anyone else knowing what I've been up to. Do you think I could spirit inside?"

"You?"

"Surely it is too early in the day for your master to be up, is it not?"

The maid opened the door, peered through the darkness, then gave a nod. "Hurry."

Though he didn't have much time, once Andrew was in Eugenia's bedchamber, it seemed as if he'd been granted a window into her soul. The room had been papered with a rose pattern in pinks and mauves. A collection of dolls filled one corner, each placed in lifelike positions—standing, seated on a chair, pushing a toy pram, two propped atop a miniature settee seemed to be deep in conversation.

The furniture was white with gilt trim and a writing table was positioned near the window to make use of the light. There was even a blank sheet of paper atop with a splotch of ink as if Eugenia had started a letter before being called away. The bed was clad with ivory lace, feminine and expertly crafted. He ran his fingers over the duvet. "This is her work."

"Do you know it?" asked the maid.

"A wee bit. At the castle, Miss Radcliffe wore an overdress that was incredibly stunning."

"Ah, yes. That piece was among her finest." The woman gestured to a small trunk at the foot of the bed that had been painted with white roses. "You'd best take that and hasten away afore someone realizes what you're up to."

"Please allow me a wee moment," he said, sitting at

the desk and reaching for the quill. "In the meantime, I'd be grateful if you would stow a few of Miss Radcliffe's dresses inside the trunk."

"How many dresses?"

"As many as you can fit."

19

It was hot in Eugenia's south-facing bedchamber,
but the temperature was to be endured. The space
papered with roses on white was adequate with a
small bed, a chair with a padded seat, a writing table,
and a washstand. Moreover, Mrs. Spencer served three
meals in the dining hall except on Sundays when
there was a late breakfast and a small dinner served in
the evening.

After purchasing a few necessities at the haberdashery, Eugenia had set to work immediately while
perspiration beaded her forehead.

It startled her when a rap sounded on the door.
When she opened it, she was even more surprised to
see Mrs. Spencer standing beside a footman who was
sweating more profusely than Eugenia, holding her
trunk.

"It appears your things have arrived, Miss
Laroux."

"How wonderful," she said, stepping aside and allowing the footman in. The only person who knew
she was staying at the boarding house was Andrew.
Running her teeth over her bottom lip, she glanced
toward the window wondering if he'd kept his

promise not to reveal her whereabouts. "Please set it at the foot of the bed, thank you."

Grunting all the while, the man did as requested and took his leave.

"Did you see who delivered it?" she asked, sliding toward the window and peering down onto the busy street, seeing no one who looked like the Highlander she'd sent away.

"The cook said a man left it at the kitchen door, saying it belonged to you." Mrs. Spencer bent over the cap Eugenia was working on. "You're a lacemaker?"

"Indeed I am. I've come to Cambridge in hopes of selling my work."

"Oh? Why not London?"

"I'm not fond of the big city with its vile smells and the sooty smoke from all the coal fires."

"I don't disagree with you there, but a woman trying to sell lace in Cambridge might have difficulty finding buyers."

"Perhaps, but I've sold my things at fetes. With good felicitations as well."

"Hmm." Mrs. Spencer slid her fingers beneath Eugenia's unfinished cap. "With this quality, I'm not surprised."

"Do you know of any ladies in town who might be in need of a cap or scarf?" she asked.

"Perhaps you might ask at the Great St. Mary's Church on Sunday. All ladies of quality attend."

As Mrs. Spencer bid her good day, Eugenia pressed her hands to her face. It might be a bit awkward attending church and asking if anyone was interested in buying her lace. To make all manner of items was one thing, but aside from annual fetes, she hadn't really thought a great deal about how to find people who wanted to buy them.

She opened the trunk and found a letter addressed
to Miss Laroux atop three of her favorite dresses,
though they'd been fairly wrinkled. Beneath her
clothing were all of the items she'd made from collars
to caps to shawls and lace gloves. Though she desperately needed the pieces to gain a foothold, Andrew
had taken too great a risk to bring them here.

With a trembling hand, she drew the letter to her
nose, closing her eyes and inhaling Andrew's scent,
lightly laced with bergamot. On a sigh, she broke the
seal on the letter and opened it.

> Dear Miss Eugenia,
>
> Since you decided against paying a
> visit to the modiste in London, I thought
> you might appreciate it if I not only sent
> your cache of lace, but also a few of your
> dresses. Also of note, your mother and
> Harriet have not yet returned to Aubrey
> Hall. Furthermore, I feel it is important
> for you to know that I enquired at the
> kitchen door and asked to see your lady's
> maid whom I convinced to spirit me
> inside.
>
> She was bereft with the news of your
> death, so it may please you to know your
> mother has fulfilled your wishes. Your
> maid was elated when I told her you
> were not dead. She also immediately

guessed that you have decided to become a lacemaker. She chose the gowns packed within.

I swore her secrecy, of course. I did not tell her where you've gone or the name you have assumed. She knows only that you are alive and happy.

I truly do wish for your happiness as well as success. Of all the people I know, I believe you are the most deserving of the joys this life has to offer.

Aye, you told me enough times that you do not wish to hear from me again, and though I do not return your sentiment, I shall endeavor to honor your wishes. If you at any time should reconsider your ill feelings toward me, I hope that you will write me a letter.

I would so dearly love to hear from you.

Your servant,
Andrew MacGalloway

A tear splashed onto the parchment as Eugenia folded the missive and pressed it against her heart.

～

THE WEEKS PASSED, swiftly at first, but the longer Eugenia went without gaining a foothold with one of the modistes in Cambridge, the more time began to slow and worry set in. She had been so blindly certain that she'd be able to sell her lace creations that she'd never once considered how difficult doing so would be.

There were five modistes in Cambridge and four of them had all but pushed her out their doors. The other had asked Eugenia to leave a card as to where she could be contacted should she need a lace piece for one of her gowns. Thus far, the woman hadn't sent a caller.

Eugenia had even darkened the doors of the local tailors—three of them, all of whom told her to go away.

Mrs. Spencer's suggestion about enquiring at St. Mary's had been a good one. Eugenia managed to sell a cap and a shawl, but that wasn't going to be enough to pay the rent at the boarding house. She secretly thanked Andrew for paying the first three months. She should have shown more gratitude at the time. Though she had softened toward him somewhat, especially after he'd gone out of his way to send her trunk, she was still hurt. Merely the memory of being betrayed by Philip cut her to the quick. If only she could forget that she'd ever been to Stack Castle or had ever been introduced the MacGalloway family.

Suspicion that Andrew continued to meddle in her affairs still plagued her. Specifically, there was a man named Mr. Smythe who always seemed to be loitering about the town square. Eugenia couldn't be sure if the chap watched all young ladies when they walked about town, but he certainly seemed to be underfoot more often than not. He was an affable fellow with good manners and a pleasant demeanor. But given Andrew's persistent intrusiveness, she couldn't prevent herself from suspecting that Mr. Smythe might be keeping an eye on her to ensure an incident akin to the one with the drunkard didn't happen again.

She hoped Andrew hadn't gone to such an extreme. She truly did.

But she couldn't help but wonder...

Presently, the only person left in town for her to present her lace creations to was Mr. Willis, the proprietor of the haberdashery. Honestly, one would wonder why she didn't start there first if one hadn't met Mr. Willis. He was a bit of a highbrow. A tall, gaunt man with penetrating eyes and a stern countenance. Eugenia could wager few thieves ever darkened the haberdashery because Mr. Willis would stare them to death.

She'd visited the haberdashery several times to purchase supplies and never once had she felt any warmth whatsoever from the proprietor. But her time was running out, and Eugenia had no choice but to pay him a visit of the professional variety.

A bell tinkled as she entered, carrying her pieces in a basket that she'd purchased in this very shop.

"Ah, Miss Laroux, back for more thread are you?" Mr. Willis sniffed, glaring from his place behind the counter.

She noted a pair of women looking at bolts of fabric that lined the rear wall. A rush of heat flooded to her face. Truly, she'd rather speak to the man without an audience. "I think I might have a look around if I may?"

"If you must," he said with a curt nod.

Mr. Smythe followed her inside. He smiled at her as he took off his hat, then peered across the shop as if he were either inspecting the place or looking for something in particular. She released a pent-up breath when he left without making a purchase.

However, to Eugenia's chagrin, yet another chap came in while Mr. Willis was helping the two ladies, this one dressed like a dandy. He spent a great deal of time looking at the bolts of cloth and touching everything as if testing the quality and texture.

When finally the women had made their purchases and took their leave, Eugenia decided that though the dandy was still very much engrossed in the back with the bolts of fabric, she'd best step forward now or risk making a spectacle of herself because she had already strolled around the circumference of the shop a dozen times.

"Miss Laroux, have you found what you're looking for?" asked Mr. Willis, his frown making his entire face look gnarled and unapproachable.

She gulped. "Yes...I mean *no*."

"No?"

"Well, I didn't come in today to make a purchase, but rather to inquire as to if you might be interested in carrying some of my lace."

She pulled out a scarf she'd made this week, it being the most exquisite of her pieces.

"Lace?" asked Mr. Willis looking as if he'd just been forced to take a spoon of foul cough mixture.

"Yes." Clearing her throat, Eugenia exchanged the scarf for one of the caps. "It hasn't escaped my notice that you do carry a small assortment of lace caps and I thought—"

"Wrong, Miss Laroux. You thought wrong."

"I beg your pardon?"

"I only buy the latest laces and fabrics manufactured by the most esteemed and established weavers and lacemakers in Christendom."

"I see," she said, not understanding at all. She needed him to at least look at her things before he booted her out of his shop. "But would it not better serve your haberdashery if you were to carry something unique, made by a local woman perchance?"

"My patrons are not looking for lace caps and shawls made by locals—especially made by local *women*. They want to adorn their dresses with laces and ribbons in the latest fashions from London and Paris." The shopkeeper opened a jar and tilted it toward her with a dismissive, crooked-toothed smile. "Now won't you have a peppermint stick? They're delicious."

"No thank you," she said, dropping the cap into her basket and giving it a pat. "Good day, sir."

When she stepped onto the footpath, Eugenia was shaking so much, the lace in her basket trembled. She drew in a few deep breaths and blinked back tears. Was she never to gain a foothold? She had been certain that after giving him a sample of her work, Mr. Willis would have been delighted to see her things displayed in his front window. Everyone—her friends, her family, the servants at Aubrey House—had told her she could sell her lace. And she'd done so at a few fetes over the years.

But the coin in her reticule wasn't going to last if she couldn't find a buyer. The problem was Mr. Willis had the largest haberdashery in Cambridge and if he didn't want her lace, then the others most likely wouldn't as well. Heaven help her, she might be forced to try her luck in London of all places.

As she started to cross the street, the dandy came out of the shop. "Miss Laroux?"

She startled at being addressed by a stranger. "Do I know you, sir?"

"Forgive my impertinence." He handed her his card. "I am Mr. Richards—a fabric merchant."

She turned the card over, finding an address on the back. "You're from London?"

"I am," he said, nodding at Mr. Smythe who happened to be leaning against a lamp post down the way and staring straight at them both. "I only got a glimpse of the pieces you held up for Mr. Willis. Would you mind letting me see your work?"

Though she felt utterly deflated, showing him the pieces in her basket couldn't hurt. She held up one of her caps while a suspicious notion made her take a step back. "Are you familiar with MacGalloway muslin?"

The man again looked to Mr. Smythe, his jaw twitching before he took the piece. "Indeed, I represent the MacGalloway Mill along with a great many British weavers."

Eugenia bit down on her bottom lip. Too many times she had been helped by Andrew, regardless of how much she needed to sell her things, she couldn't abide him meddling in her affairs. "He didn't send you, did he?"

"Who?"

"Sir Andrew MacGalloway," she replied, unable to keep the irritation from her tone.

"Sir Andrew? Oh, no. I rarely ever have the occasion to speak to one of the brothers—though I did have the privilege of meeting them when I paid a visit to their mill a few years past. But, no. I usually correspond with their clerk." His gaze shifted sideways. "The man in charge of shipments and whatnot."

"I see," she said, somewhat relieved when she

noted Mr. Smythe had moved on. "And you carry lace, do you?"

"Lace ribbon, though I hope to add more lace articles to my line." He held the cap to the sunlight and turned it in his hands. "Your workmanship is quite good."

"Thank you." Eugenia held up the ornate scarf she'd tried to show Mr. Willis. "This is one of my most recent pieces."

He took it. "Oh, this is exquisite."

"I do a great deal of specialty work as well. In fact, I made an overdress I wore to a ball, and more than one person asked me if it had come from Paris." Of course, two of her admirers had been Andrew and Mama, but this was the first person of influence who had shown interest in her lace and compliments were compliments no matter who they came from.

"Lace overdresses are made to order, of course, though any modiste in England would be delighted to engage a lacemaker from whom they could place special requests." Mr. Richards pulled a jabot similar to the one she'd made for Harriet out of her basket and examined it. "How many modistes are you selling to now?"

"Unfortunately, none. I've only recently arrived in Cambridge and I have yet to find someone who will —" Again, Eugenia bit her lip. Would Mr. Richards still be interested in her work if she admitted that she didn't have one single regular customer?

"Hmm, that is a conundrum that must be rectified." He dropped her items into the basket. "Tell me, do you have drawings of your overdresses along with samples you can give me?"

"Do you require a sample of a complete overdress or samples like these caps and scarves?"

"I would require a complete overdress, of course. I'd also like caps and scarves as well."

She twisted her lips. The only completed dress she could give him was hers—the one she wore to balls. But then, as a mere lacemaker, Eugenia doubted she'd be invited to any balls in the near future. "I can fetch you a sample today and provide you with a drawing or two. But...what about payment? How do I know you are not trying to take my pieces without compensating me?"

He smoothed his fingers down his pristine lapels. "All of my weavers gladly give me samples."

"Perhaps, but I am not familiar with you, sir." *And I will not be able to live forever on the coin I've saved.*

"Very well, if you bring back the dress and it is as well-made as the lace in your basket, I'll purchase the lot for ten pounds."

"Twenty."

He frowned. "You are rather persistent are you not?"

Eugenia stood a bit taller, tipping up her chin for good measure. "Twenty. You'll see why once I return."

After the bargain had been struck, it only took a moment for her to come back with the overdress as well as a couple of sketches she would easily be able to replicate. He paid her as she'd asked and suggested she set to work, insisting that soon she would have more orders for Laroux Lace (Mr. Richards' words) than she could possibly manage on her own.

20

After Andrew arrived home, he steered clear of Philip for more than a fortnight, which meant staying away from the mill. He'd ridden the property's border at times when he knew Philip would be making his loom inspections—something they usually did together.

In all honesty, both of them had made a fortune and neither needed to tend to the daily operating of the factory. They had overseers, clerks, and secretaries to handle all of it aside from the major decisions that required a meeting of the board of directors, which happened to be Andrew, Philip, and now Frederick.

Still, the past fortnight had been utterly miserable. He'd all but smashed his head against the wall trying to come up with some way to convince Eugenia of his affection for her. He had drowned himself in a bottle of whisky, bringing on the unpleasantness of wall-smashing. But given all the torture to his brain he'd still come up with nothing. Andrew had been certain that she'd write to him and thank him for sending her trunk, but no.

He had received no word whatsoever.

He might as well be invisible. He might as well be a cockroach beneath her tiny little feet.

What he needed to do was stop thinking about Eugenia Laroux, nee Radcliffe, and move on. Sitting idle in his manor drove him to the brink of insanity. He'd grown up a twin, all but connected at the elbow. Until now, he and Philip shared evening meals at least twice a week. He missed their Wednesday night chess matches. He missed riding the perimeter with Philip and bantering with him about the mill and horses and family, and whatever demands they'd received from Martin.

Of course, it wasn't until Mama's house party at Stack Castle that Andrew realized what a complete mutton-heid his brother could be. Not only had Philip lost Eugenia, they both had conspired in an adolescent plot and turned the woman away forever. How could he have expected her to write after he'd sent her the trunk?

She hated him.

The only person he heard from about her welfare was the chap he'd paid to keep a close watch to ensure she did not come to harm or fall victim to someone like the drunkard in the square. And now, why did Andrew feel so entirely guilty about employing a man to ensure she came to no harm?

To ensure her safety?

Even though Eugenia would be furious if she discovered she was being watched, it was for her own good. She had only known a privileged and sheltered life. The lass had no idea how deceitful men could be. Once Mr. Richards made contact and if he agreed to carry her lace, then Andrew ought to be able to tell Mr. Smythe that his services were no longer necessary.

But at least in the interim, it gave him a modicum of peace to know that the lass was safe.

Today the rain drizzled with a looming sky, reflecting the darkness lurking in Andrew's soul. It definitely was not a good day to ride the property line or walk it for that matter. After reading the newspaper, Andrew donned his boots and headed to the stables. Randolph had not yet been turned out and was in his stall, attacking a rack of hay. "No ladies to entertain this morning, aye, stud?" Andrew asked, admiring the stallion's sleek, chestnut coat.

"We havena received as many stud fees as we expected," said the stablemaster, stepping out of a stall with a pitchfork in his hand.

Andrew should have known his wager would backfire. "This fella sired Beatrice, did he not?"

"Aye, but mark me, she may have lost her first race, but that filly will become a legend."

Randolph snorted and glanced over his shoulder, his jaw ruminating as if he felt insulted that the stablemaster even had to verbalize the greatness of any of his offspring.

Andrew admired the horse's exquisite form—the muscular shoulders, straight back, and perfectly curved buttocks sprung with so much power, few other horses could match him off the starting line. "You reckon?"

"So, here he is, the destroyer of betrothals." Though the voice had come from the open stable doors, Andrew could pick Philip's tenor out of a crowd of a hundred yelling men.

He glanced to the stablemaster. "Leave us." Then he eyed his wayward brother, obviously still holding onto his ill begotten grudge. "Och, you did that all on your own, ye numpty."

Philip ignored the slight and held out an apple to Randolph.

"Feeding *my* horse are you?"

"I thought I'd pay the lad a visit. God kens you're likely to turn him into a napper nag." Chuckling at his own tomfoolery, Philip regarded Andrew out of the corner of his eye. "You havena asked how things ended at the house party."

Honestly, Andrew hadn't thought much about it. He hadn't thought much about anything aside from Eugenia. "So? Is Grace engaged?"

"As a matter of fact, Prince Isidor finally summed up the courage to propose."

"I hope he'll make her happy."

"She'll be the darling of Lithuania and a princess. Her wildest dreams are coming true."

Andrew nodded. Grace had talked about becoming a duchess all her life. Now she was reaching even higher. "Have they set a date?"

"Not as of yet. Evidently, the prince must make arrangements with his family first."

Andrew sighed. "So, the waiting begins."

Philip pulled another apple out of his sporran and gave it to Randolph. "At least someone will be happily married." Within the blink of an eye his twin's nostrils flared, stance rigid. "Because of your meddling, not only did Beatrice lose her first start, I have to visit your barn to bring *my* stallion his apples, and you...you are solely responsible for making my betrothed rescind our engagement!"

"Meddling?" God's stones, Andrew should have anticipated his brother's attack. Furious, his heart pounded in his ears. "You bloody ungrateful wretch!"

"What the devil have I to be grateful for? I have lost *everything*!"

"Oh, aye? You should have expressed to me the... No, I restate...you should expressed the depth of your affection for Miss Radcliffe to your bloody self! You didna care a whit about the lass, except that she was bonny and would keep ye warm on a cold Highland ni—"

Andrew's jaw crunched as Philip's fist slammed into it. His head snapping aside, he stumbled backward, slamming his shoulder blades into the wall. Pushing away, Andrew bent at the waist and hurled his entire body into Philip's midsection as together they crashed to the dirt.

"Ye didna love her!" Andrew shouted, aiming a jab to the chin.

Philip countered by arching up and twisting, throwing a hook. "You werena supposed to talk to her about flowers. Ye werena supposed to walk along the beach, or kiss her, ye bastard!"

"If you think about it for half a minute, she thought it you doing the kissing. And I never would have been lulled by those magical blue eyes if you would have owned to your duty in the first place. Och, you'd be happily wed by now."

Philip raised his fist, then dropped it. "Get off me."

Andrew jutted out his chin. "Are ye no' going to throw another click to the muns?"

"I ought to."

He slid away and sat against the wall, catching his breath while rain pummeled the slate roof above. "What happened with the baroness?"

Philip crawled beside him, brushing the dirt off his doublet. "Once she received Miss Eugenia's letter from Inverness, she decided it was best to feign the lassie's death."

"The unfeeling wretch."

"Aye."

"She doesna deserve Eugenia as her daughter."

"Nay," Philip agreed.

"You dunna deserve her either."

"Mayhap you're right." Philip dug his heel into a clump of hay. "But *you* made a cocked-up mess of the whole debacle."

Andrew nodded. His brother was right. No matter how much he tried, he'd failed miserably. "Not that I didna try to fix it. 'Tis just Miss Eugenia doesna want to go back to her old life. She wasna joking when she thanked you for setting her free."

"Where is she?"

"I canna say."

Philip narrowed his eyes. "Canna or willna?"

"Both, really. I gave her my word I'd not reveal her secret and I'll take it to my grave if I must."

"So, what are you doing moping around here? And dunna think I havena noticed you trudging about our lands like a wounded bear."

Andrew leaned his head against the wall and closed his eyes, the sound of the rain reminding him of the storm on the ship to London and how he'd tended Eugenia's seasickness—of how he'd longed to take away her suffering and endure it himself.

"Ye ken." He groaned and crossed his ankles. "It was all in the letter she left. She doesna want to ever see the likes of me again."

~

THREE WEEKS HAD PASSED with no word from Mr. Richards when Mrs. Spencer knocked on Eugenia's door and slipped inside. "You have a gentleman caller waiting in the parlor."

"A gentleman?" Eugenia immediately thought of Andrew, her palms perspiring, her heart thumping so hard, she was certain Mrs. Spencer could hear it. "Did he give you his card?"

"Yes." She searched in the pockets of her apron. "Oh dear, I seem to have misplaced it."

"Not to worry." Eugenia put her work aside and pushed to her feet. "I suppose I shouldn't keep him waiting."

"No." Mrs. Spencer fingered the lace. "Every time I come in here I admire your work."

"Thank you. I sold a few pieces to a merchant who does business with Mr. Willis. Since the haberdasher won't buy from a woman, I'm hoping I'll be able to sell my things incognito."

Mrs. Spencer's shoulders shook with her knowing chuckle. "I most certainly understand your conundrum, my dear. Twenty years ago when I purchased this house with my dower funds, I told everyone that I was a widow and had been my husband's only living heir. Please do not divulge my secret, but I have never been married. I abhorred the Season and London's marriage mart."

"You are a spinster?"

"Indeed I am."

"And you had a dowry? My heavens."

"Not a huge one, but large enough to buy this house and see to its maintenance whilst I was preparing to bring in boarders. My father was merely a knight. When he passed away, I asked my brother for my dower funds and came to Cambridge."

"Astonishing. My father is a baron, though I didn't dare ask him for my dowry. I fled, really."

"And I'm guessing Laroux isn't your real name."

"No."

"Well, your secret is safe with me—as long as you can pay the rent."

"Oh my, is it due?"

"Not for another month yet. Sir Andrew—"

"Compensated you well," Eugenia said, realizing that Mrs. Spencer had met the man. Perhaps the gentleman caller was Mr. Richards?

"Yes. A kindly Scotsman if I recall."

Eugenia couldn't deny it. Andrew had always treated her kindly. But the fact that he had agreed with Philip to deceive her still weighed heavily on her conscience. She gave a nod and looked to the door. "I suppose I oughtn't keep the gentleman waiting."

Of course, not many gentlemen knew she was there. It couldn't be her father. Because of his crippling gout, he never left Aubrey House. He hardly left his suite of rooms and often conducted the estate's affairs from his fourposter bed.

It had to be Mr. Richards.

She brushed her hands over her hair and smoothed out her skirts as she made her way down the stairs and peered through the gap in the parlor's closed slot doors.

A smile spread across her lips. And though her heart didn't beat out of rhythm, this was exactly who she wanted to see. She pulled open the doors. "Mr. Richards, how lovely to see you."

The dapper gentleman stood and bowed, dressed in a well-tailored suit of clothes, his neckcloth tied in the ever-popular gordian knot, and his Hessian boots polished to a mirrored shine. "Miss Laroux, thank you for seeing me without an appointment."

Eugenia almost laughed. She hadn't had a caller since she told Sir Andrew to leave her alone. "I hope all is well." She gestured for him to sit as she took the settee across from his chair. Of course, she wanted to grab him by the shoulders and shake him until he told her that the Prince Regent himself had ordered her lace to adorn all his shirts, bed curtains, linens, tablecloths—

"I wanted to let you know that I have secured orders from a number of tailors, haberdashers, and modistes in Town and I believe you are going to need to bring on an assistant soon."

She clasped her hands together, trying not to look too ecstatic. "A number?" she asked, sounding far more skeptical than she felt, but being a single woman trying to sell lace in a society dominated by men, she needed to be careful.

The gentleman pulled a list from the inner pocket of his waistcoat. "'Tis all here. I believe there are dozens of caps—very popular with widows. At least fifteen scarves, and..." From his doublet side pocket, he retrieved a letter, sealed with red wax and tied with a pink bow. "I showed your lace overdress to Madame Genevieve."

Eugenia didn't even try to downplay her gasp. Madam Genevieve was the most celebrated modiste in London. To wear a Genevieve dress to court or to a royal ball almost certainly brought with it a host of marriage proposals. Of course, a gown made by Madame Genevieve or her house, might cost upwards of five hundred pounds, a ghastly amount only afforded by a few.

Her hands shook as she untied the lace, opened the envelope, and read. "Oh my."

Mr. Richards tapped the missive. "Can you do it?"

"Three unique overdresses by November?" she asked, finding a second sheet of stationery containing drawings with detailed measurements showing exactly what Madam wanted—a full overdress in white silk similar to the one Eugenia had made for herself, a half skirt in apricot silk, and a sleeveless pelisse overdress with a train in lavender and a note asking for three buttonholes in the front, buttons to be applied by the modiste. At the bottom of the page was written the sum of three hundred pounds. "Yes."

Though her admission stunned her, Eugenia could make the items if she worked all hours and hired an assistant, or an apprentice straightaway.

Before he left, Eugenia gave him the caps and scarves she'd made in the past three weeks, then went to find Mrs. Spencer to see if she might have any suggestions as to an apprentice. To her surprise, Mrs. Spencer confided that she had dabbled in a bit of lace-making from time to time and offered to be of assistance.

Eugenia would love to have her help, however, she needed someone who could start immediately and work all hours. "But are you not far too busy with the boarding house to be of any help to me?"

"I don't know." Mrs. Spencer shrugged with a sparkle in her eyes. "I have a cook, a housekeeper, a scullery maid, and two upstairs maids. If I were to go on an expedition to Africa for six months, I doubt anyone would notice."

Eugenia couldn't believe how suddenly everything was falling into place. "Very well, if you can commit to making the caps and scarves, I'll be able to work on the overdresses, and then I'll be able to pay you for more than just my room and board."

"Oh, you don't have to pay me. It will be a welcomed diversion."

"Tell me that after we've met the deadline." Eugenia clapped her hands, wishing she could throw them about Mrs. Spencer's shoulders and hug her as she would do to Harriet. "Thank you ever so much, and please do keep watch for an apprentice. You may be looking forward to the adventure now, but I'll wager by the end of the Season, you're going to want to return to your duties as lady of the boarding house."

21

The very next day, Eugenia dashed across the street to purchase the thread she'd need for her orders. Typically, Mr. Smythe was occupying the corner, leaning against a lamppost, and he tipped his hat, smiling as he always did. What a strange fellow. He never seemed to be in his cups, but always cordial. It was as if he enjoyed watching people mull about Cambridge.

Very odd little man indeed.

Before she entered the shop, she noticed a familiar lace cap on display in the window. She stepped nearer and examined the workmanship—*her workmanship*.

"Miss Laroux. Good morn," said Mr. Willis, scowling from his place behind the counter.

She wanted to grab the cap and throw it in his face. The demure Miss Eugenia Radcliffe would scarcely think of such a thing. The new, assertive, Miss Eugenia Laroux most likely ought to let the slight pass as well. After all, she needed Mr. Richards to represent her work in places where she could never ever in all her days be considered. She bid the shopkeeper a good morn and put in her request for more thread than she'd ever ordered in her life.

Mr. Willis gaped at her over the rims of his spectacles. "That much lavender silk will have to come via special order. It will be very dear, mind you."

"Then you must order it straightaway."

He picked up his quill, wrote down a number, and turned it to her. "Are you certain? I'll need half payment up front."

"Yes, I am quite sure." She opened her reticule and pulled out a handful of gold guineas. "How soon can it arrive?"

"Dunno. I'll have to send to London, mayhap France."

She deposited the money on the counter. "I must have it within a week."

The man shook his head and made another note. "You'll be taking my entire stock of white and apricot. I'd best place an order for that whilst I'm at it."

"Excellent."

"Tell me," he said, not bothering to look up. "You're not making lace with the harebrained notion of selling it are you?"

Eugenia could have sworn her jaw hit her chest. "I...ah..." She glanced back to the window where her cap was on display. "I wouldn't dream of it."

"Good, good."

"Might I enquire if you procure your thread from the same merchant who sells you bolts of cloth, and other items?"

"Mostly." Mr. Willis wrapped her order in brown paper, tying it with twine. "Though I work with a great many merchants."

"Are they all trustworthy?"

He sneered as if this were a very unsavory topic. "Not a one, which is why it is best to have more than one supplier. Any man who has run a haberdashery as long as I have knows a chap must never show his hand as it were. Always barter for a lower price, always let them know someone else will be along in short order."

"What if there won't be another supplier?"

The man chuckled sardonically. "Well, I wouldn't own to it, would I?"

Eugenia took her package and headed for the door. As soon as her fingers brushed the latch, it opened and she stumbled directly into Mr. Smythe. His arms wrapped around her, until she steadied herself, then he quickly let go and stepped away. "Ah, Miss Laroux. I was beginning to worry that something ah...*untoward* might have happened to you."

Confused, she looked back to the door. "In the haberdashery?"

"Yes, well...um...you were in here for quite some time."

She clutched her parcel against her chest. "Pray tell, sir, why is it you are always here?"

"Always, miss?"

"Yes. Whenever I step out of doors I see you. It is as if you have nothing better to do than idle away your time in the square."

"Hmm..." The man rubbed the back of his neck and glanced away, not providing an intelligent explanation.

Narrowing her eyes, she poked him in the arm. "You're watching me are you not?"

A lady and a young boy walked around them and entered the shop while Mr. Smythe stood stunned. "Me? No, I would never—"

"Are you perchance being paid to ensure I don't come to any harm?"

"Paid?" he asked, his voice higher pitched than it had been.

"Yes, paid by a devious Scotsman named—"

"Andrew MacGalloway?"

As Eugenia turned toward the sound of Sir Andrew's voice, she clutched her hands over her heart. His deep bass rumbled through her, turning her knees into mushy bread dough, her head swimming, her heart thumping, all within the amount of time it took to blink. With her exhale, she reminded herself that she was not smitten by this man. Heavens, he was the very scoundrel to whom she'd been referring. She clutched her package tighter and looked him in the eye. "Yes." She thrust an upturned palm toward Mr. Smythe. "You have been paying this man to spy on me."

Andrew dismissed the fellow with a flick of his fingers, then offered his elbow. "I wouldna call him a spy, but I did ask him to watch out for you, especially after you were accosted by a drunkard only minutes after arriving in Cambridge."

Without taking his arm, Eugenia started to cross the street, only to be nearly run over by a passing phaeton and forced to step back onto the curb. "I do not need a keeper. Tell him he's done or I shall do it myself."

"If that is what you wish."

"It is." After dismissing Andrew with a sharp nod, she looked both ways before gathering her skirts and starting across the busy street, careful to avoid a wagon heaped with barn refuse.

"Eugenia," he called, following. If only the manure cart had upturned on him, but the Highlander managed to cross the road without a single mishap. "Might I have a word?"

She didn't stop, walking as fast as she could toward the boarding house. "I'll have you know, I have found a buyer for my lace and thus there is no need for you to pay Mrs. Spencer, or anyone else. I am happy to report that I am completely able to support myself."

"That is fabulous news."

At least he recognized her achievement and didn't assume she was a featherbrained nitwit as Mr. Willis had done. She stopped outside the door, considering inviting him into the parlor, then thinking better of it. He was not her friend, nor her ally. Must she continually remind herself that he wasn't a nice person? "What are you doing in Cambridge?"

"Well I..." He dragged his fingers through the rich auburn hair that she'd so desperately wanted to touch and hated herself for still admiring it. Though his hair was thick, she was quite certain it was softer than silk. "Look, I henceforth want only to be honest with you. Truth be told, I came down from Scotland to see you —to ask if you received the trunk."

"I did, thank you." She really ought to invite him in. He'd ridden all the way from Scotland? And it had been ever so kind of him to send her things.

"You didn't write," he said, sounding utterly deflated.

"No," she replied. She had been too full of conflicted emotions to put pen to paper and thank him, especially when she really, truly wanted to forget him. "How far is it from your manor on the River Tay to Cambridge?"

Eugenia could have kicked herself. Asking such a question indicated that she cared. Which she did not. Even if she did care, she mustn't allow him to know.

"'Tis a six-day ride give or take."

"Six days just to say hello? I would think a letter would have sufficed."

"Aye, but I reckoned you wouldna send a reply

would you?"

She sighed. "I suppose not."

He glanced to the busy street, shod horse's hooves clomping the cobbles. "Do you think we might find a quiet place to talk?"

She glanced to her parcel and cringed. Indeed, she would dearly love to sit down with him over tea and discuss the weather. However, she most definitely did not want to discuss the health of the stallion he'd won at her expense, or his scheming brother. "Honestly, I think it would be best if we agreed to be strangers."

He walked beside her to the stoop at Mrs. Spencer's Boarding House, then tapped her elbow. It wasn't much more than a brush of his fingers, the touch sent shivers all the way up her arm and across her neck. "Eugenia," he whispered, his voice thicker than molten honey. "I've missed you ever so."

She opened her mouth to issue a rebuff but was rendered speechless when the fingers that had brushed her elbow now gently cupped her cheek. "Och, lass, I ken you may never forgive me, but—"

It took a herculean effort, but Eugenia batted his hand away. "Did you send Mr. Richards to see me?"

Andrew's gaze shifted ever so slightly, making her stomach roil.

"You know him do you not?" she demanded.

"If you would have asked him, Mr. Richards is one of the MacGalloway Mill's most esteemed buyers. He is verra good at what he does."

"But did *you* send him to Cambridge?"

"I'll say this: if Mr. Richards took any interest whatsoever in your lace it would have been because it was of *supreme* quality. The man has built his reputation on providing only the most exquisite fabrics and haberdashery items to shops across the southeast of

England. He does *not* acquire anything that does not meet his standards."

Eugenia considered Andrew's reply. He'd side-stepped but had done a very good job of it. Honestly, if Andrew had provided any other answer, her lace-making endeavor would be entirely ruined. His words were spoken with such conviction that she had no difficulty believing him. To support his assertion, Madame Genevieve never would allow Mr. Richards in her door if he didn't supply the best fabric in Britain. And Mr. Willis wouldn't buy lace caps from Eugenia, but he not only purchased them from Mr. Richards, he put them on display in his window.

"You must believe me," Andrew continued. "I only want what you want. If you wish to spend your days making beautiful things, then I say, do it—though nothing can ever be as beautiful as your eyes when you're standing on the shore, feet bare, wading through the shallows between the Stacks of Duncansby." He took her hand and kissed it, the whisper of his breath melting her heart. "I came because I cannot stop thinking of you. You torment my every waking hour. I cannot sleep at night. The food on my table is tasteless. Sunshine no longer brings joy."

Eugenia slowly drew her hand away and clutched it over her parcel. "Thank you for all you have done to help me. I was a bird in a gilded cage. However, now I need to fly or I'll never know if I can."

He bowed and stepped away. "Then I wish you all the success you deserve. I do hope that one day when your lace is known by every member of the *ton*, that you will write to me and tell me of your success."

"I shall." As she stepped into the boarding house, closing the door on Andrew's handsome face was the hardest thing she'd ever done.

22

After leaving Cambridge, Andrew didn't go home straightaway. He first visited his mother who was spending the autumn in Newhailes while Martin and Julia opted to remain at Stack Castle until the Season began. Of course, Grace and Modesty were there and the house was agog with excitement over Grace's recent betrothal to Prince Isidor.

At Newhailes, Andrew managed to feign the carefree bachelor. He arose no earlier than midday, staying up all hours which were usually spent alone, reading, drinking, and, most of all, brooding. But he could only stand so much of his mother's tea parties, or house parties, or visits by Edinburgh's most esteemed modistes all vying for his sisters' attentions. Grace was quick-tongued and full of self-importance while Modesty took it upon herself to attempt to fix everyone and everything, including Andrew. She visited him daily with a new tincture she had concocted, having found it in some ancient publication dug out of the recesses of the library, insisting it was exactly what Andrew needed to mend his melancholy.

But in truth, there was nothing in all of Christendom that could make him happy—save for a lovely blonde lacemaker who never wanted to marry and who scarcely could bear to set eyes on him.

More downtrodden than he'd ever been, Andrew went back to the River Tay and sent a lad with an invitation for Philip to resume their Wednesday chess matches. Even if he didn't feel like rejoining the living, he could at least make an attempt at reestablishing his pursuits.

Philip responded by showing up on Andrew's stoop precisely on time with a bottle of Islay whisky in hand.

"Islay?" asked Andrew, showing his brother into the drawing room. "Have you something against our uncle's stills?"

"Not at all, but this was a gift from Mr. Richards, thanking us for introducing him to Miss Laroux."

Andrew's face burned. He hadn't expected the merchant to speak to Philip about Eugenia. "I promised her I would never reveal her new identity."

"Not to worry." At the sideboard, Philip opened the bottle himself and poured two glasses. "I assumed she wasn't planning to dig a hole and hide for the rest of her days."

"She has an incredible talent. A good eye for design as well."

"Is that so?" Philip gave Andrew a glass and took his usual seat at the chessboard. "Lace work would have fit in nicely with the MacGalloway muslin business."

"Aye, but as a wife her work would have been seen only by family, I'm afraid."

"Such is the lot of married women, bearing children and running households."

As Philip's words struck a chord, Andrew's heart

squeezed to the size of a walnut. He'd never marry. He'd never have children of his own—wee ones who climbed on his lap and called him Da. Children he once dreamed of putting to bed at night, teaching his son to shoot, practicing reels with his daughters and forbidding them to waltz—waltzing was far too scandalous for any of Andrew's daughters. If he were to have daughters..

He pulled a folded slip of paper out from inside his doublet and handed it to Philip.

"What's this?"

"Randolph's papers. He's yours."

"But you won him fair and square."

"You didn't seem to believe so when you were feeding the horse apples in my barn."

"Aye, well I was still sore from Eugenia rescinding the engagement."

"But you didn't truly love her did you?"

"Love?" Philip asked as if he'd never heard the word before. "Of course not. She was bonny and after her mother accused me of salacious behavior, as implausible as it was, I figured proposing to the lass might not only solve the problem at hand but save me the trouble of searching for a wife."

"She would have made you happy."

Philip examined the chessboard which was already set for play. "I dunna ken about that."

"I beg your pardon?" Andrew coughed out a guffaw. "The woman is talented and funny, and full of life. She loves the sea, and hunting for seashells, and is enamored with every variety of flowers." Andrew glanced to his dog asleep by the hearth. "In fact, she adores Skye."

"Those are not the reasons she might have made *me* happy." Philip drank his whisky and licked his lips.

"However, those are all reasons why *you* would have been her ideal match."

Andrew slumped in his chair. "I think my heart has shrunken thirteen times smaller than it was before I met her."

"You are such a romantic. Always have been. I never would have believed that a man could fall in love with a woman in a mere three days, but you surely proved it can be done."

Swirling his whisky, Andrew could only shake his head. Did he love the woman? If he did, it mattered not a whit. "I need a diversion."

Philip pulled out his pipe and tobacco pouch. "You need Eugenia Radcliffe."

"Laroux."

"Whatever name she's going by. You love her."

"So? Many men have fallen in love with women who want nothing to do with them." Not bothering to savor the whisky's peaty flavor with a sip, Andrew threw back the entire contents of his glass. "Mayhap I'll write to Gibb and sail on his next voyage to the Americas."

"That willna be until spring, ye ken."

He was well aware that his seafaring brother never crossed the Atlantic during winter. Sighing, he pointed to Randolph's papers and changed the subject. "You're the horseman, not I. Besides, that was one wager I wish I'd never won."

"HAVE you given thought to letting a cottage of your own?" asked Mrs. Spencer, sitting beside Eugenia on a worn settee in the attic which had been transformed into a small withdrawing room where she could store her growing assortment of supplies as well as baskets piled with finished items of lace.

"I've scarcely had a chance to sleep let alone think about tomorrow," she replied, though it wasn't exactly true. When one spent their days making lace, aside from endless counting, her mind did wander a great deal—unfortunately it tended to fixate on one particular Highlander. "I'd love to find a little cottage nestled somewhere on a country lane, but then I'd lose you. I've come to rely on your help ever so much."

"Hardly." Mrs. Spencer's hands stilled. "You know as well as I do, we have to tear out almost as much as I make."

"But you are getting better."

"I am, however, in time you'll be better served if you bring on a younger woman with nimbler fingers and sharper eyesight."

Eugenia had managed to finish the overdresses on time while Mr. Richards had returned with more work —almost too much work. If he were to bring in any more orders, she would need help from a lacemaker or two far more skilled than her friend.

She expected things to slow down a bit after the London Season was over. Perhaps at that time she could think about the future—a cottage, adding more help. Of course, if she were to move into a cottage, she'd need a housekeeper who could also cook. Who knew how long Mrs. Spencer would put up with Eugenia taking over the attic?

One of the housemaids' feet tapped the stairs and, when she reached the top, she cleared her throat. "There's a gentleman caller for Miss Laroux."

"Another?" asked Mrs. Spencer. "My heavens your popularity is growing by the day."

Eugenia set her work aside, also wondering how

long the lady would tolerate having her parlor used for the conducting of business transactions. "I'm so sorry."

"Don't be. I'm ever so happy to see you turning your works of art into a successful endeavor." Mrs. Spencer looked to the maid. "Please take a tea service to the parlor."

"Oh, you needn't—"

"It is only right."

"Thank you." Eugenia patted the woman on the shoulder as she headed down the two flights of stairs.

On first glance, she was certain that the man standing in the bay window with the sun illuminating the lacy curtains behind him was Andrew, but as he shifted, she noted the difference in hairstyle. Philip's was always combed more severely and held in place with an ample application of pomade. "Sir Philip?" she asked, gripping her hands tightly across her midriff, stopping in the doorway.

"Miss Eugenia," he replied moving across the room. He reached for her hand, but when she didn't place her fingers in his upturned palm, he bowed. "Forgive my sudden appearance."

"I should have known Sir Andrew wouldn't have been able to keep my secret. Who else knows I'm living here?"

The maid came with the tea service and Eugenia dismissed her. "I'm afraid Mr. MacGalloway will not be staying."

Philip waited until the maid disappeared, then closed the sliding doors. "Andrew did not tell me you were here. I learned of it from Mr. Richards."

Eugenia clapped a hand to her forehead. "Good heavens."

"Not to worry. The merchant believes you to be

only Miss Laroux. I deduced your identity on my own."

"Is that so?"

"Aye."

"So, why have you come? Surely you do not wish to renew your affections so that you can have your brother impersonate you any time you feel as though you need a reprieve."

He gestured to a chair. "Will you sit?"

"No, I do not think I will."

"Verra well," he said, sounding a great deal like Andrew. He clasped his hands behind his back and began to pace. "I came to talk to you about my twin brother."

She groaned, rolling her eyes to the cracked plaster in the ceiling above. "You can spare me the details. I think I have garnered enough about his character."

"No, you obviously have not." Philip moved to the window and looked out upon the busy street, the people in the passing carriages and wagons clueless as to the intensity of the ire pulsing through Eugenia's blood. "Andrew is nothing like me. If you harbor resentment toward him, you are grossly mistaken. Yes, it was callous of me to ask him to step in on my behalf at Mama's house party. Andrew even tried to talk me out of it. When he wagered for Randolph—my stallion— he thought I would renege for certain."

"But you didn't."

"Nay." Philip continued to watch the traffic. "You must realize that my brother went along with my ridiculous request because he didna want *you* to feel affronted by my unfeeling actions."

Eugenia crossed her arms tightly and closed her eyes. Did she want to hear more?

"Where I am a wee bit of a tyrant, Andrew is completely opposite. It sometimes amazes me how selfless my brother can be. If anyone asks for a favor, he's always the first to volunteer. He cares deeply for his family. He's loyal to a fault, and when he's not proving his loyalty to me by stepping into my ghillies when I'm off watching my horse lose a race, he's the most honest person in all of Christendom—makes for rather a lousy businessman, truth be told."

Eugenia considered this. Actually, Andrew seemed like quite an adept businessman. No matter how much it irritated her to think about it, she knew he had sent Mr. Richards her way, though she had found no reason to doubt him when he'd said her work had been what led the man to agree to represent Laroux Lace.

"Do you not see?" Sir Philip continued. "The debacle at Mama's house party was *my* ill-conceived deception. Andrew was only trying to protect me. Except somewhere along the way you so charmed him that he fell in love with you."

He did? Eugenia could scarcely breathe. And how was she to respond? She'd pushed him away at every turn. "You rode for six days just to tell me your brother is a decent man?"

Philip turned from the window, his gaze intense. "I'd be lying if I didn't admit that Beatrice is running in Newmarket two days hence."

She chuckled. At least her former betrothed had told her the truth this time.

"Well," he said, rubbing his palms together. "I'd best take my leave."

She touched his arm as he strode toward the door. "Thank you."

"I only wish my words could adequately express

the type of man my brother is. He still pines for you—
he's a right brooding boar—horrible to be around. I
ken it would mean the world to him if you would write
—tell him in your own words how successful you've
been, mayhap how happy that success has made you."

Gasping, she pulled her fingers away and drew
them over her heart. Was she happy?

Yes.

Was she content?

Not exactly.

Did she miss him?

Terribly.

She dashed after him. "Sir Philip?"

He accepted his hat and cane from the butler.
"Aye?"

"Do you truly believe that I ought to write to Sir
Andrew?"

"Truly, a letter from you is exactly what my brother
needs."

23

F rom his library, Andrew faintly heard the front door knocker. But Skye's barking as if he was a demon possessed was completely unignorable. Minutes later, the butler appeared bearing a letter on a silver tray while Skye ran circles around the man, scarcely allowing him to enter the room.

"Come behind," Andrew commanded firmly, only to have the dog sit at his feet, wagging his tail excitedly as if there were a half pound of roast lamb inside the wee missive.

"For you, sir," said the butler, holding out the tray. "If I may say, it smells *heavenly*."

"Aye, well, when I was visiting Newhailes, Grace was trying every new fragrance from Paris. She even doused *me* with the vile concoctions, the pretentious imp." Andrew took the letter from the tray and drew it to his nose. Indeed, the paper smelled slightly fragrant, with a fragile quality about it, but the letter had certainly not been heavily scented. He dismissed the butler with a wave of his hand. "Thank you."

The dog continued his antics, nosing the letter and yowling impatiently.

Andrew slid his finger beneath the seal. Only then did he notice the return address.

A lump swelled in his throat. His hands shook as he unfolded the missive while a pressed yellow pansy dropped to his lap.

> *Dear Sir Andrew,*
>
> *It dawned on me the other day that I had not properly thanked you for collecting my trunk from Aubrey House and forwarding it to me in Cambridge. At the time I was truly grateful for your kindness. The items in the trunk helped me to meet the orders so generously placed by Mr. Richards. In addition, I truly thank you for not revealing my location to my family (I know this because no one from Bedford has inquired about me).*
>
> *I am also extremely grateful to you for sending Mr. Richards my way. Yes, at first I was a tad incensed, but I now realize that had we not crossed paths, I doubt I, as a mere female, would have ever been able to sell a thing aside from the odd cap or scarf at the annual fete. I shall forever be in your debt.*
>
> *I am pleased to say that I have received orders for overdresses like the one*

I wore at Stack Castle. Madame Genevieve in London has become quite demanding and I have had to enlist help. Perhaps one day I might find a cottage nearby. One providing enough space for a half-dozen lace-making ladies.

I trust you are well.

I've oft thought ashamedly about our last meeting. I should have been cordial enough to ask you in for tea, but I'm afraid that at the time I was still too hurt to see beyond my own humiliation. I now realize the extent of the pains you endured to prove the depth of the kindness in your heart. I behaved badly and hope you will forgive me.

Should you ever pass through Cambridge again, I should be delighted to serve you tea.

Fondly,
Miss Eugenia Laroux

Skye popped his nose against the paper. Andrew laughed and patted the dog. "You ken it's from her do you not?"

Skye turned in a circle, his tail wagging.

"She made quite an impression on you, laddie," he said, carefully retrieving the yellow pansy from his lap and breathing in the subtle fragrance. He didn't need to refer to his library's flower encyclopedia to understand the meaning behind the bloom.

Eugenia Laroux, nee Radcliffe is thinking of me!

For the first time in months, Andrew smiled so widely, his face nearly split in two. He jumped up and caught Skye's front paws, dancing a jig. "She misses me!" he shouted, not caring if he sounded like a lunatic. Skye bounded around in circles while Andrew kicked up his heels and danced madly.

He must think a great deal about how he should respond. Indeed, a wee jaunt to Cambridge ought to give him enough time to think it all through.

I do believe I shall take you up on your offer for tea, Miss Laroux!

~

SNOW HAD FALLEN in the wee hours, and the noises from the carriages and carts that usually rattled Eugenia's street-facing bedchamber window were eerily muffled. She pulled away the curtain and gazed down at the men shoveling the cobblestone road, their stocking-capped heads bent while snow dusted their shoulders. Shivering, she pulled her shawl tighter about her and looked northward toward the post office.

Mr. Smythe hadn't been loitering in the square for months.

It was just outside that building where Sir Andrew had fought the drunkard. The Highlander had been so fierce and strong, fighting in her honor, yet she'd scarcely thanked him. When she'd first fled from Stack Castle and decided to become a lacemaker in her own right, the man had come to her rescue many times, and not once did she properly thank him. Not once did she recognize his chivalry.

He'd initially followed the mail coach to take her back to the house party, but once he realized that's not what she wanted, he still endeavored to protect her. The poor man had suffered a shot in the arm. In pain, he'd slept on the hard floor outside her bedchamber at the tavern where women were not allowed. He had booked passage to London wanting her to travel in comfort. And when she'd ended up seasick, he'd remained at her side, caring for her. Andrew MacGalloway had emptied her vile bedpan for heaven's sakes.

And Eugenia had been too wrapped up in her own woes to show any appreciation whatsoever.

Then Sir Philip had come to visit. Thank goodness she hadn't married *him*. Though the gesture had been thoughtful on his part, Eugenia couldn't imagine herself married to such a man. He was too stoic and terribly unromantic. She'd thought his suggestion to write to Andrew had been good advice, but now sennights had passed with no reply. Christmas would be upon them soon, and she would spend it alone. Eugenia loved Christmas, loved the greening of Aubrey Hall and the scent of cedar and pine wafting through her halls. A hollow void filled her chest as she realized the holiday would never be the same.

Well, she wouldn't exactly be alone. Mrs. Spencer was lovely company.

After all, this was what she wanted—to live her life on her terms. Though she'd always dreamed of having a family, a young woman couldn't have everything. She couldn't imagine running a household, heavy with child while making lace at all hours.

Down below, a carriage pulled up outside the boarding house. A liveried footman hopped down from the rear and placed a stool on the footpath before opening the door and standing back. Though Eugenia expected him to offer his hand to a lady, a man wearing a black great coat alighted, gave a nod to the footman, and headed directly for Mrs. Spencer's door. Eugenia craned her neck, willing the visitor to look up, but he did not.

On a sigh, she put the quizzing glass around her neck—a recent purchase from the haberdashery since she'd suffered eye strain after hours upon hours of tying tiny knots. Indeed, she still loved making lace, but it was now a duty rather than something to pass the time, something to occupy her days of privileged idleness.

"Miss Laroux?" said the housekeeper, ascending the stairs. "You have a gentleman caller."

She stopped as gooseflesh swarmed up her arms. "I do? Did he give you his name?"

"Sir Andrew Mac-something. He said you invited him for tea." She tapped her finger to her lips. "I thought that was rather odd."

Eugenia's feet barely touched the floor as she hastened to the front staircase. "I did invite him for tea. Would you mind bringing in a service?"

"I'll have to ask Mrs. Spencer for her approval first."

"Of course, do that. But please hurry!"

After racing down the stairs, Eugenia stopped at the landing, patted her hair, and smoothed out her skirts. She hadn't had a lady's maid curl her tresses since leaving Stack Castle and now it was pulled into the severe bun of a working woman. Obviously, Sir Andrew had seen her looking so plain before, but suddenly she was entirely self-aware.

Had he received her letter? *Yes, yes, of course he had,*

he'd told the housemaid that he'd come for tea. She took in a deep breath and slowly, as gracefully as possible, descended the remaining stairs.

In the parlor, Andrew wasn't watching the traffic pass by beyond the bay window as Philip had done, he was watching her, and as she moved through the entrance hall, a grin spread across his lips. He'd shed his great coat and stood like a Highland chieftain, a black woolen doublet over a crisp white shirt, his neckcloth neat and tidy. His kilt was perfectly pleated over which he wore the sporran she remembered with its silver clasp. The most memorable part of his costume was the tartan sash slashing diagonally across his chest and pinned at his shoulder with the ruby brooch which was uniquely his.

But nothing in his appearance attracted her as much as the smile on his face with those deep blue eyes reflecting the light, his white teeth, his expression speaking volumes about the character of the man—a man who had helped her achieve her dreams no matter what. A man who cared for her, who now focused on her as if she were the only woman in all of Cambridge.

"Sir Andrew," she said, her voice cracking and filled with nerves. She dipped into a curtsy.

He slid his foot forward and bowed. "Miss Eugenia."

She warmed at his use of the familiar. After all, at one time they'd completely dropped the salutations. Glancing over her shoulder, she gestured to a chair. "The tea service should be along in short order."

Together they sat. He crossed his knees, his kilt sliding up his thigh a bit. Trying not to notice, she crossed her ankles and folded her hands atop her lap.

"I imagine the journey to Cambridge must have been cold, given the snow."

"It was none too warm, though I didna—"

She waited for him to finish his sentence but he just swiped his fingers across his mouth, looking rather uncomfortable. "You did not what?" she urged.

"I arrived a fortnight ago."

"In Cambridge? Did you have business dealings here?"

"No...er...yes."

The tea arrived, giving Eugenia something to do with her hands, thank heavens. Though when she moved to the low table to pour, the teapot trembled so, the lid rattled as if she suffered from palsy. It disappointed her that Andrew had been so nearby and hadn't come to see her sooner. "Something to do with cotton, I assume?"

"Hmm?" he asked while she poured milk into his tea.

"You were about to tell me the nature of your business dealings in Cambridge," she said, handing him the cup and saucer with a sugar biscuit neatly placed on the side.

He took a sip, then set the tea aside. "Well, after I received your letter, I got to thinking about Frederick."

She nodded with intent seriousness. Had she already added a spoon of sugar to her tea? Unable to remember, she scooped another and watched the white crystals slowly sprinkle into the milky liquid. "Is Frederick in Cambridge as well?"

"No, oh no. I was also thinking about my manor house on the Tay."

Though she had absolutely no idea how Andrew's house and his brother tied together, she said, "By the mill, across the moor from Philip's home?"

"Aye...that's the one."

"Ah," she said, still failing to grasp the direction of the conversation. She sipped her tea, finding it extraordinarily sweet. How many spoons of sugar had she put in it? The entire contents of the bowl? Goodness, things had grown awkward. "I still cannot quite understand what brought you to Cambridge."

"*You* did," he whispered, his gaze unblinking and staring directly at her. "I've found a cottage...well, it's much larger than a cottage, but it is a cozy home and it has a rather large ballroom."

Had he lost his mind? "Ballroom? In Cambridge?"

"Aye, well, it is a space which I believe might transform well into a lacemaking operation."

Ah-ha, now she was beginning to realize why Andrew appeared to be so inordinately nervous. Nonetheless, after everything, she didn't want him barging in and making decisions for her. She didn't want anyone making decisions on her behalf. "You've bought a cottage that's not really a cottage and you intend to turn the ballroom into a lacemaking mill? I thought I made it clear that I did not wish for your charity, sir."

"Good God, I am making a muddle of this." He stood and paced. "Mayhap I've put the cart in front of the horse as I oft do, but please understand that I have *not* purchased the cottage—castle really." He kneeled at her side and grasped her hand. "I found an estate with a loch and a castle, but it's nay a monstrosity like Stack Castle. It is a homey place, a tad like Barrogill Castle on the road from John o'Groats to Thurso. And it's nay a medieval spectacle. It was modernized by the esteemed John Nash and has large windows that usher in light, a modest six bedchambers, a rather large dining hall, an adequate library, a drawing room, two parlors, one of which might make an excellent music room and a rather impressive—"

"Ballroom?" she asked, since that had been what he'd begun with.

"Aye. For your lacemaking endeavor."

"*My* lacemaking?" Eugenia slipped her hand away from his. "It sounds like a dream come true, but I'm afraid I'd not be able to afford such a grand home."

He retrieved her hand and kissed it. "Would you consider having a wee walk through?"

"Why would you want to raise my hopes?"

He groaned. "Forgive me. This isna exactly proceeding as I'd planned." A brilliant blush spread across Andrew's dashing face. "However, if I've learned anything when it comes to you, carefully laid plans are oft flawed."

She bit down on her lip, trying not to agree, but knowing he was exceedingly correct. Eugenia had thwarted him at every turn. Why not now?

Again, he kissed her hand, then turned it over and pressed her palm against his warm cheek. "I love you. I have been utterly miserable without you. Skye as well. You should have seen the dog's excitement when he sniffed your letter."

"Truly?" Though she could imagine the lad bashing the furniture with his swishing tail, Eugenia's stomach had fluttered exceedingly. Sir Andrew Mac-Galloway loved her?

"Aye, but the deerhound's heart wasna beating nearly as erratically as mine." He shifted her palm lower, covering his heart. "Miss Eugenia, I love your passion for lacemaking. I love your passion for flowers and seashells. I love how much attention you gave to Skye, recognizing him as a wee beasty with feelings and intelligence. Would you..."

She scarcely could breathe with his heart thrumming rapidly beneath her fingertips. "Would I?"

"Marry me? Marry me and make your lace—become the most renowned lacemaker in all of Christendom. Hire dozens of assistants, work your fingers to the bone if you wish."

"You would be content with a woman who, heaven forbid, works at something aside from running a household and raising the children?"

"Aye, I want nothing more. We can hire nurses and nannies to help with the children, and my housekeeper runs my home, I dunna ken why she canna come to Cambridge and do the same. I only ask for one thing in return."

"And what is that?"

His gaze met hers, those intense blues unblinking, filled with honesty. "Your heart."

With both hands, she drew his knuckles to her lips and kissed him. "I do love you. I think I've loved you ever since you stood up to my mother when we went to stroll in the gardens at Stack Castle."

As Andrew grinned, the parlor seemed to flood with the light. "No words have ever made me hope more. Will you..."

"Marry you?"

"Aye."

Eugenia wanted to say yes more than anything in her life, but this was so sudden. She'd be able to make her lace, just as she'd hoped when she was betrothed to Philip. She'd be able to live in Cambridge. Moreover, she had no doubt that Andrew would allow her to be a party to decisions that affected them both.

"If you need more time—"

"No, no." She squeezed his hand. "Take me to see this castle."

24

Andrew didn't feel the cold during the carriage ride to Caledonia, as he'd dubbed the estate. Love swelled through his heart while he and Eugenia sat close together beneath three woolen blankets as they ambled into the country. The sun made an appearance and, as if by magic, it melted the thin blanket of snow that had covered everything with white that morn.

Though he had provided the man from the realty office with a deposit, Andrew had been clear that his bride-to-be must give her approval before the deed could be transferred and his final payment made. Still, he had received a key to the front door in good faith. Andrew himself had lit the fires in many of the castle's rooms. Eugenia would be far more inclined to approve of the home if it weren't freezing within.

The coachman signaled with two raps when they turned onto the sycamore lined drive. Andrew pushed aside the curtain and pointed out the window. "Can you imagine how glorious our drive will be in summer with a canopy of leaves?"

Presently, icicles hung from the fingers of naked

branches. "And in autumn with oranges and golds, and in spring with the brilliant greens of new life." Eugenia craned her neck. "I think the boughs will be stunning when they're heavy with snow."

"And seeing the afternoon sun glistening off the icy crystals?" he asked.

"Exactly."

As the carriage meandered onward, Andrew pointed through the passing gaps between tree trunks. "The loch is yonder."

Eugenia gave him a playful nudge. "'Tis *lake* in England."

"But not in Caledonia—as the Romans dubbed Scotland." He kissed her temple. "You wouldna deny me the honor of naming our estate, would you, love?"

"I thought you said I would have the final say?"

"Indeed I did. Forgive me for my impertinence."

"Caledonia, hmm?" she mused, drawing out the name and giving him a coy grin. "I think it could grow on me."

His heart swelled. At last he had found the key to Eugenia's heart. All it had taken was to consult with her prior to making sweeping decisions that might affect her life. He glimpsed the loch, now fully in view as the carriage entered the corner leading to the castle doors, looking like glass, covered with a thin sheet of ice. "Do you skate?"

"I'm a bit too clumsy for skating."

He winked. "You skate."

"You're fairly confident are you not?"

"A woman who makes lace as exquisite as yours, and who dances as gracefully as you do—"

"I am not graceful."

"You certainly were when you were in my arms in the orchestra's withdrawing room."

"That's because..."

"Hmm?" he asked.

"I was with you."

He kissed her then, their lips joining in an exquisite dance. His hands gently clamped her face as he delighted in her sweet taste, the soft sigh escaping her throat.

No matter how much Andrew wanted to nestle beneath the blankets and kiss Eugenia for the rest of his life, the carriage rolled to a stop. He gently ended the kiss and ran his fingers over the bow securing her bonnet. "Your castle awaits, my love."

THE CASTLE WAS FURNISHED. Every room was more marvelous than the next. The furniture was hardly worn and the upholstery coordinating with the wallpaper, the colorful rugs, and lovely window treatments. The entry posed an example of exquisite chinoiserie, complete with a life-sized statue of a Chinese courtier and a chandelier of lanterns above. A blue parlor, a deep burgundy drawing room. The dining hall had been decorated in rich golds. And though Andrew had said the library was adequate, it was spacious. All four walls contained bookshelves that touched the ceiling, and in one corner an ornate writing desk was situated to take advantage of the morning light.

After leading her down a long gallery, Andrew grasped the knobs of two double doors. "This, my love, can be your new lacemaking workshop."

He opened the doors and stood back while Eugenia moved inside, taking in the enormity of the space, the brightness ushered in by the entire row of windows along the south-facing wall. There were no fewer than five ornate chandeliers overhead. She drew her hands over her mouth while her eyes filled with tears.

"Is this not what you wanted, lass?" Andrew asked quietly, a hint of vulnerability in his voice.

"I'm a bit overwhelmed is all. I've always imagined working in an old barn with a wood-plank floor and nothing but a brazier for warmth."

He took her into his arms and began to waltz. "Your lace...Laroux Lace will be more sought after than Mechlin from Flanders."

She followed his lead as if they had been partnering for dozens of years. "I would be content only to supply Madame Genevieve with her demands."

"Then so it will be. Whatever you want, you shall have." Andrew twirled her into a circle. "What about your family? Do you wish to reunite with them?"

"Continuing to hide might prove difficult, considering your eldest brother is a duke...unless you, too, fall off a cliff. Figuratively, I mean."

"I'd prefer to remain with the living. My mother wouldna take too kindly to rumors of my death circulating about London."

"Perhaps I ought to make up a story about washing up on the shore somewhere and being taken in by—"

"A braw Highlander?"

Eugenia threw back her head and laughed. "Mayhap a milkmaid or a washing lady, and it took some time for me to recover from a bout of amnesia."

"Verra well. I'll wager your mother will be pleased with such a tale."

Eugenia pirouetted from his arms and turned in a circle. "Are you certain we can afford this extravagance?"

"Quite certain. In fact, you need never concern yourself with money again. Any coin you earn from your lacemaking endeavors shall be yours to do with what you will."

"But once I am married, all that is mine will legally become yours."

"Not if I give it to you." He tugged her into his arms and kissed her. "I shall have my solicitor draw up the papers on the morrow."

She threw her arms around his neck and smiled up at his beautiful face. "You are the most astonishing man I have ever met."

Andrew leaned his forehead against hers. "Och, lass, I believe that is the best compliment I've ever had."

"Surely not."

"Because it came from your lips, my heart is full. I love you. Your happiness is all I desire."

"I love you as well, but what can I do to make you happy?"

"I'm a simple man. With you at my side I shall be the happiest man in all of Christendom."

Eugenia drew his face downward until his lips met hers and joined in a slow kiss, expressing all the love she held in her heart. Her entire body came alive as her eyes fluttered closed.

Never in all her days had she dared to hope that she might find a man as perfect as Sir Andrew Mac-Galloway.

Growling soft and low in his throat, he trailed delicious kisses along the sensitive skin of her neck. "If I take you above stairs, I mightn't be able to keep my hands off you, lass. But I want to wait until we are properly wed before I take you to bed."

Her breath caught as her gaze trailed upward.

"Then let us start our marriage pure and holy akin to my love for you."

25

One of the fortunate things about being the brother of a duke, was that it took but a fortnight to obtain a special license. While they waited, Andrew had taken Eugenia to Aubrey Hall and met with her parents. Though Baron Bedford was immediately full of gratitude that his daughter had returned, it took the baroness a time to come to grips with the news. She grappled with the challenge of devising a plan of how she might reveal her daughter's return to the *ton*, not to mention Eugenia's untoward engagement, swapping one twin for the other. But once Her Ladyship warmed to the story that Eugenia had suffered a bout of amnesia and was later discovered in Cambridge by Andrew, she welcomed them both with open arms.

Truth be told, Andrew suspected that the baroness was secretly proud that her daughter had founded Laroux Lace, though Her Ladyship assumed (incorrectly) that her daughter would pass the business to her husband as soon as they were married.

Andrew cared little for what polite society might think about stealing his brother's betrothed. Whenever anyone asked, he'd just say that theirs was a love match. After all, love conquered all, did it not?

Of course, *his* mother took the news with her usual flair. At first she'd suffered one of her spells, followed by a flurry of wedding plans, hurried invitations, and letters to the papers.

The wedding was a much larger affair than either Andrew or Eugenia wanted, but with a dowager duchess and a baroness for mothers, they both decided that, in this final instance, it was best to let them take charge. The wedding ceremony was held at the Great St. Mary's Church in Cambridge with all the guests invited to a reception at "Caledonia" where they used the ballroom for the first and final time before it was turned into a lacemaking shop.

To the music of an orchestra hired from the university, the wedding party enjoyed a seven-course meal in the dining hall. Even Baron Bedford's health was good enough for him to attend. After the meal, Andrew and his new bride danced and made merry with their guests, but he wasn't entirely content until the final waltz, when he at last held his wife in his arms.

"Have you enjoyed your day?" he asked, placing his hand on the arc of Eugenia's waist.

"*Our* day, mind you."

He chuckled to himself. Most women of her ilk live their entire lives with excited anticipation of their wedding days. But this woman had discovered so much more substance in the commonplace living of her dreams.

Together they danced as if they were alone in the orchestra's withdrawing room at Stack Castle, their movements perfectly mirrored as if they had been waltzing as a married couple for a score of years or more.

Mozart's Waltz in F major was performed to perfection. The ballroom was dreamlike, the candles overhead casting an ethereal, amber glow. They were joined by family and close friends. Grace looked lovely, of course, though Prince Isidor had been unable to attend. His Majesty sent his regrets, citing that there hadn't been enough time to clear his schedule and sail across the North Sea.

When the final waltz came to an end, Andrew was filled with wonder, he had to look down to ensure his feet were still on the ground. There was only one thing he wanted more than to dance the final set with Eugenia, and at long last, the time had come for the guests to bid them good night as they ascended the stairs to their marriage bed.

Though Andrew had been staying at Caledonia, this would be Eugenia's first night in the house. He wanted everything to be perfect for her. To tend her, he'd even hired away her lady's maid from Aubrey Hall. He'd never forget how the woman had cried when she thought Eugenia dead. And she had clearly kept her secret after she'd learned the truth. Such a woman was an invaluable servant.

Though he wanted to rip the pale blue lace gown from Eugenia's shoulders, he exercised self-control and patiently waited for her in his chamber, sipping only a finger of whisky, and staring into the fire, reliving visions of his bonny wife smiling as she'd stared into his eyes and recited her vows.

His glass was empty when the door between their bedchambers slowly opened.

Andrew stood, his breath seizing within him. Unable to move, he stared, gazing upon the most stunning woman he'd ever seen. Eugenia wore her hair unbound, flowing in golden waves down to her waist. She wore a night rail trimmed with fine lace caressing her neck.

She fingered the top button, glancing back into Her Ladyship's bedchamber. "Would you have preferred it if I had knocked?"

"God, no." In two strides, he crossed the floor.

Before he reached her, she held up her palm, bidding him to stop. "I feel as if I've waited my entire life for this night."

A slow smile spread across her lips as she slowly unfastened the six buttons which hid her treasures from him. As she dropped her hands to her sides, the fine muslin cloth parted ever so slightly giving him a peek at a full, creamy breast.

Andrew's knees buckled as he closed the distance and wrapped her in his arms, sealing his lips over her mouth. He pressed the length of his body against hers, showing her exactly how she affected his arousal. And Eugenia didn't disappoint. A tiny mewl escaped her throat as she returned his fervent kisses as if she would die if they were apart for one more second. That's how Andrew felt—as if he had to be inside her to be whole again.

But this was her first time. He'd reminded himself over and over, he could not act out his passions without making it the most astoundingly memorable night in all her days.

As the kiss ebbed to tiny nibbles, their bodies rubbing, touching, yearning, Andrew leaned away a tad and inclined his head to the sideboard where his valet had left two glasses and a bottle of madeira. "Would you care for a wee spot of sweet wine?"

Eugenia glanced at the bottle before she slowly

shook her head and scraped her teeth over her bottom lip. "First..." She unclasped his ruby brooch and let his sash drop to the floor.

"Hmm?" he asked, sliding the pin from her fingers and tossing it on the table.

"I want you to make love to me," she whispered, almost inaudibly, a bonny shade of rose flooding her cheeks.

Andrew's heart stopped. His eyes rolled back while his cock lengthened. It took all the self-control he could muster not to shove the night rail from her shoulders and back her onto the enormous fourposter bed. He forced himself to take a deep breath. "It might hurt."

"I know." The lass stood a bit taller. "I'm not afraid."

He twirled a lock of her silky hair around his finger. "I'll try to be gentle."

She slowly tugged away his neck cloth, making self-restraint pure torture. "I want it. I want *you*."

Andrew tugged up the hem of her gown. "I've been waiting months to hear you say that," he growled, nibbling her neck. "I need to be inside you."

Eugenia gasped. "Naked?"

He slid the hem higher until his fingers brushed the downy hair at her apex. "This is where I desire to be. Naked. In bed. With you."

"You'll be naked too?" she asked, her eyes dropping.

"Aye," he croaked.

Her breath came in sharp inhalations as she nodded her assent, holding her hands over her head and letting him remove her night rail, sending it sailing to the floor in a heap. Andrew stood back and drank her in—breasts fuller than he'd imagined, a slim waist, a tapering curve to her stomach supported by feminine hips. "There are no words to express how you make me feel."

Another lovely blush spread over her face as Eugenia folded her arms over her breasts, her legs crossing. "I've never felt so exposed."

"No, my dear." He pulled her into his embrace and kissed her forehead, her eyes, her cheeks, her lips. "You must never be shy with me."

"I might feel better if..." Eugenia's fingers slid to his belt and released it, making his kilt drop, his weapons clanking to the floor.

Within two clicks of the mantel clock, Andrew stood naked before her, his cock standing erect, which happened to be commanding her full attention. He stroked himself. "This is what you do to me."

At once, they collided in an embrace. Their lips fused, their bodies crushed together as in a frenzy while their hands explored, rubbing, caressing. Andrew urged Eugenia toward the bed and slid his fingers up and down her glorious waist, his mind all but blinded with the power of his need.

"I worship you," he growled, pulling her against his erection, sinking his fingers into her luscious, soft bottom, his eyes crossing as she rubbed against him. Rocking his hips forward, he bit his lip and pressed harder. Until his thighs shuddered, his cock so hard if he didn't regain a modicum of control, he'd spill before he gave her pleasure.

In one fluid motion, he swept her onto the mattress. Waves of exquisite blonde hair sprawled across the pillow, her body lithe, naked, and prone to him. Before this night, Andrew considered himself a connoisseur of female breasts, but Eugenia's bosom was by far the most enticing, stunningly beautiful he'd ever seen. Tipped with light rose, they weren't too large, nor were they extraordinarily small. They were a perfect handful. A perfect mouthful.

"Perfect," he whispered, climbing over her and worshipping them with kisses.

Eugenia moaned, writhing with the swirl of his tongue.

"Lady MacGalloway, you've enraptured me mind, body, and soul. Seduced me. I am yours to command," he said, his gaze meeting hers as his hands toyed with her nipples. Heaven help him, he needed her. He needed her now.

"I beg to differ, sir, it is I who have been seduced." She giggled. "Quite thoroughly!"

But as she teased him, her expression grew serious. She took his hands and slowly moved them from her breasts to her belly, downward to the nest of light curls.

"God save me," he groaned, sliding lower, spreading her legs with his shoulders. Dazed by her scent, he slid his finger along her core. "You have bewitched me and I am under your spell for all eternity."

As if schooled in the wiles of women, she arched into his hand. "Yes," she whispered.

Dipping his chin, he watched her face as he licked her. With a feral moan, an expression of unfettered passion crossed her face, from her slightly unfocused eyes to the parting of her lips. Loving every second, Andrew swirled his tongue around her sensitive button.

"Oh my," she cried, moving in tandem with his mouth.

"Mm-hmm," he urged, sliding a finger inside.

"I am the one who has been bewitched, Sir Knight!"

Chuckling, his cock leaking seed, he slid his finger faster while his tongue relentlessly licked.

Eugenia's breathing sped until she gasped. Her body stiffened, then her thighs quivered. Crying out, she tugged his hair and came undone in his mouth.

Clenching his gut against his urge to release his seed, Andrew continued to lick until her breathing ebbed.

"You are a fiend," she said, laughing as she pushed up on her elbows. "We have not yet consummated the marriage."

He coaxed her back to the mattress, giving her a devilish grin. "Then we must remedy that at once, wife."

As SHE PULLED Andrew over her and kissed him, Eugenia's insides quivered with pleasure. "I love you. I love you. I love you."

"I love you more than...*everything*," he sighed, cupping her cheek. "Though we'll both agree that Philip's scheme to have me stand in for him was adolescent, you must admit that if it weren't for my twin's fanatical fondness of horseracing, we would be spending the rest of our lives in utter misery staring longingly at each other across the hall at dinners and family gatherings."

She slid her fingers into his soft, thick hair, kissing him. "I cannot imagine being married to anyone but you."

"I'm ever so close to spilling my seed," he throatily whispered while the thick column of his manhood jutted between her thighs. The pull of wanting filled her again. But this time, she needed to find out what it would be like to have him inside her.

Eugenia moved against him, her nether parts ever so slick with want. "It's time, my love."

"I do not wish to hurt you."

"I know." She said, tugging him to her, not knowing what else to do. "Please."

Andrew's thick column filled her, stretched her.

"See," she said. "That's not so bad."

"Are you ready for more?"

More? Gulping, she nodded.

Slowly he slid farther while Eugenia held on to his shoulders.

"Are you all right?" he asked.

"Yes," she replied, squeezing her eyes shut against the pain.

"Just a bit more."

She nodded even though Andrew's head was beside hers, making it impossible for him to see her face. "Can you just stay where you are for the moment?"

His body tensed. "Aye," he said, his voice strained.

Together they took deep breaths while her insides adjusted. "I think the worst of it is over," she whispered, rubbing her hands along his back, urging him to resume.

"I'll proceed slowly." He filled and stretched her, his manhood caressing a spot that made her ravenous once more.

God bless him, he did not rush. Gradually, as they kissed and explored each other, the tempo increased.

Higher their passion mounted. Only when Eugenia cried out and bucked against him, did he topple off the edge into a wild storm of frenetic passion. And she met him thrust for thrust, cry for cry. Every inch of Eugenia's skin craved more of her Highlander until she froze at the pinnacle of ecstasy. In one earth-shattering burst, Eugenia came undone around him while with a guttural roar, Andrew thrust deep and spilled within her, his entire body shaking.

As their impassioned frenzy ebbed, he gazed into her eyes and swept the damp locks from her face. "I am yours to command, m'lady."

"Lady," she mused. As the wife of a knight, she was now a lady. She found it odd how the title hadn't tempted her one way or the other as it would with most brides. It was this man with whom she fell in love, and he was the only thing that mattered. "I promise to be a fair and congenial master, my husband." Giggling, she cupped his face and kissed him. "I quite enjoyed our...um...."

"Lovemaking?"

"Mm-hmm." She glanced down to his member which was not quite as large now. "When can we do that again?"

He blessed her with a dazzling grin. "As often as you wish, my love."

EPILOGUE

JUNE, FIVE YEARS LATER

"Come behind, Skye!" Andrew called, standing while the deerhound raced toward him, eyes wild, tongue lolling to one side.

After taking his morning jaunt about Caledonia's grounds, Andrew led the dog through the woods and used the boot scraper at the servants' entrance before heading inside. Though in most households it was unusual for the master of the house to enter through the kitchens, Andrew still wasn't one to stand on convention.

"'Tis a good thing you came in afore the rain started, sir," said Cook, turning from the enormous cast-iron hob. He was a bit of a crabbit Scot, but he made the best mulberry tart Andrew had ever tasted.

Andrew swiped a biscuit from the table as he walked past—yet another benefit of venturing this way. If he used the front door, he never would have had the opportunity to eat a wee biscuit still warm from the oven.

"You'd best not give that to the mangy hound," barked Cook.

Andrew chuckled and swiped another, just to raise the man's ire. Skye yowled, rubbing his long body on his master's leg until they reached the servants' stairs. "Sit."

The dog immediately lowered his haunches.

"Good laddie," Andrew said, holding out the treat which the deerhound swallowed in one gulp.

"That wee beasty is so spoilt, you'll be building a castle for him soon."

"Och, I pay you to mind your kitchen, ye glaiket fouter."

Cook laughed as he wiped his hands on his apron. He was the only man in the castle with the cods to be audaciously impudent. But Andrew had come to enjoy their daily banter. Of course, there were two women in the castle who took the term *audaciously impudent* to celestial levels, one being his wife, the other he was presently dashing up the stairs to see.

A shrill scream from the top of the tower. "I not hungry!"

Andrew grabbed Skye's collar to keep him from racing ahead.

"If you do not eat your luncheon, I'll have to send the biscuits back down to the kitchen," said the nursemaid.

"No!"

As his three-year-old daughter stood defiantly with her hands atop her little hips, Andrew stepped into the nursery. "What's this I hear? My wee Eloise wouldna be answering back to her nurse, would she?"

Startling, the lassie turned red in the face, looking exactly like her mother, sky blue eyes, shiny wheat-colored hair. "Da!" she said, running to him and wrapping her arms around his leg. "Nanny mean."

Andrew gave the nursemaid a wink as he picked the child up and propped her on his hip. "I disagree.

Your nanny is right. You canna eat biscuits for every meal."

"Why?"

"Because you need good food to help you grow tall like your mother."

"But I no like saniches."

"No?" Andrew carried Eloise to the child-sized table and set her down. Alas, the sandwich hadn't been touched and the sugar biscuits were now out of reach on the windowsill. "Then I suppose Nanny will have to take the biscuits away."

"No!" Eloise stamped her foot. "No, no, no!"

"What say you to a wee wager?"

The lass pursed her lips. "You eat sanich."

"If you take two bites, Nanny will give you one biscuit."

"Sir—" Miss Aston interjected, but Andrew stopped her by raising his palm.

"Two bites. Good sized ones—as large as Skye's."

Miss *Audaciously Impudent* slid into her little wooden chair and huffed as she picked up the sandwich and took a tiny bite while the dog stood gape-mouthed across the table, watching and waiting for his opportunity.

"Och, that wasna a bite, lass."

Eloise scrunched her nose and took another, then held the entire sandwich out to the deerhound. Before Skye could pounce, Andrew snatched it away. Then, with a point of his finger, commanded the dog to sit by the hearth. "Another bite, Empress Eloise."

The child complied and Andrew gave a nod to the nursemaid. Who took a biscuit from the plate and set it beside his daughter. "You spoil her so."

"She'll soon find out what it is like to have a wee

bit of competition," he replied, tapping Eloise on the shoulder. "Are you ready to go see Mummy?"

She pointed her now soggy, half-chewed biscuit at the plate in the window. "More."

"Oh, no. Only young ladies who eat all of their sandwiches are allowed more than one biscuit."

Luncheons for his strong-willed daughter were oft a battle of wills which was why Andrew frequently made an appearance in the nursery at this particular time of day. Eventually, Eloise ate her sandwich and was allowed two more biscuits before they headed down to the lacemaking shop.

Stepping through the open doorway, Andrew held his daughter's hand, panning his gaze across the baker's dozen lacemakers all sitting with their heads bent, their hands working in a blur. At the far end of the room, Eugenia stood at a table where he oft found her, though presently in profile, the bairn in her belly was making himself known. Using a pencil, she made a notation and then discussed it with the overseer.

As Andrew and Eloise moved inside she looked up, her face brightening. Eugenia's lacemaking endeavor had taken London polite society by storm. In her first two years of operation, she had received so many orders that she'd been forced to turn some away, which only made the demand for Laroux Lace grow.

Now, five years later, they employed thirteen of the best qualified lacemakers in England and only took orders from modistes who made gowns for the upper crust with Madame Genevieve being their most loyal client. For the first two years, Eugenia had made a great deal of the lace herself, but once Eloise was born, "Miss Laroux" hired enough laborers to enable her to spend more time with family, though she did oversee the creations of new designs herself.

Eugenia smiled as Andrew approached. "There you are," she said, glowing.

"Nanny mean," said Eloise, obviously still upset with being asked to eat her luncheon before her treat.

Andrew shrugged. "Mayhap the biscuits and cakes ought to remain in the kitchens until the empress finishes her meals."

"No!" Eloise said, earning a very stern expression from her mother.

"I beg your pardon? Is that how young ladies behave when they are in the presence of anyone, let alone their parents?" asked Eugenia.

Eloise's bottom lip jutted out. "Sorry."

Andrew released the child's hand. "I'll have you know, though your daughter did put up a wee fuss, she did end up eating every last morsel."

Eugenia clapped her hands. "You did?"

"I did, I did!" Eloise replied, jumping up and down.

Andrew picked her up and offered his hand to his wife. "I believe the Moss Provence are blooming, my dear."

Eugenia smiled as she laced her fingers through his. "Are they?"

"I have it on good authority."

"I also have heard we have two rows of peonies in full bloom."

Eloise squirmed. "I don't like peenies."

Andrew tweaked the babe's nose. "How do you know?"

"I happen to like them very much," said Eugenia.

"I like them, too," said Eloise as if she'd been utterly convinced.

Together the threesome, which would soon become four, strolled out through the French doors and

across the grass to the rows and rows of flowers—roses
of all colors, irises, peonies, bellflowers, freesia, and
more. Hand-in-hand they strolled along the fragrant
flower beds, examining them, discussing their colors,
discovering new blooms planted by the gardener.

After bending over to sample the fragrance of her
most favored Moss Provence rose, Eugenia straightened with a sharp gasp, her hands snapping to her dis-
tended stomach.

"What is it?" Andrew asked, wrapping his arm
around her shoulder. "Is it time? Your water? A con-
traction?"

She giggled and moved his hand over her belly.
"The babe must like roses."

Beneath his palm, the child in her womb kicked.

"Let me, let me!" said Eloise, pushing between
them.

And there they stood, all three of them in the
midst of their colorful garden, the miracle of new life
astounding them. Only when the unborn bairn's prods
ebbed, did Andrew surround his family in his arms.
"Thank you for making me the happiest man in all of
Christendom."

AUTHOR'S NOTE

Thank you for reading *Kissing the Highland Twin*. It has been fun to combine the genres of Scottish historical romance and Regency romance in this witty series about the children of a dukedom. The MacGalloways and the Dunscaby empire are fictitious, though in all my books I do try to create a world that is relatable to my readers and that has as much historical accuracy as possible, spending hours poring over historical texts and websites.

If you have read the previous books in the series, you might have found some familiarity with the dukedom's properties of Newhailes and Stack Castle which also have a mention in this story. In book one, *A Duke by Scot*, Martin purchases the land on the River Tay on behalf of his twin brothers who are about to graduate from university. It was fun to take a look a few years on to see Philip and Andrew as prosperous businessmen, settled in their manor houses.

When embarking on this series, I worried about introducing the cotton industry as the foundation of the family dynasty because of the American South's history of using slave labor. During the Regency era, the cotton industry in Europe had grown by more than 1200% and it made sense for Philip and Andrew to establish a mill, but only if they could obtain cotton grown by free people. During this era, the Irish flocked to the Americas (including one of my own ancestors) and even more so after the 1845 potato famine. They were generally poor and hardworking folk. Also, after the Civil War, African Americans and Irish Americans engaged in cotton sharecropping. Because of the importance of the present-day movement for equality, I took literary license and created the Irish sharecroppers who have been mentioned in previous books and will continue to be a part of this dynasty.

In 2017, I visited John o'Groats as well as the Stacks of Duncansby on the northern tip of Scotland and was surprised not to see a castle overlooking the sea and the astounding monoliths dominating the water just beyond the shore. Though there is a lighthouse where whales, seals, and puffins are often spotted (most frequently by multitudinous flocks of sheep), I saw no castle remains. I believe that a prominent family ought to have held that point for king and clan. Who knows, maybe they did at one time, only to have their fortress razed by the Vikings?

If you haven't already guessed, the next story in The MacGalloways series is *A Princess in Plaid* about Lady Grace and a man who claims her heart, but not before her entire world shatters. I'll share one tidbit with you: the reclusive Laird Buchanan makes himself known.

ALSO BY AMY JARECKI

The MacGalloways
A Duke by Scot
Her Unconventional Earl
The Captain's Heiress
Kissing the Highland Twin

Devilish Dukes
The Duke's Fallen Angel
The Duke's Untamed Desire
The Duke's Privateer
The Duke's Secret Longings

The King's Outlaws
Highland Warlord
Highland Raider
Highland Beast

Highland Defender
The Valiant Highlander
The Fearless Highlander
The Highlander's Iron Will

Highland Force
Captured by the Pirate Laird
The Highland Henchman
Beauty and the Barbarian

Return of the Highland Laird

Guardian of Scotland
Rise of a Legend
In the Kingdom's Name
The Time Traveler's Destiny

Highland Dynasty
Knight in Highland Armor
A Highland Knight's Desire
A Highland Knight to Remember
Highland Knight of Rapture
Highland Knight of Dreams

ICE
Hunt for Evil
Body Shot
Mach One

Celtic Fire
Rescued by the Celtic Warrior
Deceived by the Celtic Spy

Lords of the Highlands series:
The Highland Duke
The Highland Commander
The Highland Guardian
The Highland Chieftain
The Highland Renegade
The Highland Earl
The Highland Rogue

The Highland Laird

The Chihuahua Affair
Virtue: A Cruise Dancer Romance
Boy Man Chief
Time Warriors

ABOUT THE AUTHOR

Known for her action-packed, passionate historical romances, Amy Jarecki has received reader and critical praise throughout her writing career. She won the prestigious 2018 RT Reviewers' Choice award for *The Highland Duke* and the 2016 RONE award from InD'tale Magazine for Best Time Travel for her novel *Rise of a Legend*. In addition, she hit Amazon's Top 100 Bestseller List, the Apple, Barnes & Noble, and Bookscan Bestseller lists, in addition to earning the designation as an Amazon All Star Author. Readers also chose her Scottish historical romance, *A Highland Knight's Desire,* as the winning title through Amazon's Kindle Scout Program. Amy holds an MBA from Heriot-Watt University in Edinburgh, Scotland and now resides in Southwest Utah with her husband where she writes immersive historical romances. Learn more on Amy's website. Or sign up to receive Amy's newsletter.

CPSIA information can be obtained
at www.ICGtesting.com
Printed in the USA
BVHW040835300123
657433BV00020B/789